Breaking Amish Tradition

by

Sandra Becker

First published in United States in 2016
Copyright © Sandra Becker 2016

ISBN: 978-1541084667

This book is a work of fiction and any resemblance to actual persons, living or dead, events and locales is purely coincidental.

All rights reserved. No part of this publication may be reproduced, stored in or introduced into a retrieval system, or transmitted, in any form, or by any means (electrical, mechanical, photocopying, recording or otherwise) without the prior written permission of the author or publisher. Any person who does any unauthorized act in relation to this publication may be liable to criminal prosecution and civil claims for damages.

TABLE OF CONTENTS

1. Breaking Amish Tradition I — 1
2. Breaking Amish Tradition II — 37
3. The Wildflower Blooms — 73
4. A New Life — 122
5. The Mysterious Stranger — 156
6. Having Second Thoughts — 187
7. Twin Hearts — 239
8. Growing Up In Love — 289
9. Truth or Bare? — 340

1: BREAKING AMISH TRADITION I

Chapter One

"Mother, father, come back", Miriam yelled.

"No." her father shouted back. "The fire is spreading. We have to save our house."

Miriam watched from a distance as her father and mother rushed to fill buckets of water from the well. They had been working in the field when they saw the smoke coming out from the house. The fire had started in the kitchen, and her parents went there to dowse it. She saw them rushing to and fro in an attempt to quell the fire that was raging in the kitchen and spreading fast.

"Mother, father, please..." Miriam repeated. The fire had spread to the roof.

There was a tremendous creaking noise from the inside of the house. The whole house shook, and instantly imploded, with her parents still inside.

"No!" Miriam screamed.

The scream echoed in her ears as Miriam's eyes flew open and she sat up straight. She looked around. It was still dark, and she was sleeping in her uncle's house. She could hear her aunt mumble in the adjoining room. "Were you screaming in your sleep again, Miriam?"

Miriam found herself drenched in cold sweat. Her heart was still thudding wildly, even though she realized that it was a dream. It had been three months since her parents had died in the fire, but she couldn't escape the traumatic nightmare that visited her every now and then.

Miriam had been forced to move in with her Aunt Sarah and Uncle Isaac after her parents had died. Sarah was her mother's youngest sister and the one with the least children, although she had five. Moving into their home was when things took a turn for the worse in Miriam's life. It wasn't that she didn't like her relatives, because they were good people, but she simply loved and missed her parents.

She tried to close her eyes and go back to sleep, but she could still hear her parents' voices calling her, "Miriam..." The smell of burning wood lingered in her nostrils. Images of her parents running through the flames were permanently etched in her mind and in her heart. God had allowed her to live through it all but why? *Is there a purpose for my life?*

But there was no answer to her question. All alone in her room, Miriam cried herself to sleep.

The crowing of the rooster woke her up. Miriam started her chores according to her aunt and uncle's strict mandates. There was the usual collecting of the eggs, the milking of the cows, feeding of the animals, and tending to the garden. She did each chore mechanically, with no joy whatsoever, but not a soul noticed. She knew that she was depressed but despite her own frequent attempts to remind herself to be grateful, she couldn't seem to pull herself out of her mood. A tired plea escaped her lips. *Lord, please help me.*

At first, she had a problem actually accepting her parent's death and she secretly expected that they would reappear at any time. She had walked around at night, shivering with fear and sometimes calling out to them. But as the days went on and after the burial, she began to accept their fate, still wondering why her life had to be like this, why her parents had suffered such a horrific and untimely death. Every day since then, she tried to reconcile it in her mind but it never turned out right.

No matter what anyone told her and no matter how anyone tried to comfort her, she could never accept it. Their death never made any sense to her and she quietly expressed her sadness all the more. Eventually, the family members, neighbors and friends stopped coming. So her grief was only intensified by her loneliness. Why would *Gott* let such a thing happen? She never dared to say these words aloud, but Miriam carried it in her soul every day.

By this time, she was numb from crying and grieving and pouring her heart out for God. *Why has God forsaken me?* But none of that would bring her parents back, especially at this delicate time in her life. It was supposed to be a time of exploration and celebration, but not for Miriam. While her friends were busy courting, playing games and going to singings, Miriam sat at home sulking and questioning God. She often looked up at the sky and dreamed of seeing her parents again.

"Miriam, stop all of the daydreaming; it's time for church and your baptism meeting," her aunt Sarah said in an effort to cheer her up.

But in Miriam there was no cheer. In fact, she hated that *Rumspringa* was over for her and that everyone was expecting her to be baptized, forever accepting the Amish ways as her way of life.

"I will," she said, looking at her aunt's weathered face and wondering if she would look the same way in eighteen years.

Still, consistent with Amish tradition, she was obedient and kept her thoughts of rebellion to herself. Every other Sunday during the first thirty to forty minutes of the church service, she separated from the singing congregation and joined her peers for a baptism meeting. They met for nine weeks and each time they listened as the elders reviewed the two articles of Dordrecht Confession. Yet, in her heart she was emotionless. She went through the motions, and then slipped back into the regular church service beside her aunt and uncle.

Aunt Sarah patted Miriam's folded hands and Uncle Isaac smiled at her. Miriam forced herself to smile back. Her demeanor was cool but in her heart burned a fiery passion for change.

When the church service was finally over, Miriam piled into the back of the buggy, waiting for Sarah and Isaac.

Sarah said, "Miriam dear, aren't you staying for the singing?"

Miriam slowly shook her head, and then answered, "No, I'm not staying."

"Why not, dear?" Sarah asked.

Miriam shrugged. "I would rather not stay; that's all." she said solemnly.

"But how will you ever find a suitable mate if you don't attend any of the social activities for people your age? It is *Rumspringa*, after all." Her aunt smiled, gently. "And it's almost over for you."

"I'd rather not," Miriam said. "There is much work to be done at home."

Her aunt and uncle looked at each other and shook their heads as their under aged children piled into the buggy next to Miriam. Sadly, the cousins who were closer to her age were already married and out of the house. So she was stuck with ten year old Mary and eight year old Jacob, playing in the back of the wagon. Miriam rode in silence all the way home, knowing that there had to be a better way to live than this.

Upon arrival at home, Miriam proceeded to go out to the garden. The garden was her favorite place. It was always so peaceful; full of beautiful flowers of different colors. She loved them all: the roses, the daisies, the marigolds and even the daffodils. The flowers gave her an escape from the ugliness she considered her life to be. She would sit amongst the flowers and smell them and dream of the time when she was happy and dream of the time that she would be happy again. Sadly, however Miriam didn't really believe that time would ever come again. Yet, she didn't share this with anyone.

On the day before the baptism, she was about to go for a final and special session. There she would be given one last opportunity to change her mind and she looked forward to doing just that.

When her friend's buggy pulled up for her outside, her aunt nudged her to hurry along but she wouldn't budge.

"I don't think I can do it," Miriam said, respectfully.

"What do you mean you can't do it?" Sarah asked.

"You owe us an explanation don't you? Isaac asked, with a hint of anger in his voice.

"After all we've done for you, don't you at least owe us that much?"

Miriam took a deep breath before she answered, knowing that whatever came out of her mouth at this point would be unacceptable. "To be honest, I don't believe that I can make a commitment to be Amish right now and to follow the rules of the *ordnung*. How can I be baptized when I no longer have the faith?"

Sarah put her hand up to her forehead in despair. "What do you mean by you no longer have faith? Following *Gott's* law is the way to faith."

"I'm sorry but I'm very confused right now and I cannot make a decision based in confusion. I don't know what I want to do with my life. I don't know what I believe about *Gott* right now." Miriam said. "But I do know that I owe it to myself to find out.

Miriam's uncle stormed out of the room, so upset that he could not even speak. With only her aunt still standing by her, Miriam expected more of a lecture but her aunt only shook her head and walked away as well. They left her standing there in the living room pondering her fate.

Finally, she left for the session. Once she was there, when asked if she was certain that she wanted to commit her life to the Christian values, she found the courage to say no.

The bishop asked, "What did you say,

Miriam?"

And Miriam said it again, in a whisper this time, "No."

Once the others noticed Miriam's response, the looks on their faces changed from smiles to frowns. Normally Miriam would have been ashamed, but at this time in her life the only thing she felt was pain. *Maybe this confession will end my turmoil.*

After the meeting, the elders surrounded her. Then the bishop came up to her and spoke in a stern tone, "Miriam, what you are doing is unacceptable. But because your parents were such good and committed people in our community, and it is so sad that their lives ended so tragically, we are willing to give you a chance. Now you have three months to get yourself together and you may get baptized in the fall. Otherwise we will have no choice but to shun you."

"Do you understand?" One of the elders by the name of Father Graber asked.

Miriam closed her eyes and nodded, resigning herself to an uncertain fate.

Shun. The word rang out in Miriam's ears for the rest of the day and night; over and over again, making her plight worse than what it was before.

Chapter Two

John Calhoun sat in the small Philadelphia café, eager to hear more about what his friend was talking about. Curiously enough, they were discussing the Amish and the simple lifestyle that they led. Having never heard of these things before, John was amazed.

"Are you kidding me? Is that how they really live?" John asked.

"Yeah man, I'm telling you that I know a friend of a friend whose family is Amish. They're a very close group." His friend David nodded as he bit into his hamburger. "Lots of community."

"It doesn't sound too bad to me. I wouldn't mind having some community. Sometimes out here in the big city, even though you are surrounded by lots of people, it can get really lonely. It's like you're really all on your own." John looked around for dramatic effect. "Then when you really need help, no one is around." John bit into his chili hotdog and took a handful of ketchup drenched fries.

"Tell me about it. But they're really serious about family and the Christian values. And they won't let the world distort them," David explained.

"Wow, you've got to respect that, huh?"

John continued to pick at his food because he was deep in thought. "I mean as a Christian you really have to respect them."

John had been born in a very religious family. He had accompanied his parents to Sunday church every week, and had been brought up with strong Christian values. When he had grown up, he had decided that he would spend his time doing God's work. And he had been doing that selflessly for a year during his spare time.

Lately, John had been wrestling with which direction he should go with his ministry. Struggling with all kinds of obstacles, he often prayed and questioned God about where he should go from here and what exactly he should do.

When David had heard about the Amish, he was sure that John would be interested in them. And John was keenly interested. John felt as if a Higher Power was urging him towards knowing more about the community. Their lifestyle was refreshing and he admired their faithfulness.

David's words broke into his thoughts. "The Amish have a rare purity of character, and they are really grounded. They don't seem to be from this world."

John smiled. "They appear to be from heaven itself."

"My thoughts exactly."

John closed his eyes and thought of the work he had done so far. He thought about the Amish, and he felt that he could learn a thing or two from them.

John opened his eyes to find David peering down at him. "What do you think?" David asked.

"I don't know, David. But I don't feel like I'm doing enough out here in the world. I mean I go to church and I serve on committees but at the end of the day I'm not sure I'm taking enough of a stand. The Amish people are taking a stand. You know what I mean?"

"I guess I do. It sure is hard to concentrate on ministry with so many distractions around you," David said, pointing out at the traffic, bright lights, and people on the streets. "The Amish sure have a way of separating themselves from the distractions; I'll say that."

"Exactly," John said.

"Well, if you feel so strongly about it, why don't you take a day tour to an Amish community and spend some time figuring it out. You know sometimes things seem better from the outside than from the inside."

"You know what? Not a bad idea at all. Maybe I'll do that. Maybe I will go for a day and check things out for myself." John began to grin. "I'll meet the Amish face-to-face."

"That sounds like a great idea to me then. At least you'll know for sure."

"You're right," John agreed, nodding. "Right."

So David helped John to set up a day tour for himself in a nearby Amish community in Lancaster, Pennsylvania. Since John was only accustomed to the big city, he knew he was in for quite a culture shock, but he was certainly up for the challenge. John was ready for a slower pace, and a simpler lifestyle. He often questioned the ills of society and the negative effects that advancement had created.

Progress is controversial he thought as he prepared himself for the journey. Luckily, he convinced David to come along with him on the tour. And David, having nothing else better to do and also being more than a little curious about the things that he'd heard, agreed to take the tour as well.

Finally the day came when John would get to meet the Amish he so admired and to see if there was anything hidden underneath this polished Christian surface.

Chapter Three

"Wow!" John pointed at the endless spread of farms. "Look at that."

David nodded happily. The clear blue sky complemented the lush green grass of the farms. It was a lovely spring day. John and David were in a tour bus on a visit to Lancaster County. "I am sure glad I came along. I always feel wonderful whenever I see nature resplendent in its beauty. It's a pity I don't travel often to the countryside."

"We are almost there. Hey look, there's an Amish farmer." And, sure enough they could see a man in a straw hat working on his farm. They saw four teenagers joining the farmer at his side, obviously his sons. John looked at the farms passing by, and couldn't help smiling. It was already looking to be a great trip.

The bus eventually stopped and the group trooped out. Their Amish tour guide, Abram, was helpful in showing them how and where they lived and worked, what they wore and even how they made do without many of the conveniences of the modern world. Then at one point, the tour guide allowed them to separate so they could explore the land for themselves. They were told not to go far, but to remain within the general area.

"This is so cool." Josh looked at the Amish people around him going around their daily work. "I finally get to experience the Amish life."

"Please don't," a female voice floated across.

John turned around to see a fellow tourist pestering an Amish girl to let him take her photo. John watched from a distance as the man stood in front of her, then to the side of her as the girl dodged the camera.

"But one little picture won't hurt," the persistent man said.

Then as the man was about to snap her picture anyway, the girl covered her face and head, dropping the bundle of firewood that she was carrying.

John immediately ran to her rescue. "That's no way to treat a lady." He admonished the man.

The fellow tourist took off in a huff. John shook his head and picked up the firewood. "I apologize for his behavior. He was very much out of line."

"That's all right and thank you." The Amish girl turned towards John, he noticed the softness of her face and the brightness of her eyes.

John extended his hand and said, "My name is John."

She ignored his hand but said, "Hello,

John. You're very kind for an *Englischer*. I am Miriam." She smiled at him.

"Please let me help you carry the firewood to your house," John said, studying her face. "You see I'm here on a tour to see how the Amish live."

"That is very nice of you but it's not nec-"

"Consider it done." Before she could finish her sentence, John lifted the firewood and followed her to her house.

She walked ahead, but continued to look back at him as they walked. He couldn't help but notice that the girl was young and very beautiful. Although her hair was hidden underneath a white *kapp*, he could see that her loose golden strands glimmered in the sunlight. John felt drawn to her and by the way she returned his glances, she seemed to be taken with him as well. They exchanged engaging conversation along the way. That was when he found out that her parent's had perished in a house fire and that she lived with her aunt and uncle.

Once they reached the house, her aunt and uncle were outside working in the field. She introduced John to her family and explained to them that he was on a tour. Then she ran inside to bring him some fresh water to drink.

John expressed his gratitude to Miriam and drank the water quickly.

When John was done drinking, he began

to talk about his dream of spreading God's word.

They all listened carefully with blank looks on their faces. He continued, "I see that you all like to work on the land and that's good because I read somewhere that the Amish believe that God is closest to those who toil upon the earth. "

"Is that so?" Isaac eyed him, suspiciously.

"Yes, Sir, I'm giving a lot of consideration to the pure way you live. Is it true about the farm and the simple life?"

"I'd say so... yes. Farming provides a good life for me and my family," Isaac said.

John said. "I think I may like to learn more about God and these simple ways from the Amish.

Sarah, too, looked hesitant to trust him.

"Well, it was very nice meeting all of you and I hope to see you all again." Then he looked at Miriam and was caught by the sadness in her eyes.

There was something hidden behind their beauty; he could feel it. He wanted to say something else but as he felt the stares of her aunt and uncle, he decided against it. He didn't want to start any trouble for her. Instead, he looked deeply into her eyes and hoped that she could feel his compassion. As he turned to walk away, he heard her small voice saying, "Thanks again."

And something inside him knew that he had to see her again.

At the end of the day, John joined up with his friend David and reflected on the lessons he learned about the Amish lifestyle. He also considered the beautiful Amish girl he'd met along his journey. There was something, undoubtedly, special about her.

"Maybe it's a signal from God that I should learn more of their lifestyle." John paced in front of David.

David shrugged his shoulders. "Maybe, "he said. "Maybe not."

"I'm not going back to Philadelphia," John said.

"Come on, man. It's late. What are you talking about?"

"I'm talking about getting a hotel room for the night and staying a little longer and maybe staying permanently." John clasped his hands together.

David squinted his eyes. "You're really serious aren't you?"

"Yep. Tomorrow is Sunday so I'll get to attend a Sunday service. I'm going to wait here until God gives me direction."

And with those words, the two friends parted company, with David going back to Philadelphia and John checking into a local hotel. One way or another, he had to be sure.

Chapter Four

The next morning John woke up optimistic. He yawned and stretched, then knelt down to pray. By the end of his prayer, a strange feeling came over him and he knew that he would have a fruitful day. John showered and got dressed, wearing a pair of khaki pants and a plain blue polo shirt because he didn't want to offend the Amish with any of his usual fashion statements. He looked in the mirror and noticed his budding beard which he'd recently decided to grow. He smiled as he remembered that the hair on his face would be considered a plus. He grabbed his Bible and made his way to the lobby. Taking advantage of the free continental breakfast, he grabbed an apple Danish and a cup of coffee before he started on his way.

As he walked he remembered the face of the girl he had met. That image gave him the incentive to walk faster and he hoped that he would at least be able to see her one more time.

Arriving at the community without an Amish tour guide brought on many stares and whispers, but John didn't mind. He understood their anxiety and as far as he was concerned he represented the unknown. As he walked along the side of the road beside the buggies, elders and families, he began to feel a little out of place.

Finally, he ran into Abram, his tour guide from the day before.

Abram shook his hand and said, "What are you doing here? Have you forgotten something?"

"No, but I am certainly glad to see you. I've been thinking a lot about the life the Amish live here and I'd really like to know more about it. So I came to ask permission to visit again. I was hoping to meet your bishop and attend a church service if that's at all possible."

"Come. I will take you straight to the bishop," Abram said and proceeded to walk to the bishop's house.

Once they'd arrived at the bishop's house, Abram went in first and explained the matter. John waited outside, patiently. After seeing families passing by, obviously on their way to church, he was glad that he had come out early. At last Abram came to the door and invited him inside.

"Welcome, John," the bishop said.

"Thank you, Sir." John continued, "I know there's much that I need to learn but I would like to study your ways. I believe I may be led to join the Amish."

"Ours is a good life, a life of devotion, son. But it's not for everyone, not even every Christian. You must be sure you know all you need to know if you think you want to commit."

"Absolutely, Sir. And that's why I'm here

-to learn. If of course I am given the chance to see it all from the inside-out."

"If you are really sincere, I don't believe there's anything wrong with spending some time among us or attending our church service. Yes, you may extend your visit as long as you follow our rules while you are here. I will entrust you to Abram's care and you can stay with him and his family."

"Why, thank you both. This is great." John shook the hands of both men.

He followed Abram to the church, which was being held in the basement of one member's house. John sat through his first Amish service, which he found not as enlightening as he expected. He saw Miriam sitting with her aunt and uncle and he supposed, her cousins across the room. With the very long and structured service, he realized that it was very different from his own church and that it would take getting used to.

When it was time for lunch, he was finally able to speak to Miriam. She was one of the women serving the food.

"It's so good to see you again," John said.

Miriam's eyes widened on looking at him, and then she grinned. "I am also happy to see you again."

After speaking briefly, they sat at their assigned places, which were opposite each other. John sat with the other men and boys and of course, Miriam sat with the women and girls. It was an odd setup but John didn't complain. He just finished his lunch and was grateful.

Miriam's uncle asked him what he was doing back in the Amish community but when he explained, he received no encouragement whatsoever. After introducing himself and explaining his situation to a few other people, John realized that what he was doing was not the most popular thing. Although they seemed to be excited about him wanting to join the Amish, they also expressed concern about him being able to give up his worldly ways.

After lunch was over, they continued with the service but once it was complete, Abram invited John to stay for a singing."

Abram shrugged. "You might enjoy it. It's for all of the single young people. That's how I met my wife."

"Well, can I invite a friend?"

"I see that you have your eye on an Amish girl and I don't know how well that will set with the bishop since you are an *Englischer*."

John nodded. "There's that word again. "

"You're an outsider now so just be careful," Abram cautioned him.

John nodded and took Abram's advice. But he did choose to stay for the singing and he managed to convince Miriam to do the same. There they were able to talk between group songs and frolicking. She shared her heart with him and John with her, his heart. Miriam was attracted to John's kind and God-fearing nature and John was attracted to her vulnerability as an insecure orphan.

"Trust in God," John whispered in her ear. "And your life will be filled with faith and strength."

But they noticed that they were being watched and that the faces behind those eyes were not friendly.

Chapter Five

After the singing, John walked Miriam back to her house. Miriam enjoyed John's company and Miriam even laughed for the first time since the death of her parents. Since John was very patient and gentle, Miriam felt safe with John.

John stopped walking and faced Miriam. "I think your life is about to get better."

Miriam stopped also. "It already has since you came."

John started to walk again. "I've learned so much about this way of life since I've been here."

"It's different I know," Miriam said as she followed closely behind him. "Not everything is bad, but not everything is good either."

"I can certainly understand that. But you are one of the good things it has produced," John said.

Miriam couldn't help but to smile and John smiled back at her. John's eyes seemed to dance in the moonlight and she was drawn closer to him. The more they talked, the closer she felt to him, like she had known him all of her life.

"A week ago I chose not to join the Amish

church."

"Really? Why?"

"I have quite a few concerns and I'm not sure I'm ready to commit. You don't know everything you're getting yourself into." She shook her head.

"That's why I'm here. I want to do God's will but I must know exactly what I'm getting myself into before I join." John paused. "Don't worry."

"I've been given three months to change my mind. In the fall there will be another baptism and if I refuse, I'll be shunned." Miriam looked sad. "I have already lost my parents and if I'm not careful, I'll lose everyone else too."

"Don't worry. No matter what, I'll be here for you." John took her hand and stared into her eyes. "You'll never lose me."

As they neared Miriam's house, they heard a rustling amongst the trees.

Someone was watching them.

Chapter Six

"Who is there?" Miriam called out.

A woman came up behind them. Miriam's heart beat faster as she realized it was her neighbor.

"Miriam King, is that you out here in the dark alone with a young man?"

"I apologize. I didn't know uh-" John started.

Miriam blurted out, "We were just talking. John is only a visitor."

"I know who he is. He's an *Englischer*; that's what he is," the woman spat out.

"I'm sorry but he is a very good man, a man of God and he was just making sure that I arrive at home safely," Miriam explained.

"Hmph," the woman said and turned up her nose. "We shall see about that."

Once the woman disappeared through the bushes, Miriam was relieved.

After letting out a deep breath, Miriam sped up the walk to her house. "We'd better hurry. I'm sure there will be trouble to follow."

John agreed and hurried to deliver Miriam to her doorstep. Miriam found the kerosene lamp on the porch and John lit it before disappearing into the shadows.

Chapter Seven

John found it difficult to sleep that night. Although he had been enjoying his stay with the Amish and feeling more in touch with God overall, the problem he was having was with Miriam. As an outsider, no one seemed to approve of their growing relationship. Sadly, he had the most honest of intentions and actually imagined himself settling down with the beautiful Miriam. But no one would allow him to say that or feel that about her because he was not yet Amish.

That night in the guest bedroom of Abram's home, John prayed for clarity. He was still undecided on whether or not he would join the Amish church, but mainly because of the way they were treating Miriam. He only wanted her to be happy after being sad for so long. He made up his mind to rectify the situation the next day; he would tell her that he loved her.

John woke up at the sound of the rooster crowing and hearing Abram's children running about the house. After washing up and getting dressed, he ran downstairs and out the front door. He and Abram started working out in the field while Abram's wife and children milked the cows and collected eggs.

As he worked alongside Abram, he said, "I'm thinking about telling Miriam that I love her."

"You love her?" Abram stopped chopping the crops. "What do you plan to do about that?"

"I'm hoping that she will agree to marry me." John grinned, excitedly. He was just becoming accustomed to the idea himself and he liked saying it.

"That will never happen unless you become Amish," Abram said, pulling his own beard.

"There is a really good chance now that I will become Amish." John felt satisfied with his answer.

"A really good chance is not good enough," Abram said, without even looking up.

After the crops were chopped, John walked over to Miriam's house. His heart felt light, and he imagined himself proposing to Miriam. He just hoped that she wouldn't refuse his offer of marriage. But from all their interactions from the past, he could find no cause for her to say no.

He saw the door to her house half-open. As he approached the door, he could hear a voice. "We've heard reports of you getting close with the newcomer." John peered inside and saw that the speaker was one of the elders that the Bishop had introduced him as Father Graber.

He was speaking to Miriam.

Father Graber's voice was cold. "While all people who speak God's word are allowed in our community, the young women should ensure that they are following the tradition and should mingle with their own people, rather than a stranger from outside."

John could see the solemn expression on Miriam's face. There was no smile or light there. Instead, Miriam merely kept her head bowed.

John debated whether to confront the elder or to let them close it as an internal matter. He realized that however much he loved the community, he was still an outsider. Besides, he didn't want Miriam to get into trouble.

"I hope it is clear to you."

"Yes Father."

"Good, I will take leave now, child."

John concealed himself when Father Graber left the house. Once the Father was out of earshot, he went inside.

Miriam was in tears. As soon as she saw him, she told him to leave.

"Just go, please. I don't want you here. I don't want to be seen with you. I have enough trouble with the elders. They are already against me", Miriam said.

"I'll go but I'm sorry; I can't leave you like this," John pleaded.

Miriam dried her tears and asked, "Why are you so concerned about me?"

"It's because I love you," John blurted out.

Miriam gasped in shock. John could see her crumpling her handkerchief tightly. She turned her gaze away."It isn't appropriate for us to be seen together. Please leave."

John felt totally defeated, but he could not refuse her plea. And with a sigh, he left the house. He still did not know if she shared his feelings or not. But he wondered if his straightforwardness had embarrassed her. Guilt began to infiltrate his soul.

God, what have I done?

Chapter Eight

Miriam walked around the room, thinking of what John had just said. She pondered the words in her head, over and over again. Eventually, she began to come to terms with John's disclosure.

When her aunt and uncle approached her about what they heard, she decided to defend him. Perhaps, standing up to them was the answer to these attacks.

"He has done nothing wrong and technically neither have I. If I have not been baptized yet, then I am still in *Rumspringa*," she said quietly, trembling in fear.

"You cannot claim that forever," Isaac said, shaking his finger at her. "You've been given grace until the fall. Not a moment longer."

"I understand but John is the one person who has shown that he cares about me. He may not be familiar with all of our rules but he has been trying." Miriam looked down. "He actually may want to be Amish."

"Him wanting it is not enough," Sarah said, with her lips twisted and her arms crossed against her chest.

"But for the first time since *Daed* and *Mudder* died, I am happy." Miriam turned on her heels and faced her uncle. "He is the only one who listens to me when I talk about my parents, the only one who comes to visit me. No one else comes around anymore, not since the week of the funeral."

"Is that what this is all about? You want company?" Isaac asked.

"Yes."

Aunt Sarah said, "Then do it the right way. Choose an Amish boy and get engaged, get baptized and get married."

Miriam shut down. She was tired of debating when clearly she was getting nowhere. She realized there was nothing she could say that would change their closed minds. There was nothing she could do.

She had failed.

Chapter Nine

Miriam tossed and turned all night, thinking about John's words and also the elder's words. As soon as she woke up the next morning, her decision was clear. They could no longer defend each other individually. If she expected to be happy, they had to stand together. There was no other way. So she slipped out of the house before anyone got up and walked down to Abram's house.

***

'Please leave.'

The words were still ringing in John's ears. He realized that he was foolish to let his feelings take the better of him. They were two worlds apart and just confessing his love was not enough. But if he expected to have any kind of future with her, they had to fight against these forces together. If she cared for him, she would have to stand with him just as he was willing to stand with her. He was sitting on Abram's front porch when he saw Father Graber coming.

Father Graber said, "I appreciate your intentions to learn with us, but there are certain boundaries that shouldn't be crossed."

John said, "Sure, I think I know what you

are implying. But I assure you that-"

"There is no assurance you can possibly give me," the elder said.

"I didn't come to cause any trouble," John said, humbly.

The elder said, "Good. Then I understand that you will no longer be meeting Miriam."

John was crushed at the thought, realizing that his relationship with Miriam was the icing on the cake for his Amish stay. However, she hadn't reciprocated his feelings and had told him to stay away. Maybe it was all for the better. "Yes, I will no longer meet Miriam."

"Oh, you will meet Miriam!" A voice spoke up.

John and the elder turned around and found Miriam in the doorway. She walked across to John. "John, do you really mean what you said back at my house?" Her eyes searched his face.

"Yes, I did." John nodded. He was numb, still stunned by her presence.

"Well, I am here to tell you that I feel the same way you do. It just took me a while to realize it."

John was elated. "Really. Do you love me too?"

Miriam nodded as the tears ran down her gentle face.

The elder coughed. "A moment please. The *ordung* will never accept an *Englischer* marrying our girl. I forbid it."

John was deflated. "But, I stayed here because I eventually wanted to join the Amish community."

Father Graber contorted his face. "I don't think a person who is willfully ignoring our sacred customs will be allowed in our community. In fact, I will recommend the elders against your inclusion."

John looked at Miriam's innocent face and felt like he was in a nightmare. His beloved Miriam was slipping out of his reach, and he couldn't do anything about it.

Miriam spoke up. "If John is going, so will I."

John's eyes widened in surprise.

Miriam continued. "There is no one for me here. John has been the only person in the last few months who cared enough to ask how I was doing, the only one who cared to feel what I was feeling."

Father Graber gave an angry look at Miriam. "So be it." And he walked out in a huff.

Miriam looked at John questioningly. John reassured her. "You don't have to worry. I am here to take care of you."

"Forever?"

"Forever and always."

Chapter Ten

That evening after her family tried to convince her that she was making a big mistake. Miriam packed her things while John waited outside for her. When she came outside with her bags, Sarah and Isaac followed behind her.

"I love you both," Miriam said as she glanced back over her shoulder.

"And don't worry; I will take good care of your niece."

"What do you know about taking care of her?" Sarah said.

"I know that I love her with all my heart," John replied.

Isaac stepped forward. "And what does that mean? What are your plans for her?"

"We will be getting married right away and who knows, in time, maybe we will be allowed to come back." John smiled, and then waved as he turned to his soon to be bride.

Miriam felt a sudden pang at the thought of leaving her Amish community. This had been her life and it was coming to a close. She looked up at John and felt reassured. He was her life now.

The future would be uncertain, but there was one thing she was certain of as John took her in his strong arms.

His love.

END OF PART 1

2: BREAKING AMISH TRADITION II

Chapter One

The angry clouds gathered overhead as John and Miriam fled the Amish community. Filled with fear, doubt and pain, they trudged through the puddles, past farms and buggies to come to the end of the road.

The words of the elder echoed in Miriam's head, "We will never allow you to marry an *Englischer*..." And as John held up Miriam's frail, wet body, she wept and whimpered about the implications for her future. *Had they made the right decision?* Only God knew the answer. The first thing they needed to do, however, was to find a place to stay. John went back to the same hotel that he stayed in a few days prior and checked in with two separate hotel rooms.

"Don't worry," he said. "Tomorrow we will find a place to get married; if that's okay with you, that is." John wanted to be reassuring. He knew that this was a big change for Miriam and he wanted the transition to be as smooth as possible.

"That would be perfect," Miriam said.

John opened the door and showed Miriam to her room. "I hope this is okay for you."

Miriam fluttered her eyelashes. "Yes, it's fine."

John could barely concentrate on what he was doing while looking at his future wife.

"I'm going to give you a few minutes to freshen up and put your things down, but I'll be back for you in a little while. We must find something to eat. I'm sure you're hungry."

"I am just a little."

John left Miriam in her room and went down the hall to his own room. He had a million emotions all swirling around inside him. He had won the girl of his dreams and he was excited about the new relationship. But at the same time, she had been put away, put out of her way of life; and he knew that was painful for her. Likewise, he had wanted to give the Amish lifestyle a chance and now it had been snatched from them both. Yes, it was a day of mixed emotions, a bittersweet victory. He took a deep breath, went to wash his hands and prepare himself to have dinner with his fiancé. *Fiancé*: the word rolled off his tongue easily.

John looked at himself in the bathroom mirror and saw that he looked tired. He had been under so much stress the past few hours and even the past few days. Although he learned so much from the Amish and had so much peace on one hand, trying to have a relationship with Miriam on Amish territory had caused so much stress on the other hand. He was glad that all of the hiding and whispering was over and that she had decided to come with him. He hoped with everything in him that they both made the right decision and that Miriam would not change her mind.

John went back to Miriam's room and knocked on the door. She came to the door without her kapp and he was taken aback. He almost didn't recognize her; she was so beautiful he could hardly believe it. Her golden hair bounced about her shoulders and her eyes lit up at the sight of him.

"You look amazing," he said.

"Thank you. This will take some time getting used to, though."

John smiled and took her hand. He led her out the front door and down the street to a small restaurant. There they ordered chicken entrée and sodas to drink.

The two of them sat talking and quietly staring into each other's eyes.

"Are you sure you want to get married tomorrow?" John paused. "I don't want you to feel pressured."

"I do feel a little confused about some the things that have happened and about some of the things I see out here in the world." Miriam looked around her. "But I am not confused about my love for you."

John held her hand and squeezed it.

"I just hope you can adapt to this new world." John chuckled.

But Miriam did not laugh back. "Me too," she said.

Chapter Two

Miriam woke up in a cold sweat. She looked around, and then realized where she was. Her safe Amish community was far behind and much adventure lay ahead. She smiled, optimistic about life for the first time in so long. She was glad that she had met John, even under the stressful circumstances. She leaped out of bed, not knowing what to do first.

After showering and getting dressed, she waited for John to come and when he knocked, she was ready.

"Good morning, my love," he said. "Take all your things because we won't be coming back here.

"Good morning," Miriam answered, brushing her long flowing hair out of her face.

"Well I've already called my job and told them that I won't be in for the rest of the week. So I'm all yours."

Miriam giggled. "I hope that won't be too much trouble."

"No, not at all. I've accumulated a lot of time off. Besides we need this time to get ourselves together."

"What shall we do first?" Miriam asked, excitedly.

"The first thing we must do is go home

and get a marriage license."

"Home?"

"Back to Philadelphia. I don't live here in Lancaster. My job, my apartment and my family are all in the city of Philadelphia," John explained as they walked towards the stairs.

Miriam wanted to know everything about him. "What about your family?"

"Well, there's my mom and my brother and they're both in Philadelphia. Along with my best friend, David. You'll love him because he's a funny guy."

Miriam stared at him.

"We'll take a taxi, the train, and then another taxi." And so they did until they ended up on the busy streets of Philadelphia, with honking horns and screeching tires, tall buildings, fire trucks, police sirens, more noise than Miriam could stand. Miriam was understandably overwhelmed.

Their first stop was to apply for the marriage license. "Three days," the clerk said.

Next, he took her to his mother's house to introduce her. "Miriam, this is my mother, Ms. Elizabeth Calhoun and mother, this is Miriam, my fiancé."

Elizabeth began to stumble. "Your what-fiancé? Are you out of your mind?"

"I love her, Mom," John explained.

"You're gone for not even a whole week and this is what you tell me. You said you were going to stay with the Amish to seek the Lord's direction." Elizabeth threw her hands into the air in exasperation. "Not going for a love connection."

John put both hand into his pant pockets and rocked back and forth on his heels. "I did and I suppose this too is part of God's plan."

"Oh my goodness." Elizabeth fell backwards, almost fainting, but John caught her.

"Are you okay?" he asked, helping his mother to her feet.

"I guess so." Elizabeth's face softened.

"I'm sorry but we're in love so with or without your approval, we'll be getting married." He looked at Miriam and waited for confirmation.

Miriam nodded.

John continued, "As soon as possible... so three days from now."

Elizabeth peered at them both. "What is the hurry?"

"We just want to be together as man and wife." John shrugged, smiling.

Elizabeth looked directly at Miriam. "Young lady, do you have anything to say?"

Miriam smiled. "I would be honored to be a part of your family."

"Of course." Elizabeth sighed, and then turned back to her son. "So what exactly do you need me to do?"

"Well, we have three days to wait for the

license so maybe you can help her to get ready. You know, help her go shopping. I've already told David. I'm going to call my brother and meet with Pastor Brown down at the church."

"Wait a minute." Elizabeth put her hand up. "Do you really have time for all of this? What about your job?"

"I've got some time off. Don't worry. I'll take care of everything." John reached into his pocket for his wallet and pulled out a debit card. He slipped it into his mother's hand. "Here, I've got some money saved so let her get whatever she needs for the wedding and in general."

"I don't know. What does she need?"

"She's not Amish anymore. She has nothing suitable so she'll need everything," John said, taking Miriam's hand.

Elizabeth turned to address Miriam again. "Is that all right with you, Miriam?"

"Yes, I'm excited." Miriam nodded, not exactly sure what this shopping spree would entail.

Before long John had disappeared into the city streets, leaving Miriam in the capable hands of Elizabeth. Their first stop was Macys Department Store and Miriam was so excited to actually be shopping. She tried on jeans and T-shirts for the first time in her life, capri pants and even shorts, although she giggled with embarrassment. She enjoyed trying on a number of different outfits and spinning around in front of Elizabeth who found herself caught up in the excitement as well. Shopping was a new experience for Miriam and she loved every minute of it.

Her clothes had always been sewn either by herself or by her mother. She didn't know what it was like to wear clothes that were bought from a store. She didn't know what it was like to not have her head covered or to walk with bare arms or bare legs, bright colors or designs. These things were never allowed back where she came from. It was all so different but most of it seemed harmless enough to Miriam.

She whirled and twirled and at the end of the day had a great start to a new wardrobe.

"I'm glad you're having fun but the next thing that we must do is find a wedding dress for you." Elizabeth looked her up and down. "I know the perfect little boutique on the other side of town."

Sure enough, they took the bus further downtown and went into a small wedding boutique. It was elegantly decorated and the salesperson was very friendly. She, along with Elizabeth tried to help Miriam to find something that fit her personality and style. But that task was very difficult considering Miriam had no experience with having her own individual style. In fact, where she had come from individualism was not allowed. So after trying their best to accommodate, they both helped

Miriam to choose a dress. Finally, they decided on a very simple traditional white, full lace dress; it was long in the front and had a flowing train in the back, with puffy Victorian style sleeves and a high collar. It was perfect. Miriam and Elizabeth smiled as she turned back and forth in the mirror.

Three days, Miriam thought as she headed back to Elizabeth's house to meet up with John.

Heading for home, Miriam left, complete with a wedding dress, matching shoes and purse, and even a darling pair of clip-on pearl earrings and a matching necklace. Miriam had never worn jewelry before so she felt special and glamorous.

On the way back, the excitement began to wear off as she thought of her family who would not get a chance to attend the wedding. Tears came to her eyes as she thought about her parents and how much she missed them. Would they be ashamed of her now? Had she disappointed them? Was she ruining her life?

Miriam hoped that she had made the right decision. She would know for sure in three days.

Chapter Three

When they finally returned from their shopping adventure, they settled down in the den, excited and waiting for John. Miriam tried her best to relax, although she had many things on her mind. Not long after, they heard his voice calling for them.

Miriam quickened as she heard his voice. As John approached her heart beat faster. Miriam was so happy to see him. It was as if it was a dream.

"I missed you." John said, pulling her into his arms.

"I missed you too," she said, loosening herself from his grasp.

"How did the shopping go?"

"I guess we did okay. Your mother drove me all over the city and we got quite a few things. I'm just not used to dressing like that but I imagine I'll get used to it sooner or later."

"It will take some time but I'm willing to wait." John reached into his back pocket and kneeled down in front of Miriam.

Miriam's heart began to beat harder. *Could it be?*

"Miriam, ever since I met you I've been absolutely taken by you. At first I thought that it would go away, that it was unimportant, just a fleeting fancy for a pretty girl, but after talking to you and getting to know you, I realized that it was more than that. You are the one for me."

"Oh, John."

John opened the box to reveal a beautiful gold ring accented with small diamonds. "Miriam, will you marry me?"

"Yes, I absolutely will." Tears began to run down Miriam's face.

"I hope those are tears of joy," John said, putting his hand up to her face.

Miriam grasped his hand and held tight. "They definitely are. I'm so happy that I found you. But at the same time, I'm a little sad that my parents are not here to share this with me."

"I'm sorry too." John held his head down.

Miriam put her hands into his hair and rubbed his head.

"I just want to make you happy," he said.

"You already have." Miriam batted her eyelashes.

"I know that God has brought us together." John stood to his feet. "I just want to show you everything in my world."

Miriam nodded, not knowing exactly what he meant at the time.

But by the next day, she knew. It started with dressing herself in her new clothes and as she did she felt totally inappropriate. The necklines were too low; the sleeves were too short; the hemlines were too short. At times she even felt naked; it felt so different baring her arms and legs in public.

"You look so beautiful," John frequently said, as he gazed into her eyes.

"Thanks," she always said, twirling around, shyly in front of John and his mother. But she didn't feel beautiful; she felt ashamed. She packed away her Amish garments, with their dull colors, void of design and her prayer *kapps*, the few that she brought with her. So she forced herself into the contemporary clothes, although she wasn't really comfortable in them.

Then there were the things that she saw others do. She saw children and teenagers disrespecting their elders. She watched and she saw things available to her that never were before. She got to wear her hair loose around her shoulders and John's mother even helped her to apply some makeup to her face.

"Just a little around your bright eyes and some color on your lips," John's mother. "You've got to be ready for the wedding."

She imagined her wedding and smiled. "Yes," she agreed. "I'll be ready."

Miriam and John walked a few blocks down to the theatre to watch a movie, which was both strange and scary. She wasn't really sure how she felt about sitting in the dark with strangers, while loud sounds surrounded her from all angles. With all of the freedom she had, to go and do as she pleased, without worrying how or why she was doing it made Miriam feel a little guilty.

She thought about Mudder and Daed. Would they be upset in their graves if they could see her now? They got into John's Toyota and went out to eat at a seafood restaurant. The food was tasty and being with John was romantic. But although she laughed and talked and saw her ring sparkle in the moonlight, she couldn't seem to reconcile herself to the new world.

Chapter 4

John yawned and stretched at the sight of the morning sun coming through his apartment windows. He whispered a quick prayer, and then went off to shower and get dressed. He looked in the mirror and decided that he needed to shave. He remembered how close he had come to deciding to grow a beard when he stayed with the Amish. Abram was about his age and already had quite a thick one. Now that he and Miriam had been kicked out, he wouldn't need it.

John thought of Miriam and how this change was affecting her. Then he picked up his cell phone and the first thing he saw was a photograph of Miriam's smiling face. Seeing her sent a funny feeling through him. Oh, how he loved her.

After much coaxing the day before, he had taken several natural shots of her. He and his mother had encouraged her to model her new clothes in order to get a feel for them.

"They all fit you so nicely," his mother had said.

"That's my future wife," he'd said, grabbing her and beginning to tickle her.

She'd laughed a little, and then released herself from his hold.

He'd noticed that Miriam seemed a little uneasy at times but deep inside he hoped that she would relax a little and start to have more fun. Coming from an Amish community, he knew that it would take time for her to adjust but he hoped he could help with her smooth transition into society. He knew she missed her family and he tried everything to get her mind off her problems. With only two days left before the wedding, he was determined to make her happy, at least as much as possible.

John showed up at his mother's home to pick up Miriam. She was wearing a long, flowered lavender sundress with purple flowers. "Those violets look so good on you."

"Thank you. You know I love flowers but I've never been able to wear them before." Miriam did a little spin.

Elizabeth threw her head back and laughed. "She's something special, son."

Miriam's eyes seemed to dance in the sunlight and John couldn't help himself from wanting to kiss her. He lifted her up off the floor and spun her around in his arms, then brought his lips close to hers. But Miriam, sensing what was coming turned away and jumped out of his embrace. She straightened her clothes, put a frown on her face, and then excused herself from the room.

John and Elizabeth looked at each other in surprise.

John's mother gently patted him on the back. "Be careful not to move so fast. Try to understand that she's probably not accustomed to such outward signs of affection."

John nodded. "No, I guess not…"

"She'll probably come around in her own time but will that be enough for you in the meantime?" John's mother put one hand on her hip and shook her head.

That same evening John took Miriam to his church for Wednesday evening Bible study. After service, they all gathered outside the sanctuary and he introduced Miriam to his pastor, who spoke with them privately.

"So you are the little lady who will be joined to Brother John in matrimony? I must say that I'm honored that you two chose me to do the ceremony," the pastor said.

Miriam leaned in close. "I have a question for you, Father."

The pastor chuckled. "Why, go right ahead."

"You talked about salvation being a free gift and I never heard that before."

"I'm glad I could share some enlightenment from God's word," he said.

"Where I'm from, we aren't really encouraged to read the Bible for ourselves. We get our understanding from the Bishop and from the ordnung."

"Yes, I've heard that." The pastor glanced

over at John.

John whisked her away to introduce her to a few of his friends, including David.

David shook Miriam's hand, although she looked hesitant about it. "It's so good to finally meet the girl John was willing to change his whole life for."

"It's a pleasure to meet you, David," Miriam said, dryly.

David didn't seem to mind the awkward silence and went on with his usual stream of charming anecdotes and jokes. John nudged him in the ribs but that didn't stop him. David's laughter was contagious and before long, Miriam was laughing too. John let out a sigh of relief.

"So you're his ex-best friend?"

"Ex best friend?" David chuckled. "What did I mess up now?" he asked, looking over at John.

John shrugged his shoulders. "I don't know why she would ask if you were my ex-best friend."

"Because I'll be your wife soon and I should be your best friend."

John and David laughed simultaneously but a moment of worry overshadowed John.

Chapter Five

With one more day before the wedding, Miriam began to feel more excited. She would finally be a bride and not just any bride but she would be marrying the love of her life. She was grateful that *Gott* had blessed her with a man as caring and as kind as John. In fact, the more she thought about it and the more time they spent together, the more she was convinced that he was her soul mate.

John picked her up early that morning, complete with an armful of red roses.

"Thank you; you're so sweet," she said.

John smiled. "It's easy to be at my best around you."

Miriam blushed at John's words.

John took her hand and led her to his car, then opened the door for her.

Miriam slid into the passenger seat, closed her eyes and tried to relax. She glanced over at John as he was driving and they talked along the way. As he spoke, she hung onto John's every word.

"Where are we going?"

"I want to take you somewhere special," he said.

"Anywhere you take me will be special."

"I was thinking that I'd like to take you to

an amusement park. I want to see you laugh and have fun."

"That sounds interesting I guess. I kind of always wanted to see what that would be like, going to an amusement park." Then she looked down at herself. "Is what I'm wearing okay?"

"It's perfect. You're perfect," John said, admiring her.

Miriam wore a pair of relaxed fit jeans and a white t-shirt with a daisy on it. Within minutes, they pulled up at the crowded park and went inside, holding hands.

"Let's go to the roller coaster first." John said. "It's my favorite."

Miriam nodded, and followed John onto one of the biggest roller coasters there.

"This is one of the park's main attractions," John explained as they climbed into its car.

John and Miriam whirled around on the ride, with the breeze blowing through their hair. Miriam couldn't believe the funny feeling she got in her stomach as they went speeding down the track or the sensation as they rounded the curves. Miriam squealed and screamed and clung to John's strong, muscular arms. Her heart pounded with happiness. As John and Miriam left the ride, arm in arm, they were more in love than ever.

Miriam giggled as they walked. "I had the best time."

John stopped to look at Miriam. "I'm glad you enjoyed yourself."

"Shhh." Miriam stood on her tiptoes and put her finger to John's lips. "I'm glad I'm going to soon be your wife."

"Not as glad as I am." John said, gently touching her cheek.

John turned on his heels and started to walk again, holding Miriam's hands.

They stopped at a concession stand where John bought Miriam a hot dog and fries and a funnel cake, while John ordered a hamburger and cotton candy for himself. They sat at a small outdoor table and stared into each other's eyes.

John gave Miriam a quick peck on the lips, which pleasantly surprised Miriam. She wanted to save that warm feeling for the rest of the day.

Chapter Six

As the day went on, Miriam began to take her eyes off of John and notice things that made her uncomfortable again. Once on a water ride, she saw that a few of the park's visitors wore only skimpy bikinis.

"Do you see what they're wearing?" Miriam shook her head in disgust. "They're practically naked."

John shook his head also. "Unfortunately, that's true. When I work with the youth in the community out of and sometimes even in the church, the young people seem to have no inhibitions at all."

"But look at them over there. They're practically engaging in public fornication," Miriam spat out, pointing to a teenage couple who were kissing and fondling each other by the front gate.

Miriam began to feel sick in her stomach. Seeing such behavior made her skin crawl. She remembered her loving parents and her strict, Amish upbringing.

John said, "I'm sorry but sadly, it's the condition of the world."

Miriam folded her arms across her chest as she considered the situation. "In the Amish community, this would never be accepted."

John shrugged. "I know you're right and that's one of the reasons that I was so interested in joining them in the first place. But now I guess that's not an option."

And although Miriam accepted his assessment of the worldly plight, she believed that something was very wrong with that picture. *Am I supposed to be like that?*

That evening as they drove home, Miriam was quieter than usual. This was her last day as an unmarried woman and she was having second thoughts. It was clear that John was a wonderful man but she wasn't sure she could live this married life outside in this crazy, mixed-up world.

Chapter Seven

John couldn't help but realize that something had upset Miriam. With only a half day left before the wedding, he certainly wanted to keep her happy. Not only did he feel compassion for her and the grief she'd experienced in losing her parents, but he also identified with most of her feelings regarding moral decay. He just wasn't totally convinced that the Amish had it all figured out. And from the way they'd treated them during his last visit, the Amish were no longer high on his "respect" list. Still he could feel the tension in the relationship over the guidelines. He wondered if the Amish ever felt that kind of tension.

Once they'd arrived safely back at his mother's house and Miriam went to take a shower, John took advantage of the time he had alone with his mother.

John leaned against the wall. "May I speak to you for a moment, mom?"

"Of course, dear." His mother sat down on the couch and called him over. "What's wrong?"

"It's just Miriam." John came over and sat beside his mother.

"You want out?"

"No, it's not that." John shook his head. "I

want in but I think she's confused. I don't know…"

"You think she'll call off the wedding?"

"I'm not really sure either way. I don't know if she'll go through with it or not but I'm sure she has her doubts."

"Do you want to marry someone who has doubts?"

"I want to marry Miriam. I love her. But she is so devoted to the Amish lifestyle and I'm just not sure that what I can offer her will ever be enough."

John's mother shook her head. "That's definitely not the best way to begin a new relationship."

"I want to do the right things but what can I do if she wants to go?"

John's mother looked him straight in the eyes. "If she wants to go, you'll have to let her."

John listened to his mother's words but secretly, he decided to take matters into his own hands. He would prove her how wrong the Amish had been, and hopefully, send her flying into his arms for consolation.

When Miriam came out of the bathroom, she was wearing a long maxi dress with a crop jacket and red sandals.

"I like your outfit," he said.

"Thanks." Miriam spun around quickly. "Your mother helped me to pick it out."

John rubbed his two hands together. "I

actually wanted to talk to you about going to get the rest of your things."

Miriam raised her eyebrows. "Getting the rest of my things?"

"I know you didn't have a chance to take everything you wanted to bring so…"

Miriam put up her hand. "I don't think it's a good idea to go back right now."

"Why not?" John asked, determined to show how unreasonable her people were being.

"I don't think they're ready to see me yet. They're certainly not going to be ready to accept my new lifestyle so I think it's best to just stay away."

John followed Miriam around the room. "But isn't that just avoiding the issue?"

"I don't call it that." Miriam put two hands on her hips, something she'd learned in the last few days. "I call it being respectful of their beliefs."

"But what about our beliefs and our love?" John remained right on her heels. "Doesn't that count for anything?"

Miriam spun around. "Of course it does but…"

"But you mean your aunt and uncle and the whole community have the right to throw us out for being in love and then turn their backs on us and we should be afraid to see them? I don't think we should be playing their game."

Tears began to run down Miriam's face as

her heart was breaking. "It's not a game, John. This is my life and those people you refer to are my family and friends, people I care a great deal about. Just because I've left the community to marry you doesn't mean that I don't still agree with some or most of what I was taught my whole life."

John threw both hands into the air in mock surrender. "But how can you agree with people who would keep us apart?"

"But not for bad reasons. They're trying to protect my honor. There is no honor out here in this world. Absolutely none."

John could see Miriam getting angry, but he couldn't stop himself. "That's not true. You *don't* need to be Amish to have integrity or character."

"But it seems that you *do* have to be Amish to have rules that enforce it." Miriam walked out of the room, slamming the door behind her. "Maybe I've made a mistake."

Chapter Eight

Pacing back and forth on the hardwood floors, Miriam was infuriated. She couldn't believe John's arrogance. How dare he presume that her aunt and uncle and the community that she once adored were at fault. Although she didn't agree with everything they did, she still respected their customs and their intentions. *Why couldn't John understand that?* She didn't know what had gotten into him but suddenly she was less confident about their impending marriage. How could the two of them have a life together unless they were in agreement?

Miriam sat in the guest room sulking and wishing that her parents were here to help her make the most important decision of her life. Would she still marry John? To be honest, at this point, she didn't know. Her heart felt one way but her head felt another way. But with only hours to go before the wedding, what could she do about it? She snapped her fingers as an idea struck her. She would appeal to John's mother and let her talk some sense into him.

"Mrs. Calhoun, may I speak to you for a moment, please?"

"Certainly," Ms. Calhoun continued to prepare dinner, with her back turned to Miriam.

Miriam sat down in one of the kitchen

chairs. "I want to marry your son but I don't think I can."

"Is that so?" Ms. Calhoun never stopped what she was doing. "And why not might I ask?"

"Because John and I do not have the same ideals." Tears began to stream down her face once more. "He is used to living in a more fast-paced world where there are revealing clothes, cars, and technology. But I believe in what my parents taught me before they lost their lives."

"And what exactly is that?" Ms. Calhoun peered at her. "No electricity for life?"

"The *ordnung* talks about more than just electricity and other modern conveniences being evil."

"So you do believe that the way we live is evil? Do you think this is a healthy way to start a relationship?" Ms. Calhoun threw her head back and laughed.

Miriam was surprised at her reaction and stood up.

"To tell you the truth, I don't think you two are well suited for one another. Don't get me wrong, I think you're a nice girl but my son deserves to be happy. And I think he'll be happier if he doesn't have to worry about what you're thinking and how you're feeling about the things that are important to him."

Miriam looked her in the eyes. "What are you saying?"

"It's okay to admit you two may have made a mistake."

Miriam felt defeated. It was the last hours before the wedding and her future mother-in-law was telling her to call the wedding off.

Chapter Nine

By the time Miriam returned to the guest room, she was even more distraught than ever. She didn't want to cancel the wedding; she loved John and wanted to be his wife. But at the same time she wanted the old fashioned values that she once found herself rejecting. She'd refused to get baptized a little over a week ago because she didn't agree with everything that the Amish stood for but after not agreeing with the standards of the world, she was grateful that the Amish stood for something. *Lord, give me clarity.*

She got down on her knees and prayed like she had never prayed before, pouring out her heart before *Gott*, and allowing His peace to fill her spirit. She asked God for guidance, and knew that He would be able to guide her. After a few minutes of soulful praying, she felt calm and relaxed. She decided to meet John, not to confront him, and not to call off the wedding, but simply to call a truce.

"It's time for us to stop attacking each other and work together," she said.

"I agree with that," John said, hugging her. "I'm so glad you're here. I thought I'd lost you forever."

"You almost did but what's inside me is stronger than what is on the outside. I've prayed about it and I believe the same about my people."

"What do you mean?"

"I believe that we should pray together for unity and strength."

"I think you're right. That's why I believe that you are indeed perfect."

"I'm not perfect- just focused for the first time in my entire life." Miriam stood in front of John, looking up to him. "Can't we try to reason with my people? You were interested in joining them once. Perhaps you could be interested again."

John pulled Miriam into his arms. "What do you want us to do?"

"We must pray and then go meet the elders," Miriam said.

John nodded in agreement.

The next day Miriam and John met at John's church and got married, having a very short but traditional marriage ceremony. John's brother walked Miriam down the aisle and David was John's best man. Mrs. Calhoun, although she was skeptical about the wedding, stood in as maître of honor. After their vows had been taken and they were declared as husband and wife, the celebration began.

After the wedding ceremony was over, they headed for Lancaster.

Chapter Ten

They arrived at the Bishop's house. The Bishop was surrounded with the other elders.

John spoke up first announcing their commitment as man and wife. He requested that they be allowed back into the Amish community.

Father Graber who was against them all along said, "This is an outrage, a disgrace, and a mockery of our institution. Miriam refused to be baptized, and then she ran off to marry outside. This is unacceptable."

"What harm can it do?" Miriam pleaded, "We're married now and very much in love."

Father Graber turned up his nose. "I am against inclusion. They are from the outside world. They are tainted and we do not want them to bring these evil things into our community."

John continued, "We do not want to cause any trouble, but we've been praying and seeking God's help in this matter...."

The elders began to mumble amongst themselves.

The Bishop interrupted. "Quiet down now. No matter what, Miriam was always one of us and John wanted to become a part of us. I am fine with their inclusion. Let me know what you all think."

John and Miriam looked at one another in shock. The elders continued to murmur amongst themselves. Some agreed, whereas others disagreed. There didn't seem to be reaching a conclusion. Miriam clutched John's arm tightly. Their future depended on the outcome of the discussion.

After a couple of minutes, one of the elders broke away and said to the Bishop. "We are unable to come to an agreement. Please advise what needs to be done."

"What makes you think that they are suitable or unsuitable for our community?"

Father Graber spoke up. "They went to the outside world and have lived amongst sinners. We cannot allow them in our community."

The Bishop smiled. "Think of it this way. They have seen the sins of the outside world, and indulged in it. Yet they have chosen to come back in spite of the temptations."

Father Graber said nothing. The Bishop continued. "Doesn't the holy book say that whoever has been forgiven little, loves little. And whose sins are most, yet forgiven, loves the most? As Amish we mustn't just preach it, we must live out these principles. They will be baptized in the fall and then they will join us."

John and Miriam were grateful for the Bishop's decision and hugged each other in joy.

The elders nodded their heads on listening to the Bishop and welcomed John and Miriam back into the community.

    John let out a sigh. "We've trusted God and we've been led home. I knew since the first day I met you that you were a part of my future and if we've been led here to a place of strength and faith, then the best is yet to come,"

    "Yes, my love, the best is yet to come." Miriam looked into her husband's eyes and for the first time, there was no fear, no loneliness and no doubt – only a love which came from deep within.

Epilogue

Miriam looked at the crowd that surrounded her and her chest bubbled with joy. It was finally fall and the last few months had been the happiest of her life. Now as she watched John being baptized, she realized that God had answered her prayers. John was now an Amish. She closed her eyes and thanked the Lord.

A quiet voice spoke at her shoulder. "It's your turn, Miriam."

Miriam stepped forward and glanced at John. He had a broad grin on his face. Miriam smiled back at him.

Everything was perfect.

THE END

3: THE WILDFLOWER BLOOMS

Amish Wildflower cast:

Sarah – an Amish girl

Maggie – Sarah's friend

Heather – Maggie's English friend

Ann – Sarah's sister

Jacob – an ex-Amish

Mary & Joshua – Sarah's parents

Chapter One

Wildflower was everything her parents, Joshua and Mary never expected. Named Sarah when she was born, it soon became clear that she was a "wildflower," - a beautiful wild thing that was everywhere and all at the same time. Ever since she was a young child, Sarah had been different and despite the constant attempts of her well-meaning parents, even at nineteen years old her wild spirit was never successfully tamed.

Here on the dance floor of a local nightclub, Sarah felt free and no one could contain her. After spending her entire life fighting containment in her Amish community, this was a new and exciting experience for her.

"Shake it, Wildflower. Shake it," Heather said, clapping her hands and spinning.

And Sarah moved her body to the tune of the blaring music. She'd never heard anything like this in her entire life but it was pleasant and it made her feel like moving. No music like that would ever be allowed where she came from, except the hymns or the faster paced songs they sang at the bi-monthly singings. She threw her head back and swung her hair like she saw the other girls doing.

Heather brought her a drink, and after taking a sip of it, her stomach began to turn. She had tried alcohol before but she didn't really like it. But she did like the option of being out at a party on a Friday night. Suddenly, she felt like a typical teenager and not like a sheltered Amish girl, doing her expected *rumspringa* rebellion right before choosing to get baptized. It was a vicious cycle and Sarah was determined to break it.

"Wildflower, let's go," Maggie called from the sidelines. "It's time to go." Maggie and Sarah were friends from the same Amish community.

"All right," Sarah said, pulling herself away from the crowd and walking out to Heather's car. She stumbled in the three inch stilettos that Maggie's friend, Heather had let her borrow. And she straightened the clothes that felt two sizes too small, although she noticed that all of the *Englischer* men seemed to give her compliments on the outfit.

"Aren't you ready to go?" Maggie asked, anxiously.

"To be honest, I've been ready. This dress is way too tight. It's cutting off my circulation." Sarah giggled.

Heather smirked, "I think it's a big hit."

"Are you kidding me? The men have only one thing on their minds and I'm not that stupid." Sarah shook her head. "But thanks anyway for letting me borrow it."

Heather shrugged her shoulders. "No problem. I don't know how you girls do it, wearing the same ugly dresses every day and those bonnets are hideous." Heather began to giggle uncontrollably.

Sadly, Sarah knew she was right but there was nothing she could do about changing her wardrobe at this time. She and Maggie had grown up together and were stuck in the same world, the world of being Amish.

"You'll never understand what we have to go through," Sarah said.

"Well, hopefully you'll get out of it as soon as you can, right?" Heather stuffed a wad of gum into her mouth as the three of them piled into her car.

"I'm certainly looking forward to it," Sarah answered and she meant it with her whole heart.

But Maggie was silent. It was just as Sarah thought. Maggie would probably just have a good time and in a few weeks give it all up for the same humdrum lifestyle. Sarah shook her head as she thought about it.

Heather stopped at a gas station so that they could all change clothes.

Once Sarah and Maggie hopped back into the car, their knapsacks were full of the worldly clothing, evidence that they had stepped away from their strict Amish upbringing.

Both Sarah and Maggie attempted to hand the knapsack back to Heather.

"You all can keep the clothes. It's no big

deal. I've gained a few pounds lately so they don't fit like they used to. And I've got plenty more where they came from. Besides you need them more than I do," Heather said examining their plain dresses.

"Thanks," Sarah and Maggie said in unison.

Then Maggie drove them back to the Amish community where they each ran to the fields back to their own houses, which were not far from each other. Sarah climbed up to her second-story bedroom and went into the window. Since she started doing it a couple of months ago, she had become a pro at it.

She tried not to wake her sister as she climbed inside, but unfortunately, it was inevitable.

"Are you just getting back?" Ann asked, annoyed.

Sarah lit a candle so she could see. "I'm afraid so," Sarah answered as she stepped out of her clothes. She took off her bonnet and let down her long, brown hair.

"Why must you keep going out every week, doing all of those horrible things?"

"I'm not doing anything horrible." Sarah sighed. "It's my right to go out and explore. It's *rumspringa*." Sarah pulled on her nightgown.

"But that doesn't mean you must go out to the world all of the time. It's very dangerous out there," Ann snapped.

Sarah whispered, "How would you know how dangerous it is if you've never been out there?"

"Because I've been told of the dangers," Ann said.

"Don't believe everything that you're told." Sarah rolled her eyes. "How else can I explore my options?"

"Options? The *ordnung* has all of our options," Ann spat out.

Sarah pursed her lips before speaking. "But what if I don't want to follow the *ordnung* or if I don't want to be Amish anymore?"

"Are you serious?" Ann pointed her finger at Sarah's face. "Personally, I think you're headed for trouble."

Sarah put her hands on her hips. "I don't know about all of that or whether or not I'll stay or go but I'll never know what I'm missing until I find out for myself."

"If you say so but I still don't see why you can't just pray about it," Ann huffed.

"I know you don't see and knowing you, you'll never see. Believe me, I've prayed about it. But I'm going out to search for my answers." Sarah spoke quietly, careful not to wake up her parents who were asleep down the hall.

Disgusted by her sister's attitude, Ann shook her head and pulled the covers up to her nose.

"Good night to you too," Sarah said.

She was used to having these altercations with her sister because they never saw eye to eye on many issues.

Sarah got into her own bed and drifted off to sleep, dreaming of what it would be like to not have to sneak around and dreaming about the day she'd have to tell her parents she would not be getting baptized.

Chapter Two

Jacob adjusted his tie and examined himself from all angles in the mirror. Being just six weeks away from completing his residency, he was on top of the world. For many long years he had waited to become a doctor and it was finally at his fingertips. The thought of saving lives made him tingle all over. It had been an arduous road with many valleys and rough days but in his heart he knew that it was worth it. He had sacrificed everything for the calling to heal the sick; if only his family and community had understood that.

He had a date with one of the nurses that worked on his floor but he wasn't very excited about it. No matter how hard he tried to dismiss his strict Amish upbringing, deep inside he still longed for it. And leaving the community as a teenager, he'd missed his turn at *rumspringa*. He'd missed the chance for courting and the innocence associated with it. Since he left the community, the rules had changed on the dating scene, taking on a more conditional and less commitment oriented meaning. He'd been unlucky in love a couple of times and was almost ready to call it quits. It seemed that in the outside world, romantic relationships were so complicated.

A few minutes later he was driving down the road with his date beside him. She was tall and lanky, with a traditional kind of attractiveness. From his peripheral vision, he could see that she could hardly keep her eyes off of herself. Every few minutes, she was looking at her reflection in the mirror attached to the sun visor.

He sighed as he thought to himself; here we go again – another shallow one.

"So how long did you know that you wanted to be a nurse?"

Raquel smacked her gum and said, "I didn't really want to be one but I just chose something to get my parents off my back."

"Oh, I see," Jacob said, obviously disappointed. Jacob would complete his residency soon and was considering accepting a permanent position at a prestigious hospital in the heart of the city.

"What about you? When did you decide that you would go for the big money?" Raquel joked.

Jacob didn't think that it was funny; he took his career aspirations very seriously. "Ever since I was very young, I've wanted to save lives but because I was Amish it wouldn't have been a possibility for me."

"So how did you get out?"

"It wasn't easy but I made it." Jacob didn't want to explain.

Raquel nodded and continued to chatter. The rest of the evening the date continued the same way it started, with minor conversation, empty laughs, and ended with Jacob wishing that it had never even happened. He finally went home to watch television alone. He wasn't sure what was happening to him but he just didn't enjoy the same kinds of things anymore. Despite his look of success, there was something inside him that ached for the way things used to be.

Chapter Three

The very next morning Sarah heard her mother calling them, "Wildflower, Ann, it's time to prepare breakfast."

Both Sarah and Ann came downstairs and lined up beside their mother to help in the kitchen.

"Why do you look so tired?" Mary asked, looking at Sarah.

"I guess I just need more rest," Sarah said.

"Be sure that you get your rest." Mary stared at her daughter's face, searching for clues.

"Oh *Mudder*, I doubt that," Sarah said.

"You do? Why would you doubt something like that?" Mary raised her eyebrows.

"I don't know. It's just that all of the boys I know seem the same," Sarah explained.

"One day you will calm down all of the wildness you have inside and you will want to settle down. You see?" Mary looked at Sarah skeptically.

Sarah smiled, not wanting to cause a confrontation, but she didn't respond.

Ann interjected, "I can't wait, *Mudder*. I already know how my wedding will be."

Sarah sighed so that no one could hear her and spent the rest of the day doing all the things she was told to do, and in her heart, she waited patiently for the evening.

That evening, like clockwork, Mary and

Joshua said good night and went upstairs to bed. Sarah then hurried upstairs with her sister, Ann, but as soon as Ann turned off the kerosene lamp, Sarah set out on her night's journey.

She left Ann in their bedroom, sleeping, and climbed down the side of her window once again, meeting Maggie at the same spot. The two of them waited for Heather together. But Heather was late and when she finally arrived, she didn't look so good. She was pale and complained that she was feeling nauseous and dizzy, although that didn't stop the girls from getting into Heather's car. But once that was safely off Amish property and onto the main road, Heather began to feel sick again.

Sarah eyed her curiously. "Are you sure you're okay?"

Heather shrugged. "I don't know. I'm feeling pretty bad." Heather opened the window and threw up onto the street.

"Eeeew," Sarah and Maggie said simultaneously.

"You're definitely not okay," Sarah said, pinching her nose and covering her mouth.

"Not at all," Maggie agreed. "Maybe we should go back."

Suddenly, Heather moaned loudly and fell forward in the driver seat, clutching her stomach."

"Forget about going home," Sarah said. "We'd better get her to the nearest hospital."

"I guess you're right," Maggie said, looking worried. "But how do we get her there?"

"I can drive," Sarah volunteered.

Maggie shook her head. "Are you serious?"

Sarah answered, "She showed me how to drive last time. Besides how hard can it be?"

Sarah traded spots with Heather and stared at the controls. She remembered that the left pedal was to make it stop and the right one was for the gas. It looked simple enough to her and she took over the driving for the few blocks to the hospital. She remembered passing by this hospital every single time she came out. Luckily, they were not pulled over by police because Sarah, of course, did not have a license. In fact, the only thing that she had experienced driving was her father's horse and buggy.

They pulled up by the emergency room ramp and a host of medical personnel came out to grab Heather.

As she and Maggie hurried to the waiting room, Sarah bumped into someone.

"Oh, I'm sorry," she said, looking up into one of the most handsome faces she'd ever seen. He was tall, dark-haired and dressed in doctor's scrubs.

"No, it's my fault," he said, attempting to steady her after she lost her balance. "You seem like you're in a hurry. Is everything all right, Ma'am?"

"Well, a friend of mine is sick so my friend and I brought her to the emergency room." Sarah moved around nervously.

Maggie stood behind her, covering her mouth from giggling.

"I see," Jacob said. "I hope your friend is all right."

"Thank you." Sarah smiled.

Jacob tilted his head sideways. "By the way, hope this isn't too personal but are you Amish?"

Sarah looked down at the way she was dressed. "The clothes gave me away, huh?"

Jacob chuckled. "Yep, they do it every time."

Sarah nodded.

"I remember those outfits well," he said.

Sarah squinted at Jacob. "What you mean, remember? You can't be Amish?"

Jacob grinned. "Well, no... Not anymore but I was. My name is Jacob."

"Hello, Jacob. I'm Sarah but everyone calls me Wildflower." Sarah offered her hand.

"That's very fitting." Jacob shook her hand.

Sarah blushed. "How did you become a doctor?"

"Actually, I'm a resident but in a few more weeks I'll be a full-fledged doctor. But to answer your question, I ran away to stay with my *Englischer* uncle. I was very fortunate that my father didn't force me to come back since I was under-aged. I guess he was just too grief stricken over my mother's death. I was lucky to have a way out," Jacob felt compelled to explain.

"Oh," Sarah said.

"But, it wasn't easy. My whole family still lives there," he said deep in thought.

Sarah asked, "Really?"

"Yes, I was shunned, and then excommunicated actually but I had a tough choice to make – family or medicine." Jacob swallowed hard.

At that moment Jacob was paged. "Sorry, I've got to go but it was really nice meeting you…uh… Wildflower."

Sarah was fascinated with their conversation and wanted to know more. "Wait, please."

Jacob turned around to hear what she had to say.

"What about my friend, Heather Beaumont?"

"I'm sure she should be fine but if you'd like, I'll check in on her for you as soon as I get a chance."

"Thanks; I would like that." Sarah watched Jacob walk away but wasn't sure why her heart was beating fast.

Maggie snapped her fingers in her face. "What was that all about?"

"I don't know. But I get the feeling that

I'll be seeing him again," Sarah said dreamily.

Maggie and Sarah found seats in the crowded waiting room, waiting and watching time. And there wasn't much time left because they knew they would have to leave soon. They felt so embarrassed because everyone was staring at them. Not having time to change into *Englischer* clothing made all the difference in Sarah's level of comfort. She didn't enjoy being a spectacle.

Finally, Jacob appeared, hovering over. Sarah hopped up and said, "This is my other friend, Maggie."

"Hello, Maggie. Listen, I don't have much time but I wanted you to know that your friend is doing okay now and that she'll be released shortly," Jacob said, looking just a bit agitated.

Both Sarah and Maggie sighed with relief.

"Thank you, thank you. But what was it, though? She was so sick earlier," Sarah asked.

Jacob had no smile on his face. "I'm afraid that your friend Heather is six months pregnant."

Chapter Four

Sarah couldn't believe her ears. As soon as Heather was released, Heather drove the girls back home in silence. There was nothing left to say. A night that had been planned for youthful frolicking had turned out to be a nightmare of sorts.

As Sarah finally crept into her own bed, she couldn't help but wonder what would happen to Heather. She now realized why Heather could no longer fit into her clothes comfortably and why she had chosen to give them away so quickly.

Still, the next morning was a Sunday and Sarah was up early, getting ready for the day's activities. She always enjoyed Sunday service, not only because of the Bishop's message but because she got to see her brothers, William, David, and John, and their families. Then there were the singings, in which she got to socialize with her peers; yet she thought of them all as hypocrites.

"Wildflower," Maggie whispered. "Can you believe what's happened to Heather?"

"Yes, and the same thing or worse can happen to us if we are not careful. My *Mudder* told me about *Englischers* and that's something we do not like about the world. How do they manage the mess? Like having babies without a husband?"

"It's called born out of wedlock," Maggie explained.

"I know what it's called but I don't know how she'll manage," Sarah said.

Maggie shrugged. "Shhh; here comes trouble."

And with those words, both girls closed their mouths as Ann approached them.

Ann pointed her finger at them. "My, my, my, it gets quiet whenever I come around. I wonder what in the world you two have to hide?" Ann said that as she passed by.

"What is wrong with your sister?" Maggie asked.

Sarah shook her head. "Pay her no attention. She's always been like that. There is no hope in changing her."

Maggie smirked, "But what about you?"

Sarah looked confused. "What about me?"

Maggie grinned. "What about that good-looking doctor of yours?"

Sarah blushed. "First of all, he's not mine. And secondly, I'm sure he barely remembers me."

Maggie started to giggle. "Not the way he was looking at you last night, he won't forget."

Sarah started to giggle also. "I just hope I can see him again."

"We'll see if Heather's at the spot tonight. If so we can go to the hospital and try to find him," Maggie suggested.

Sarah put her finger up to her lips and nodded. "The hospital... Yes."

"Yep, that's a good place to find a doctor." Maggie smiled.

Sarah asked, "I can find him but what if he doesn't care?"

"Oh, he cares," Maggie nodded. "I could see it in his eyes. I know that he's an *Englischer* now but I see Amish in his soul."

"Maybe you're right," Sarah said.

"Of course I am," Maggie answered.

Sarah stayed for the singings and met a boy that she'd never noticed before. They talked for a little while but she found the conversation quite boring. It was nothing like she'd had with Jacob and she soon dismissed him, sending him on his way.

That evening she and Maggie piled into Heather's car and changed clothes in the back seat. Following Sarah's instructions, Heather headed for the hospital.

The three of them burst in and scoped out the emergency room waiting quarters. They sneaked down the hallways and even peeped into the staff rooms when there was no one looking but they didn't see Jacob around.

Sarah sighed. "I don't even know if he's on duty tonight."

"Maybe he's already gone for the day," Maggie said.

"Or maybe he never even came in at all," Heather added.

Maggie put her hand up to her forehead. "Well, what do we know about him?"

"I know that he's a resident here, just a few weeks short of completion but it's really all I know about him. And I don't know his last name so I can't even ask at the front desk," Sarah explained.

"Yeah, you're right. Maybe coming here was a mistake." Maggie shrugged and turned towards the door.

Just as they were about to leave, Sarah felt a strong hand on her shoulder. "Wildflower?"

And there he was standing before her as tall and strong looking as ever. The mention of her name sent shivers through her body. "You are just the one I'm looking for."

"Really?" Jacob asked as he locked eyes with Sarah.

For a moment, it was as if they were the only two in the crowded lobby.

Then he pulled Sarah to the side and asked, "I'm on a break, do you have time to grab a bite to eat?"

"I would love to," she said, looking back at her friends for confirmation.

Heather answered, "Sure, go ahead. We'll meet back here in an hour, okay?"

"Thanks; I promise I'll be here on time." Sarah started to walk away with Jacob.

Heather and Maggie nodded and waved.

***

They settled in at a small café around the corner from the hospital. A waiter seated them in a corner booth and handed them menus.

"Maybe you could order something for me since I don't have much experience with this," Sarah said, closing her menu and pushing it away.

"I think you can handle it." Jacob pushed the menu back to her.

By the time the waiter came back, they both ordered cheeseburgers and ice teas.

Sarah smiled. "I've never met anyone like you before."

Jacob studied her face before speaking. "You look so different than you did the other day."

Sarah frowned. "Oh…uh….. I was hideous then."

"No…just different," Jacob said, while staring at her.

"You don't think I look better now?"

Jacob cleared his throat. "Well, I am able to see more of you, that's for sure," he said, referring to her bare shoulders. "But honestly, you were just as beautiful yesterday."

"Wow, you really do have an Amish soul?"

"I beg your pardon." Jacob looked

confused.

Sarah's face turned red. "I'm sorry, I was just thinking out loud."

"No, don't apologize; I like it." Jacob continued to stare.

"You do?"

"Yes, I don't usually meet people as genuine as you are. Most of the people I talk to are
very shallow and self-centered."

The waiter delivered their food and Sarah, who was extremely hungry, started to dig in.

"I can imagine," she said, taking a sip of her tea.

"So what brings you out here to the streets of Lancaster?"

"I've been coming out with my friend Maggie for a couple of months now and she introduced me to Heather…"

"Your pregnant friend?"

"Yes…unfortunately."

Jacob smiled. "*Rumspringa?*"

"Exactly," Sarah said. "But I don't want to be predictable. I don't want this to be some kind of wild experiment and then go back to the way things were."

"I can see that you're different, that you want more," Jacob said. "I understand."

Sarah leaned in closer. "You can? I thought no one ever would."

"I used to want something different. I saw people dying all around me and I wanted to be part of the solution. I watched my own mother die without a doctor's care and I promised myself and *Gott* that I would make a difference."

"That's so selfless."

"I don't know about that but I do know about being different and about wanting more," Jacob said.

"What about your friend and her baby? What is she going to do?"

Sarah shrugged. "I don't know. Heather hasn't really talked about it yet."

Jacob nodded. "I see but carrying a child is such a serious matter. Maybe she should talk it over with her parents now."

"I don't think that Heather has parents but I'll try to talk to her... I promise," Sarah said.

"I know you'll think me corny but I'm very comfortable with you and maybe that's because of the Amish in you. I miss those values." Jacob leaned over and touched Sarah's long hair.

Sarah felt her heart flutter and didn't know why. And when the evening was over, and she was safely in her own bed, she smiled because she had a wonderful evening, then cried because she was more certain than ever that she would have to leave her family.

Chapter Five

Jacob drove to work the next morning happier than ever, grinning the whole way. Then realizing what he was doing, he forced himself to stop. What was he thinking, getting involved with an Amish girl anyway?

He took the scenic route, purposely passing by the Amish community. He watched the bearded men going by in their buggies and thought about his family. Then his thoughts returned to Sarah.

He knew that Sarah was special but he couldn't take the chance of being distracted. He had to stop thinking about her and focus on his future – the future that he'd worked so hard to attain.

With an offer from one of the best hospitals in the city waiting in the wings, everything was finally falling into place. It'd taken him a long time to make up for his lack of education, to study hard and to turn himself around, to be able to fit in to society. Why would he want to give that all up now for a simple little Amish girl? He tried to dismiss her from his mind but her beautiful smile continued to appear. What was he supposed to do?

"Jacob, we've got just a few more weeks. Aren't you excited, man?" one of Jacob's fellow interns said, as he passed him in the parking lot.

"Right. Best time of my life." Jacob gave

him the thumbs up signal.

He continued to walk into the building, passing his colleagues, taking in the atmosphere. Soon he would be healing the sick and it was all he ever wanted. Was he supposed to give up the best offer of his life, sacrificing his hopes and dreams and for what? He wasn't sure.

"Hi, Jacob," a cute nurse said, waving and Jacob waved back.

"Good morning, Doctor," a nurse's aide said and Jacob loved the sound of that, "Doctor". He smiled so hard that he thought his lips would crack.

Jacob had a few brief conversations before checking in for work and his career seemed to be moving right along at a steady pace.

But with only a few weeks left to his residency, the time would come for him to sign his contracts, and he had to make his decision soon. He took out his phone and went online to check the balance of his checking account. After paying all of his bills, including the rent on his apartment, Jacob would have a zero balance.

Accepting that lucrative offer at the hospital was a no-brainer he decided. He wouldn't let anything or anyone deter him from his mission.

Chapter Six

Sarah had been daydreaming about Jacob all week but she had not seen him. So she moped around the house, doing her morning chores until her parents entered the room.

"The baptism classes will be starting next week," Mary said sternly.

"Yes *Mudder*." Sarah knew where the conversation was headed and she wasn't looking forward to it.

"Don't forget your responsibilities," Joshua said. "This is your time."

"I understand, *Daed*."

From her peripheral vision, Sarah could see Ann frowning.

"I can't wait to be baptized," Ann said. "I'm more than excited about surrendering my life to *Gott*."

"I thought it was getting married and surrendering your life to a man that you were so excited about," Sarah spat out

Ann shot Sarah a nasty look.

Mary waved her hands in their faces. "I won't stand for this foolishness. In any case, are you girls ready for the quilting?"

"I am, *Mudder*," Ann said in excitement.

"So am I," Sarah answered reluctantly.

So Sarah agreed to meet the other girls for quilting; not that she'd had any interest in the activity but with her mother nagging her to go, she found it in her best interests to agree. Once they arrived, Sarah found her way over to her friend Maggie. The ladies started to quilt, and just as she'd suspected, she was bored to tears with the whole activity. She wondered why she was never excited by the normal things that other Amish girls her age loved. Was there something wrong with her? Perhaps, she was never meant to be Amish.

But when there was a break she could finally talk to Maggie freely.

Maggie leaned in close to her. "Have you heard from Heather at all?"

"Not since the last time we went out together," Sarah said.

Maggie nodded. "What about you? Have you heard from Jacob?" Maggie began to giggle.

"Shhhh; keep your voice down." Sarah pulled Maggie further away from the group and whispered, "No, I haven't. How could I have? Without Heather coming for us, I have no connection to the outside world."

"That's not true," Maggie teased. "I'm sure Jacob would come and get you if you asked."

Sarah shrugged. "Well, I haven't had the chance to ask."

"What do you think of Heather's situation? Do you think she's okay?"

"I don't know. We won't know for sure

until we talk to her. We'll have to find a way to go and see her." Sarah was adamant about that.

"Maybe we can do that tonight," Maggie suggested.

"Fine… tonight. Same place. Same time." Sarah folded her arms across her chest.

"Don't be late." Maggie started to giggle again.

"I won't," Sarah said. "But bring some money. I have a plan."

"Good. Because being pregnant is serious business." Maggie said.

"Sure is." But Sarah never knew that Ann was lurking around nearby.

***

That night Sarah and Maggie met under the willow tree but this time it was without Heather. They walked to the entrance by themselves and then once they were out on the street, they took out the spare change from their pockets and caught a taxi to the hospital. Thankfully, the hospital wasn't too far away.

Sure enough, as planned Jacob was walking through the emergency room area but he had a blank look on his face when he saw them.

"I'm surprised to see you here. I thought maybe that you decided not to come back," Jacob said.

"And why would I do that?" Sarah didn't

know what to think of that comment but she was clearly disappointed at his lack of enthusiasm.

"I don't know; I just thought…"

"You probably thought I was just out here to party for a few weeks and then go back to the Amish lifestyle like most of us do. But I'm not here tonight to have a good time, I'm here because being pregnant is serious business and we've come to check on our friend."

"Oh, that's very nice," Jacob said. "But is she here?"

"No, we came to see you first, actually" Sarah studied his face for a reaction.

Jacob raised his eyebrows. "Me?" How can I help?'"

Sarah pulled him over to the side and whispered, "Are you going on break now?"

"Actually, since I just did a double shift, I'm off for the night." Jacob smiled.

Sarah smiled back. "That's even better. Would you drive us to Heather's house? She lives with her grandfather and we want to check on her."

Jacob looked at the faces of both girls. "Meet me outside in five minutes."

Sarah and Maggie looked at each other, then back at him and said, "Thanks" at the same time; then they headed for the exit.

Within minutes, Jacob came out in his scrubs and directed them to his car. It was parked in the middle of the parking lot and

Jacob unlocked the doors with his remote key and then held the door open for both of them to get in. Maggie sat in the backseat and Sarah sat in the front.

"Do you ladies have an address for your friend?" Jacob asked before starting the car.

"This is all we have." Sarah handed him a piece of crumpled up paper with sloppy handwriting on it.

"That's where she told us that she lives," Maggie explained.

"That's good enough and not too far from here," Jacob said as he took off down the road.

Jacob drove them to the address and since he wasn't sure that it was safe for them to go in alone, he went inside the building with them. They climbed the four flights of stairs together. Sarah was completely out of breath as she reached the top. She never had to climb so many stairs in her life.

When they knocked on the apartment door, a frail old man came to answer it and said, "What do you want?"

They looked at each other, and then back at him.

"We're here to see Heather, sir."

"Heather is gone. She ain't here," the old man said.

"Gone? Do you know where she went? We're friends of hers," Sarah went on to explain.

"Heather doesn't have any friends," the

old man said.

"Maybe that was true before but she does now, sir," Jacob responded.

"And who are you?" The old man looked Jacob up and down.

"I'm Jacob," he said extending his hand.

Without another word, the old man ignored his gesture and slammed the door in their faces.

As the three of them were walking downstairs they ran into Heather in the hallway.

She looked heavier than usual and there were traces of dried tears around her eyes.

"What are you all doing here?" Heather asked.

"We're here to see you," Sarah said, excited that they'd found her.

"We're here to help you," Maggie explained.

"What if I don't need your help," Heather said, looking at Jacob up and down.

"We think you do," Sarah said, boldly.

"Well you're wrong. Dead wrong," Heather said.

"Are we?" Sarah asked putting one hand on her hip.

"Yeah, you are. You two have been stuck in that place so long that you don't know anything about the outside world. My mama raised me by herself and her mama before that did the same," Heather said.

Jacob sighed. "Heather, I don't think that your friends are trying to offend you but sometimes you might need a shoulder to lean on."

Heather rolled her eyes but obviously reconsidering her decision, she signaled for them to follow her and they did. She invited them into her apartment, where they helped her to tell her aging grandfather about her condition.

Afterwards, Jacob took Sarah and Maggie and stopped at the designated willow tree as instructed. Maggie got out of the car and ran through the bushes towards her house. Sarah also got out.

"Goodbye, and thanks again," Sarah said to Jacob.

Jacob reached out for her. "Wait, please."

Sarah turned around and faced Jacob.

"Can you stay and talk for moment?"

"I suppose I can stay for a few minutes more," Sarah said, looking at him suspiciously.

"I apologize for not being so friendly this evening."

"I understand. You're a very busy man - a doctor at that and I'm just a silly girl taking up your time."

"No, you couldn't be more wrong. To be honest I haven't been able to get you off my mind since the first day I laid eyes on you. Believe me I've tried but there's something special about you. And to tell you the truth it scares me," Jacob explained.

"Scares you? Why?"

"Because it complicates things for me because we live in two different worlds. I'm just a few weeks away from accepting a position in a wonderful hospital that is further away from here, in the big city and it's everything I've ever dreamed of, everything I've ever wanted until now..."

"What do you mean until now?" Sarah batted her eyelashes. "What do you want now?"

"Now I'm confused about a lot of things. Meeting you has reminded me of all of the good things in the Amish community that I've missed." Jacob took Sarah's hand. "Meeting you has changed my priorities. I used to think that the prestigious position and the salary that comes along with it would be enough to satisfy me but lately I realize how empty I really am."

"I too have been confused because I've wanted to get away from the community for so long but then meeting you kind of reminds me of all the good things I love about being Amish. But I don't know how to balance this curiosity that I have and this dissatisfied way I feel," Sarah said.

"I know what you mean. I felt that way for a long time before I left and even after. And just when I thought I had it all together, you come along and mess it all up." Jacob chuckled.

"I'm sorry," she said.

"You don't have anything to be sorry about. The last few times we spent together, you've also made me very happy, even sitting with your friends tonight gave me a chance to see how mature and sensitive you really are."

"My parents are pressuring me about being baptized and it's not that I don't love *Gott* but I'm just not sure that I can stay, especially now that I've met you."

Jacob kissed Sarah gently on the lips and Sarah thought that she would soar through the clouds. Instead, they ended up talking for the next few hours and lost track of time.

"Oh no, I must hurry home. My sister usually waits up for me and she will be furious that I'm so late."

"When will I be able to see you again?"

"Meet me here at the willow tree tomorrow night at 10 o'clock," Sarah said as she ran through the woods.

As soon as she reached the walkway to her house, she noticed something amiss. There was a light on in the kitchen and she knew that meant trouble.

Sarah opened the front door to see her parents and sister sitting at the kitchen table. Her father was holding the kerosene lamp.

"*Mudder, Daed?*"

"Sarah," her mother said, "What have you done?"

Sarah noticed that Ann was mumbling

under her breath.

"I'm not sure what you mean, *Mudder*." Sarah's heart beat rapidly.

Joshua stood up and met her at the door. "Where have you been? And what is this about you being pregnant?"

Chapter Seven

Sarah was stunned. She couldn't believe what she'd walked into and she also couldn't believe what her parents were asking her.

"Answer me," Joshua demanded.

"I'm coming from a friend's house," Sarah answered.

"A friend?" Mary's eyes filled up with tears.

Ann grinned in the background.

"And what friend is that? And what were you doing there?" Joshua's usually kind demeanor was gone.

"A friend of mine named Heather." Sarah was shaking. She'd never seen her parents so angry before.

"Is she an *Englischer*?" Mary asked.

"Yes," Sarah said.

"Is she the one who helped you get into trouble?" Joshua asked.

"*Mudder, Daed,* I assure you that I'm not in trouble. I don't know where you would get an idea like that." Sarah looked her parents in the eyes.

"I heard you tell Maggie that you were pregnant." Ann folded her arms.

"I am certainly not pregnant," Sarah said.

"Are you sure?" Mary asked.

"*Mudder,* I promise I have not done anything to possibly become pregnant."

"Then it is Maggie?" Joshua asked.

"It is neither of us. No, Maggie is not pregnant either." Sarah once again looked at Ann and said to her, "You heard wrong."

Joshua and Mary also looked at Ann and shook their heads.

"I'm sorry but I know what I heard," Ann insisted.

"You heard a private conversation between Maggie and I talking about a friend of ours whose name is Heather and yes, she is pregnant. We've been trying to help her." Sarah swallowed hard and waited.

"Help her? How can you possibly help her when you cannot help yourself?" Mary asked, infuriated.

"Sneaking out all times of the night, running the streets with the *Englischers*. It's a disgrace..." Joshua said.

"But it's *rumspringa*." Sarah hoped to receive some mercy.

"And that is the only reason we've tolerated your attitude this long but this..." Mary pointed her finger at Sarah.

"I'm sorry but I do have more to tell you." Sarah took a deep breath.

"And what is that?" Joshua asked.

"While I was out there I finally met someone that I connect with. He is an *Englischer* and we're in love. I want to leave to be with him." Sarah held her breath for their reaction.

"In love? What do you know of love?"

Joshua asked.

"I know that I want more than any of these boys here can offer me. His name is Jacob and he is a doctor," Sarah told them.

"Oh my heavens," Mary said, looking up to the sky.

"What about baptism?" Joshua asked.

"If I'm going to leave then I won't need to be baptized," Sarah explained, with tears streaming down her face. "I've never been quite satisfied here so I think that leaving will be best for me."

Mary raised her eyebrows. "Best for you?"

"Jacob had to leave home years ago in order to study to become a doctor. Sometimes leaving is best. Won't you two please accept it and give me your blessings?" Sarah looked at both of her parents' faces.

"You know that is not the Amish way. We did not raise you like this," Joshua said.

"And now you break our hearts and run off with some *Englischer*." Mary wiped her eyes.

"But he was Amish once." Sarah felt that she was losing the battle.

"He *was*. But now he *is* an *Englischer*." Mary frowned at her daughter.

"But he loves *Gott* and he wants to help to heal people," Sarah said, defending him.

"But if he is an *Englischer* then he is healing out of the will of *Gott*. If you leave, you will be excommunicated." Joshua turned his back on his daughter. "We are Amish first and we cannot give you our blessings.

Sarah's heart was broken. But that evening she still met with Jacob by the willow tree and explained how she was caught.

"It's a good thing that your parents know. Don't worry; we'd have to tell them sooner or later," he said. "I love you, Sarah."

"I love you too, Jacob."

"And when we're married then…"

Sarah's face brightened. "You want to marry me?"

"Of course, I do."

Sarah forced herself not to cry. "It doesn't matter. My parents will never come to my wedding and they will never accept me or you." Sarah put her hand up to her forehead in distress.

"You must decide, Wildflower. No one can make this decision but you. You must choose." Jacob gave her one last hug for the night.

And Sarah's heart ached with feelings of indecision and failure.

Chapter Eight

Jacob was distraught over his conversation with Sarah the night before. He was glad she'd finally accepted the fact that he needed her in his life, but now that he made that profession of his love, it seemed that things had become even more complicated.

But although her parents were angry, and he had his own doubts, Jacob felt that he had the solution. He had considered the situation and decided that Sarah's similar upbringing was the answer that he'd been looking for. Sarah would be coming into the world with him so she could bring with her all of the simplicity and values that he grew up with. They would have children and raise them in the same way he was accustomed to; he had it all planned out. He would stay in the world and be a doctor and have an "almost Amish" wife. He would have the best of both worlds. And Jacob was so excited about sharing his plan with Sarah.

He even withdrew a good portion of money from his savings account and went out to purchase an engagement ring.

That evening when he met Sarah at the usual spot, he took her to a fancy restaurant and officially asked her to marry him.

Tears began to run down Sarah's face. "Oh, Jacob, you know I would marry you if I knew for sure that I was leaving the Amish."

"I understand that it's a big decision. But if you love me and I love you, we'll have to be together no matter what, won't we?"

Sarah sighed. "I suppose so."

"Of course, we will."

"So you don't have any more doubts?" Sarah squinted.

"Not since I realized I'll be getting an *almost Amish* wife."

"Almost Amish wife?" Sarah frowned. "And what does that mean?"

"It means you are the embodiment of everything I love in the Amish community and yet you're more unique than anyone else I've ever known."

"So what does that mean?"

"So you'll be living out here with me but you'll be bringing all that goodness with you." Jacob used his hands to express himself.

"So you think that I'm going to come out here and be exactly the same - dressed the same, act the same? That's impossible. And once I leave the Amish, it will truly be gone. I will no longer be the same girl. I'm already different," Sarah snapped.

In fact, she couldn't believe that she was snapping; it wasn't like her at all.

"But Wildflower... "

"My name is Sarah but all my life they've called me Wildflower and they've called me that for a reason. Now you also want to take away my identity. And the one reason I want to go is the same thing you want me to give up – my freedom." Sarah stood up. "Well, I won't do it. Not even for you."

"Wildflower, wait...."

But she was gone. By the time he caught up with her, she was jumping into a taxi.

Jacob was devastated that his plan had not worked, that she hadn't been impressed with his ring or his proposal and she hadn't accepted either of them outright. Instead, it seemed to only upset her. Yet, he only had a short time to make his choice and she only had a short time to make hers. The job in the city was waiting for him so he had to move fast if he wanted to stay on track.

But in the meanwhile, Sarah had put their engagement on hold. She had crushed him and he wasn't sure their relationship would ever recover.

Chapter Nine

When the taxi dropped Sarah off at the entrance she walked, and then ran through the bushes to her house. As she approached the walkway, she could see from the kitchen window that the kerosene lamp had been left on for her. So she went to the front door quietly and looked around for her parents. When there was no sign of them she tiptoed up to her room. Her heart was heavy but she knew what she had to do; she had to pray.

She entered her bedroom where her sister was waiting.

"I want to apologize for today," Ann said. "I never meant to hurt you."

"Don't worry about it," Sarah said.

"You'll probably be leaving soon and I just wanted to say that I'm really sorry I never understood you. I don't think I ever tried to."

"I think that's the nicest and most sincere thing you've ever said to me." Sarah hugged her sister and in that tender moment, she didn't want to leave. She knew that she would miss Ann, even with all of the differences. Yet, Sarah knew that leaving meant she would leave her entire family behind forever.

"What are you going to do?" Ann asked, sitting straight up in bed.

"I'm going to do the only thing that I can do and that is to pray." Sarah dropped to her knees beside her bed and spent the next thirty minutes there. She needed to pour her heart out to *Gott* but more importantly; she needed to take wisdom in.

By the next morning Sarah had peace. Knowing the sacrifices that she had to make, she went downstairs to talk to her parents. She told them that she did indeed love Jacob, and that she had to work things out with him before she could make her final decision. Her parents agreed that she could take the buggy to go and meet Jacob.

So Sarah took the buggy and headed down the road to the hospital where Jacob was completing his residency. She didn't know his work hours and she wasn't even sure that he would be happy to see her but she knew they had to work their issues out together.

Once she arrived she went to the information desk and had him paged. Jacob came right away but he looked annoyed.

"I'm sorry I had to page you but this matter of ours is an *emergency* and I honestly don't know if I'll see you again after today. But I know that we've got to work things out together."

"I agree with you. You're absolutely right that we have to talk and work things out so we can go on with our lives."

Jacob and Sarah left the hospital and walked across the street to a small coffee shop. Jacob ordered two lattes, which they sipped on as they talked.

Jacob looked into her eyes. "I was going to come to your parent's home after work this evening."

"Really?" Sarah was pleasantly surprised.

"Yes, I wanted to tell you that I prayed about us and about the decision that I've made," Jacob said.

Sarah crossed her arms in front of her and put a guard over her heart. "I'm listening."

"I've decided that I was wrong in thinking that I could make you into something other than what you are. I was wrong in thinking that you bringing a piece of Amish life into the world would be enough for me."

Sarah studied Jacob's face as he was talking. "What are you saying?"

"I'm saying that I want to go back home and get baptized. I want to be Amish again," Jacob said.

"What about healing the people?"

"Can you think of a better place that could use a doctor than in the Amish community? I began to think that maybe it is my calling to go back and to heal my people. I was Amish once and deep inside I have never let go of it. I would like to go back but I would like to marry you if you will have me."

"Yes, Jacob, I will. If you will sacrifice the job of your dreams to do *Gott's* will, so can I. We understand each other so perfectly and I feel so totally comfortable around you. I've never felt this way about anyone before..."

"Neither have I..."

Sarah continued, "I now believe that it is my calling to be a doctor's wife and that it was *Gott's* plan from the very beginning. Maybe that's why I was so different and so wild. Maybe I was just waiting for the right person to understand me, to tame me and to heal me. I believe that you are that person." Sarah took Jacob's hand and squeezed it, gently.

"And you are the person for me." Jacob kissed Sarah and the staff at the coffee shop clapped their hands.

And they sat in the coffee shop, making plans for their future until Jacob's short break was over.

"Tonight we will tell my parents and they'll be so relieved," Sarah said as tears welled up in her eyes.

"Imagine the joy of my family when I tell my *Daed* and brothers that I'm coming back. I haven't seen them since the year *Mudder* passed away."

Jacob and Sarah were excited as they looked forward to sharing the good news with their families.

Chapter Ten

Jacob and Sarah told their families that that they would be getting baptized and then married. Everyone was happy with their decision and welcomed them with open arms.

Jacob went to the Bishop, and then stood in front of the congregation to repent before taking his baptism. The Bishop and the deacons were happy to see him again and glad that he decided to come back. Sarah was baptized too. And the official forwarding announcements were made.

Sarah was proud of Jacob for doing the right thing, for choosing right over money and prestige, and for choosing God's will over his own. She only hoped that she could meet his lofty expectations as a wife. She prayed that her love and respect for her husband would help to quench the need for adventure inside her.

Finally, the day of the wedding came and celery was spread all over everywhere. The ceremony took place at Sarah's home and the Bishop happily performed it. Maggie and her family were in attendance but Sarah was disappointed that Heather could not come.

Still, Sarah was the happiest that she'd ever been and nothing was humdrum or boring. The two of them enjoyed the occasion, eating and drinking and celebrating their love with family and friends. It was a perfect day.

A few weeks prior, Jacob had managed to secure a small piece of land on the other side of the creek where they had their house built. They also built a guest building in the back for Jacob's medical practice.

When the evening came and the wedding guests dispersed, Sarah and Jacob piled into their new buggy and rode to their new home.

Sarah looked at Jacob's face in the moonlight. There was a quiet happiness radiating through his face as he loosely held the reins. She clutched his arms and rested her head on his shoulder. "Thank you," she said.

Jacob smiled at her. "I should be the one to thank you. You have made my life complete."

Sarah looked up at him. "No one would have accepted this wildflower except for you. For a long time I used to think I was different and I used to somehow feel guilty about being different."

Jacob touched her cheek. "Even wildflowers are a creation of God. Maybe we have to just wait for it to bloom fully. And then, someone would come along to take good care of it."

"I don't think this wildflower would have accepted anyone but you."

Jacob pulled her close. "And that is why I love you. Because we were made for each other. It was God's will for us to come together."

Sarah smiled as she looked ahead. In the

distance she could see their new home. Her chest swelled with happiness.

It was the start of a new life.

END OF PART 1

4: A NEW LIFE

Chapter One

Jacob pulled the carriage to a stop in front of their new home. He couldn't have been happier. He had finally married the girl of his dreams Sarah today. He glanced at Sarah. *My wife.* The word felt wonderful. It would take him some time to get used to the fact that he was married.

Jacob got out of the buggy and assisted Sarah. It was dark and he lit a candle to aid them in walking to the door. They walked arm in arm up the front steps, excited that they were finally entering their new home as man and wife. But before Jacob could open the cedar wood door, they heard a strange gurgling noise.

"What's that?" Sarah was perplexed.

"I don't know." Jacob was confused.

"Look!" Sarah pointed.

Sarah and Jacob could hardly believe their eyes. There beside the front window, wrapped in a thin blanket was a newborn baby.

"It's a baby." Sarah gasped.

Neither Sarah nor Jacob could believe that someone could leave an innocent baby on their doorstep and on their wedding night at that.

Jacob looked around. "There is no one here. What do we do?"

"Well, we can't let him lie outside. The baby will freeze in the cold night air."

"You are right. God help the poor little child." Jacob examined the baby and discovered that he seemed to be healthy, although maybe a little underweight. He lifted the baby and the three of them entered the house.

"I can't believe that someone would actually do something like this and here in our community too," Sarah commented.

"Amish people have problems too," Jacob said.

"I know that but usually this is not one of them. I mean there are usually family members to take care of the child even if the parents aren't able to for some reason."

Jacob looked at the baby. "That's very true but we don't know the circumstances yet so…"

Sarah looked into the child's eyes and was instantly connected. He seemed so helpless that the situation almost brought her to tears. "I could take the baby to my parents' home tomorrow."

"That won't be necessary. We have a perfectly good home here and the baby will be just fine for the night. Tomorrow we'll find out who he belongs to and what the problem is."

Sarah nodded in agreement.

All throughout the night the baby woke up because he was hungry and Sarah held him close to her heart and fed him. Early the next morning, instead of continuing their marriage celebration, the two of them went to the Bishop so he could put the word out in the community about the mysterious baby.

"No one seems to know anything." Sarah plopped down in a wooden chair, frustrated.

"That's how it sounds but that's very hard to believe. It's hard to hide a nine-month pregnancy," Jacob said, running his hands through his hair.

"You're right about that," Sarah said. "If only we knew where he came from."

"With all of our planning for the wedding, the baptism and everything the past few months I haven't had time to notice much of anything except …wait a minute," Jacob said. "I think I know where the baby may have come from."

Sarah opened her mouth wide. "Where?"

"I could be wrong but it makes sense." Jacob nodded. "We've been so busy with our own plans that we forgot about the outside world."

"What do you mean?"

Jacob continued, "I believe this just might be Heather's baby."

Sarah raised her eyebrows. "Heather's

baby? But how could she possibly know where we live and how to get out here?"

"That's the easy part. Maybe she asked Maggie for our new address while claiming to send you a card or wedding gift or something."

"I guess that would make sense, wouldn't it?" Sarah thought about it for a moment. "It definitely would explain why we haven't been able to find the mother *here*.

"Yes, because the mother is not *here*. She's out *there*." Jacob pointed out at the window.

Sarah nodded. "You know what; I think you may be right."

"Unfortunately, I know I'm right," Jacob said.

"So what do we do now?" Sarah pouted.

"Now we must take the baby back to her and help her decide what she really wants to do," Jacob explained.

Sarah nodded, and then looked over at the bundle of joy beside her. "But how could Heather do something like this?"

"I've seen it done one million times before while working at the hospital. A young girl gets caught up in a relationship that her body says she can handle but her mind can't. Next thing you know her heart tells her to keep it, but sometimes she just can't."

"Are you saying that Heather is giving up her baby permanently?"

"We won't know for sure until we see

her," Jacob said.

Chapter Two

Sarah and Jacob went to see Heather at her home. They entered her apartment building and went up the steps. When they reached her apartment Sarah knocked on the door.

"Let me handle this," she said.

Jacob stood back, holding the baby and waited for the old man to come to the door. But instead Heather finally cracked the door open herself.

"Heather, you're here." Sarah looked surprised.

"Of course I'm here. Where else would I be?" Heather spat out.

"No, it's just that I thought that your grandfather would answer the door like last time," Sarah explained.

"He passed away from a heart attack last week. So I'll be the only one opening the door here from now on."

"I'm so sorry to hear that," Sarah said. "May we come in?"

"We?"

"Yes, you know that Jacob and I got married so..." Sarah turned to face Jacob.

"I heard. Come on in." Heather held the door open wide.

"I'm sorry you couldn't come to the

wedding," Sarah added.

"Yeah, yeah." Heather yawned.

Heather looked at Jacob holding the baby but did not comment. Sarah and Jacob sat besides each other on an old couch.

"We wanted to talk to you about…" Sarah started.

"About this?" Heather pointed to the baby.

"Yes," Sarah answered.

"What about it?" Heather asked in a matter-of-fact tone.

"Is this your baby?" Jacob asked.

"Well, he *was*, but he's not anymore."

"What you mean he *was*?" Jacob asked. "You can't just walk away from your own child."

"Oh yeah. That's not what I've been told," Heather said.

"I mean you can't just leave him on anyone's doorstep," Sarah said.

"I didn't leave him on just anyone's doorstep. I left him at your doorstep because I know you two can give him a good home. Can *I* give him a good home? The answer is no." Heather shrugged her shoulders.

Jacob and Sarah looked at each other in astonishment.

"You can give him love," Sarah said.

"Babies can't live off that. They need milk and diapers and stuff. And I've got none of that, especially now that my grandfather is gone. He was my only family. After that I've got nothing and no one," Heather explained.

"That's not true. You have us and Maggie too."

Heather shrugged her shoulders again. "Are you kidding me? You guys are Amish and that means you won't be able to deal with me soon. Once your people find out that you're helping me, they'll ban you. So you'll go back to your isolated lives and forget that I ever existed." Heather stuck a wad of gum into her mouth and started chewing.

"I doubt if we'll ever forget you," Sarah said.

Heather frowned. "Yeah, right."

"But what about this baby?" Jacob said, getting back to the point.

"I can't take care of him. But I'm sure you guys will do a great job." Heather looked directly at Jacob.

"But we can't just go around taking other people's babies," Sarah said.

"Even I know that but you can legally adopt him," Heather said.

Jacob asked, "What about his father?"

Heather handed Jacob a Pennsylvania birth certificate, which had no father listed on it. "See there is no father."

"But that's impossible. Just because you have not listed the father's name doesn't mean that he doesn't exist. Now where is he?"

"Dead, okay? Are you happy now?" Heather rolled her eyes.

"Oh, I'm so sorry. How did it happen?" Sarah leaned in to hear what she had to say.

"I don't want to talk about it if you don't mind. He's just dead, okay. So if you want this baby, you can have him outright. I'll sign the papers at any time terminating my parental rights." Heather blew a bubble. "I've already talked to someone about it."

Visibly shaken by Heather's nonchalant attitude, Jacob gave Sarah a signal. Then they both stood up and headed towards the door.

"Heather, I think you just need a little more time to come to your senses. So we are going to go now and we'll be in touch," Sarah said.

Heather followed them. "I know what I'm doing. Please, don't come back."

Chapter Three

Sarah and Jacob were unsure about what to do with the baby that Heather had abandoned. Whatever they did or didn't do might have legal repercussions if they weren't careful.

Sarah pouted, "What do you think we should do?"

"What can we do? She's not being levelheaded. We can't keep her baby," Jacob reminded his wife.

"But why not? She has a good point. We can give them a good home."

"Wildflower, that's not a good idea. You are not thinking clearly right now," Jacob said.

"But she gave up the baby because she can't take care of him. With her grandfather gone, who will help her now?"

"I know that you want to keep him and I know that this is hard for you but I just don't know if that is the right thing to do."

"You don't know if it's the right thing to do?"

"Listen to yourself. We just got married ourselves. I mean I just rededicated my life to *Gott* and surrendered my life in service to him. But I don't think it's our place to raise this child."

"But if not us, then who?"

"I'm sure the social workers can find a good home for him."

"Why don't you at least give him a chance? I mean what if Heather changes her mind next week and wants to keep him. Can't we just keep him for a little while longer?"

"I'll think about it. But we will have to first meet the Bishop about this," Jacob said.

"Fair enough. If you will give me just a little more time to try to find him a good home then I'll be satisfied."

"What if his father wants him?"

Sarah shrugged. "If his father wants him, then he can have him."

"All right then. I'll give you a little longer to see if we can find him a good home or if we can find his father. That should give Heather enough time to get over whatever postpartum depression she might be having. But if not, then we'll give him to the state. I'm not convinced that it's our place to raise him."

The baby smiled and Sarah's heart began to overflow with love for him. Although his name was listed as "Baby" on the birth certificate, she secretly called him John. "You look like a John to me," she whispered. She could feel his heart beating against hers and tears came to her eyes. "He's so little."

Jacob turned his head sideways to look at him. "That's how they are when they are just born."

Sarah threw her arms around Jacob. "I can't wait until we have children of our own."

"Why wait?" Jacob took the opportunity to kiss her passionately. Just as he began to caress her soft skin, the baby started to cry and Sarah pulled away from him.

"I'll get him," she said.

Jacob let out a long sigh of frustration. When was he going to finally have some quality time with his new wife? He wanted to hold her and to touch her and to feel that she was his. When he was an *Englischer*, he was no saint. But now that he was married, he fully intended to enjoy the benefits of their union. He looked over at Sarah and saw how beautiful she was, with her long brown hair and shapely figure. She was the kind of girl that men in the "world" liked to exploit and display in magazines. But he intended to treat her like a queen.

Seeing Sarah struggle, he said, "Here, let me help you with that." He took the diaper away from her. He gave her a quick kiss on the lips and was satisfied. For now just being with her was enough.

"Thanks for being so helpful. You'll make a wonderful father," Sarah said, rubbing Jacob's back.

"One day." Jacob said, as he completed the diaper change.

"*Denki*." She kissed him on the cheek and

then took up the baby.

"I've got an idea about what we can do now. Why don't we figure out how we are going to arrange the office?" Jacob grabbed Sarah's hand and led the way to the door.

"Now that's a good idea," Sarah agreed, following him.

Once they stood in the small empty house, Jacob had a vision of the place filled with Amish patients from all over.

"There is so much to do. I've got to get my business license and get some furniture built for this place."

"You can put a counter and chairs over there," Sarah pointed out.

"And in the examination room I'll need a bed of course," Jacob added.

"Maybe we can plant a few flowers out front to make it colorful."

"Spoken like a real wildflower." Jacob smiled.

"I am what I am."

"And I wouldn't change who you are for anything in the world," Jacob said.

"Do you mean it?"

"No doubt about it." Jacob grinned.

Sarah teased, "Even if I want something that maybe you don't want?"

Jacob was intrigued. "And what could that possibly be?"

"A baby."

"I will gladly give you one of those if you ever slow down long enough." Jacob chuckled, then reached for her but she slipped away from him.

"No, I mean this baby." She pointed to baby John now asleep in the bassinet.

Jacob's playful expression ended. "To be honest, I don't think it's a good idea to get attached because he'll probably be going back soon."

"Do you mean give him back to his mother?"

"Or back to the state; either-or"

Sarah placed her hands on her hips. "How can a man with such a big heart to heal people say such a cruel thing?"

"It's not cruel. It's just the truth," Jacob said.

"You've been gone a long time and you've forgotten how we do things in the Amish community. Everyone pitches in and helps."

"I haven't forgotten. But perhaps you've forgotten that our community doesn't usually put out a welcome mat for *Englischers*."

"Even a little baby?"

"Even a little *Englischer* baby."

Chapter Four

Three weeks had passed and Sarah had managed to convince Jacob to hold on for a little while longer. But each day was getting harder and harder to persuade him to listen. Each day Sarah told Jacob how sweet, how cute, and how innocent he was, constantly pleading her case.

Jacob sat down on their bed next to Sarah. "You're going to have to start gathering his things."

"Jacob, please just one more week," she pleaded, getting down on her knees.

"No. Wildflower, this has to stop," Jacob demanded. "I mean when will this ever end? We're dragging this thing on but there's no more time. If Heather does not want her son by now, we must get the authorities involved."

Sarah stood up in front of Jacob. "But maybe she's been depressed..."

"I'm sure she has been, but nevertheless she hasn't come by or tried to see him, not even once in the whole three weeks." Jacob took Sarah's hand and guided her to sit back down on the bed.

"But maybe there's a good explanation for that," Sarah grabbed Jacob's hand.

"We can't keep making excuses for her." Jacob loosened his hand from Sarah's grasp.

"She's a mother but when is she going to start acting like one?"

"Look, I know that it looks bad but…"

"We can't keep covering for her. I don't believe that she wants this child. Nor do I believe that she's capable of taking care of him." Jacob shook his head and walked away.

"Isn't that where we step in?"

Jacob did not look Sarah in the eyes. "No, that's when the state steps in. This will be his last night here. Tomorrow we will take him back."

"I guess you're right," Sarah said.

"Sadly, I know I'm right. I know it is not easy but it's the best thing for him." Jacob nodded. "It is the best thing for all of us."

That night Sarah and Jacob were cuddling up together, as married couples do, when they heard the baby start to cry.

Without hesitation, Sarah got up to tend to him as she had been doing for the past few weeks. She changed his soiled diaper and fixed him a bottle of warm milk. When she was done, she lifted the baby gently in her arms and took him back to bed with her.

"I see that we have a visitor," Jacob said, looking annoyed.

Sarah smiled and started to feed the baby but he would hardly drink from the bottle. He just kept crying, louder and louder until finally Jacob took him away from Sarah. Jacob felt his forehead.

"This baby is burning up with fever." Jacob frowned. "Didn't you notice he was?

"No, I didn't," she said.

"Hurry and get me some cool towels," he instructed.

Jacob got up and went out to the guesthouse and returned with some of his doctor's gear, including the thermometer. He checked the baby's temperature and vital signs, including his breathing.

"His heartbeat feels a little erratic. We'll have to bring that temperature down or I'm afraid that we'll have to take him to the hospital."

Sarah closed her eyes and a single tear fell down her cheek. "But if we bring him there to the emergency room, they will probably take him away from us tonight."

"Then that's the way it has to be."

Chapter Five

Jacob and Sarah kept a close watch on the baby but with his temperature steadily rising during the next half an hour, despite Jacob and Sarah's attempt to bring it down, it soon became clear that they would have to visit the emergency room.

"It's time to go," Jacob insisted after taking the child's temperature for the last time.

Sarah's heart felt like it would drop. "All right, if you're certain..."

Luckily, the hospital wasn't far away so Sarah and Jacob bundled the baby up and loaded him into the buggy. Since Jacob had given up his car, he wasn't used to parking a buggy in the parking lot, or driving a buggy for that matter. Yet, he finally found a suitable spot for the horse and buggy to fit, grabbed Sarah's hand, and they sped into the hospital with the baby. The intake nurse looked at the baby, whose cheeks appeared flushed, and asked them a series of questions which made Sarah very nervous. Sarah didn't want anything to happen that would jeopardize their chances of keeping the baby, at least as long as they could. When she told the nurse that they were not the baby's parents or legal guardians, and that they were merely babysitting, the woman asked that they call Heather.

Sarah took out a folded sheet of paper which had Heather's address and phone number on it. She'd never called Heather before because she wasn't allowed to use phones, nor did she own one, but now it seemed necessary. She handed the paper to the nurse and stood by as she called. Heather listened as the nurse explained to Heather that her baby was in the hospital and wondered what Heather was thinking. While the nurse continued to talk to Heather, Sarah leaned in to check on the baby. By the time the nurse hung up, she looked at them and said, "She denied that she ever had a baby."

Sarah and Jacob looked at each other and sighed. The nightmare had begun and Sarah didn't know how it was going to end.

The nurse curled her lips. "I'm afraid that it is our policy to have the parent's consent to care."

"But Ma'am, the mother is surely suffering from post-partum depression and as you can see the child is ill," Jacob explained in a very humble manner.

"And who are you?"

Jacob leaned in. "I am Dr. Jacob Miller and I completed my residency here a few months ago."

Sarah held her breath as he spoke. "Please ma'am."

The nurse looked back and forth at the two of them. "Well, since this is an emergency, I guess we can figure it all out later," she rationalized.

Sarah let out a breath of relief, grateful for whatever mercy they were given. Hopefully, it would be enough time for a miracle. Sarah mouthed the words, "Thank you," before completing the paperwork.

"I told you so," Jacob whispered once they left the front desk.

"I know; I know but I was hoping that…"

"I know what you were hoping and so was I. You have a good heart and you want good things to happen. But I'm afraid that sometimes it doesn't work out that way," Jacob lectured.

And within minutes they were called to the back and another nurse examined the child.

"Has there been a difference in the baby's behavior? Like poor feeding, difficulty breathing, listlessness or persistent crying?"

"Well, he's been crying off and on all night," Sarah said.

"He has a temperature of 103 and that's dangerously high for anyone, and especially for an infant." The nurse proceeded to check the baby and referred him to the doctor.

Sarah and Jacob waited nervously while the medical staff gave John the much needed attention.

"We want to take a blood sample," the doctor said.

Sarah gasped.

"Don't worry, ma'am; given the circumstances this is standard procedure," the doctor explained.

Sarah turned her head while the nurse stuck little John with the needle; she couldn't stand to see anyone hurt him.

Jacob tried to comfort Sarah about the various procedures as everyone shuffled about.

"I can't wait until this is all over," Sarah whispered, putting her head onto Jacob's chest.

Jacob kissed her on the forehead. "It will be over soon; I promise."

"I hope you're right." Sarah closed her eyes in despair.

All of a sudden a quiet fell over the examination room and Sarah opened her eyes just in time to see the doctor walking directly towards them. Sarah's heart began to beat faster with anticipation.

The doctor looked up from his clipboard. "I'm afraid that we have bad news…"

Chapter Six

Sarah held Jacob's hand as she prepared herself for the worst. Yet, after hearing that the baby would have to be admitted to the hospital for observation, she was almost relieved. She let out a deep breath and said, "After seeing horrible worst scenarios in my mind, I'm really glad he'll be getting twenty-four hour care."

"So am I. He will be in good hands, looked after by pediatric doctors."

Sarah smiled. "That's good. And I will stay with him until he's better."

"Wildflower, you can't do that." Jacob shook his head. "You're not his mother so I don't think it's a good idea."

"Why not?"

"Because you must break this bond you seem to be building with him. He is not our child; he belongs to Heather." Jacob appeared frustrated.

"But Heather doesn't want him," Sarah whined.

"That much is clear but we cannot take him."

"Why can't we? Why can't we just adopt him?"

Jacob used his hands to express himself.

"Because it would just complicate things."

"Complicate things? Are you really afraid of the challenge, Dr. Miller? If you hadn't gone against the rules, you wouldn't even be a doctor today."

"That's true but –"

Sarah interrupted, "But don't you think that he's worth it? Besides he's sick and you are a doctor. Shouldn't you have a sense of loyalty to your patient?"

"Jacob started, "I do but –"

"I thought you wanted to heal people and to do *Gott's* will."

"You know I do," Jacob agreed.

"Well how do you know that this baby wasn't sent to us to raise as Amish? Heather is not able to and there is no one else around to help her except us. Do you think that it's just a coincidence?

"I don't know; I haven't had a chance to give it a lot of thought."

"Perhaps, Heather's baby coming to us was God's plan all along," Sarah suggested.

***

Jacob couldn't help but to consider Sarah's words. Despite his initial perspective, he began to think of himself as being one of the sole caregivers for the abandoned infant. What if it was God's will that he and his wife raise the child as their own? The thought of bringing a non-Amish child into the community made him anxious but he decided that he was up for the challenge. If he was to be a healer, then why not start with healing his own wife's heart and an innocent little baby?

"We can speak to a lawyer about our options," he said. "But I'm not promising anything."

"Do you mean it?" Sarah jumped up and down with joy.

"Yes, but I know it won't be easy. We must be ready to fight."

"Where will we start?"

"Heather has already signed over her rights so we must take the legal steps to ensure that he can become ours."

"That doesn't sound so bad."

"That's not the bad part. But first we will have to tell the bishop what we're planning."

"And that's where the trouble comes in," Sarah spat out.

Jacob nodded in silence.

Chapter Seven

As planned, the hospital admitted baby John so Sarah and Jacob spent the night in his room. Sarah kept waking up in the middle of the night, and looking through the glass window of the incubator. The nurses also kept a close watch on him during the night.

But by the morning, his lab results were in and they were informed that the baby's condition wasn't as serious as the doctor originally suspected that it was. Baby John only had a mild ear infection and was given a prescription for it. Surprisingly, he was discharged to Jacob and Sarah in the afternoon and they brought them straight to the bishop's house.

Neither of them was looking forward to this visit but it was necessary. They parked their buggy right next to the bishop's buggy and started walking up the walkway.

Sarah whispered, "How do we explain it?"

Jacob shrugged his shoulders but never stopped walking. "*Gott* must give us the words," Jacob said as he knocked on the front door.

The bishop's wife, Miriam, answered the door, politely invited them in, and then disappeared.

Holding baby John in their arms, Jacob and Sarah whispered to themselves as they waited. After a few minutes, the bishop finally entered the room.

"And how may I help you two today?"

Jacob started, "Well, sir, it's about this baby..."

"Yes, yes, the baby that was left on your doorstep. Why do you still have him? I heard that you'd found his parents outside of our community."

"Well, uh...that's true, Bishop but you see there are no suitable parents," Jacob continued.

"No suitable parents?"

"If I may, Bishop..." Sarah looked down, humbly.

Bishop nodded.

Sarah explained, "This baby was abandoned by his mother and there seems to be no father. The mother tells us that he is deceased and there is no record of a father on the birth certificate. In fact, the child was not even named."

Jacob interrupted, "So we were wondering, Bishop, if it might be possible for us to keep the child and raise him as *Gott* sees fit."

"I see. This is a most unusual request. We are not in the habit of mixing the *Englischers* with our world even when that *Englischer* is a baby." The bishop rubbed his beard.

Sarah asked, without thinking, "But what

harm can one small baby do?"

The bishop frowned. "I suppose that one baby in and of itself may not be able to do harm but it's the mindset of the people that do the damage. If we start with one thing, then we end up bringing in more things from the world."

Jacob looked at Sarah before speaking. "But with all respect, Bishop, we don't regard this little one as a thing nor do we believe…"

"You are out of place and quite mistaken in thinking that I care what you believe. I am sorry about the mother's misfortune but I believe that you must return this child at once. He has no place here amongst us." The bishop walked towards the front door and held it open.

Before Jacob or Sarah could make another point, the bishop dismissed them as easily as they had been invited in.

"What do we do now?" Sarah asked.

"Find a good lawyer," Jacob said.

Chapter Eight

Jacob and Sarah headed home, confused and disappointed about what had just happened. How could the bishop be so uncaring? How could someone who was usually so right be so wrong?

In any case, Jacob reached out to one of his *Englischer* friends for an attorney referral.

"I'm not certain that I want to take on such a case," he said.

"Why not? I don't understand."

"There are a lot of political issues involved when I take on an Amish adoption of this sort. Often the media gets involved and to be honest, I don't want to be a part of the backlash."

"What could possibly be the problem with wanting to raise an unwanted child and give him a home that he otherwise, wouldn't have?"

"I know that you see it like you're giving him a loving home and I have no doubt that you will give that to him but to the public it is a travesty. They will want to know how you can take care of a child without giving him the use of electricity or exposure to higher education."

With tears in her eyes, Sarah started to explain, "But that is just the Amish way; the *ordnung...*"

"Rest assured that the world does not care about your way or why you believe what you believe. They will judge this adoption as will your own people. I've been down this road before," the attorney said. "I'm afraid that I will have to turn down the case."

Jacob put his arm around Sarah's shoulder. "Can you refer us to anyone else?"

"I'm afraid that won't be possible," the attorney said.

So Jacob and Sarah once again were at a stalemate. The bishop had told the deacons and the other members of the church about their desire to adopt an *Englischer* baby and the word spread through the community in no time. Everywhere they went; they were questioned and harassed, even during Sunday church service. It was obvious that they had all been tainted by the bishop's opinion.

"I can't believe that it's this hard to adopt one baby. Sometimes it seems like everything is against us," Sarah said, holding the child to her chest.

"Tomorrow I will find another lawyer for us, one who believes in our cause and one who is brave."

Sarah nodded. "But what if we can't find one?"

"Then we will wait on Gott's will to reveal itself to us," Jacob said.

"What do we do in the meantime?" Sarah asked.

"In the meantime we will keep trying. We can't stop now, not if a child's life depends on us," Jacob said.

Sarah threw her arms around her husband and squeezed. "That's what I love about you, Jacob -your heart."

The next few days proved themselves to be very challenging but after doing much research and prayer, they finally found an attorney who would accept the case. He met with them to discuss everything and to start the paperwork. He also advised them that it could become quite a lengthy and exhausting process. But Sarah's heart was set on adopting John and it didn't matter how much it would cost or how long it would take. Jacob followed suit.

The community seemed to give them the cold shoulder but since they hadn't officially been forbidden to adopt, they continued with their plans and hoped for the best. Their attorney proceeded with the case but did advise them that given the possibility of a public outcry, it could be risky. Jacob and Sarah understood the risk but were more than willing to fight against the odds.

The stress took quite a toll on their marriage though. Jacob, who had opened his practice and had started to see patients, began to come home less and less. Sarah spent more time with the growing John than she did with her husband. And when she did get together with Jacob, they usually ended up arguing over the bishop or the incidents resulting from the bishop.

"I feel that the bishop has a right to express what he believes because he is our leader," Jacob said.

"I don't believe that at all. Just because he is our leader doesn't mean that he has the right to influence the entire congregation against us." Sarah threw her head back, wildly. "It's just not fair."

"Some things are certainly not fair but it doesn't mean we can change the situation," Jacob rationalized.

Sarah looked out of the window and saw a figure walking towards their home.

"Hush." Sarah whispered

"What?" Jacob looked at her.

"The Bishop is coming here."

Chapter Nine

Jacob went to meet the bishop at the door and invited him in. Sarah stood back and waited to hear what he had to say. Would there be more trouble than there had already been? She picked up the child and held him protectively against her chest.

"How may we be of service to you today, Bishop?"

"Based on our last conversation and the things that I've been seeing and hearing, I felt the need to meet with you two again."

"I don't understand," Jacob replied.

The bishop paced their wooden floor, occasionally peeking at the child, whose head was covered with a thin blanket.

"Several things have come to my attention since the last time we spoke and one of those things is that we Amish are to be an example to the world. The second is that we have some of the strongest families and therefore, the strongest communities," the bishop explained.

Sarah could feel herself shaking and she loathed the power that the bishop had over them and their lives.

The bishop continued, "Perhaps, I was too harsh in judging the situation." The bishop smiled. "The two of you will be good parents."

"Respectfully, Bishop, I do not know what you're saying," Sarah said.

"I'm saying that you have my blessing," the bishop said. "I believe that with the right guidance and grooming, this child can easily become a pillar of our community."

"*Denki, denki,*" Jacob and Sarah said in unison. The bishop wished them a good day and left.

Jacob picked up his wife and spun her around.

Finally, they'd received the answer they'd been waiting for and after so many struggles, everything was falling into place.

Chapter Ten

After the bishop provided his consent, Jacob and Sarah stopped arguing every day. They started to spend time together again, to laugh again and their marriage was finally able to move forward.

John grew stronger every day and Jacob and Sarah adored him. And despite the stress that was initially caused by the situation, they were now happy that the baby was finally accepted in the community.

Jacob said, "Look, John is moving his hands just like me."

Sarah teased Jacob, "Yes, after a few days, I won't be able to tell the difference between you two."

"You are just being jealous."

"No, it is called imitation. And babies learn that way." Sarah reached over and took the baby in her arms. The baby looked at her and gave a gurgled laugh.

"Oh, isn't he adorable?" Sarah watched the baby clutch her finger.

"You are both adorable," Jacob said as he hugged both of them.

Sarah mouthed a word of prayer. God's will had been done.

END OF PART 2

5: THE MYSTERIOUS STRANGER

Prologue

Jacob and Sarah grew closer to John by the day. Each day they seemed to forget that he did not yet belong to them. Each day he became more and more like their son.

Now that the bishop had finally decided to be supportive, Jacob and Sarah stopped arguing every day. They started to spend time together again, to laugh again and their marriage was finally able to move forward.

"We must hurry." Jacob helped Sarah into the buggy. It was Sunday and church service was being held at one of the neighbor's barn.

Sarah held baby John close to her and sniffed his baby fresh scent. "I am so happy that the bishop changed his mind. It means the entire world to me," she said.

"It was surely tearing us apart," Jacob confirmed. "There is no escaping from the Bishop's influence as long as we are Amish."

Sarah wasn't certain of whether she agreed with him or not but she decided to let it go. Once they arrived at the church service, she quickly gathered together with the other women, including her mother and sister.

Right before the sermon portion of the service, a strange young man entered the basement and walked straight up to the front where the bishop was standing. He was dressed in jeans and a t-shirt and he had a snake tattoo on his arm so it was obvious that he was not one of them. He also looked vaguely familiar but Sarah could not remember where she'd seen him before. Within minutes, he was introduced by the bishop as a visiting *Englischer*. Everyone looked around and mumbled amongst themselves, wondering why the bishop invited such a man into their church.

As the man came forward to speak, the people assumed that he wanted to convert. But not Sarah; she did not feel that in her heart. Once the man stood next to the bishop and between the two deacons, he opened his mouth to speak. She'd seen that man before. Sarah's heart began to beat faster; something wasn't right. He looked out into the congregation, then at Sarah and said, "I am the father of the baby you found here."

Sarah took one last look at the man and dropped to the floor

Chapter One

When Sarah woke up, she was being fanned by Jacob and her mother.

"Are you all right?" Jacob asked as he helped her to her feet.

"Just a little wobbly," Sarah whispered. She couldn't believe that she'd fainted in the midst of the congregation nor could she believe that a mysterious man had shown up to claim her baby. After discovering him abandoned, loving him and nursing him back to life, John was all hers; at least he was in her heart.

Even as she got her bearings, she continued to lean on Jacob for support.

"Right this way," one of the deacons said as he led them downstairs to the basement.

Sarah and Jacob went downstairs and peeped around the corner cautiously. There they saw the bishop and the man he'd introduced earlier.

"We've been waiting for you two," the bishop said as he turned to leave. "This is Drew and he has come looking for his son." The bishop's look was a stern one and Sarah felt betrayed.

Drew extended his hand to Jacob but looked more nervous than gracious.

Jacob shook his hand but Sarah did not;

she just didn't see the need for it. Instead, Sarah sat down on the bench, and then leaned over to Jacob and whispered," They've got the same eyes."

"May I see my son?" Drew kneeled down and touched the baby's head.

"How do we know that he's yours? The birth certificate has no father's name listed and not even a name for the child," Jacob said, reluctantly handing over the baby.

"I didn't know that. In fact, I didn't even know that Heather was pregnant until a few days ago." Drew sighed. "But Heather …I don't know, man. I heard her grandfather recently passed away so when I went to visit, that's when she broke down and told me." Drew looked back and forth at Jacob and Sarah.

Jacob shook his head. "That's too bad that she never told you. She told us that you were dead."

Drew nodded as he held the child to his chest. "Sounds like something she would do."

Tears began to fall down Sarah's face. She looked at the young man and asked, "Are you here for your son?"

She had fallen in love with the child and the thought that she might have to give him up was tearing her apart. Jacob held Sarah's hand as she held her breath.

"No, I'm not here for my son," Drew said, looking at both of their faces.

Sarah let out a breath of relief. "You're not?"

"Not yet. I know that you two have been taking good care of him and I am here to see him for the first time but I will not sign over my parental rights," Drew said.

"You won't?" Sarah asked, obviously heartbroken.

"I will come back for him as soon as I get a job and my own place," Drew explained.

Jacob stared at Drew. "You're not even working?"

Drew kissed the baby's cheek and Sarah cringed. "I was in my second year of college but I've decided to drop out to take care of my son."

Jacob cornered him. "Drop out of school? What do your parents say about all of this?"

"They think that I can't take care of a baby." Drew placed the baby back into Sarah's arms. "My parents would kill me - not help me - if I decided to keep him. But I can't let him go..."

Sarah pushed Jacob aside and stood face to face with Drew. "Why don't you just let us adopt him?"

"Believe me, it's nothing personal. Heather has explained to me about you two and I believe that you'd give him a good home if he had no parents." Drew walked towards the door. "But he does have a parent... at least one left."

"But are you sure that you know what

you're doing? I mean taking care of a young child is a big responsibility, day and night? Are you sure that you're ready for that?" Sarah asked in desperation.

"No, I'm not sure I'm ready but I guess I'll have to get ready." Drew chuckled.

Sarah didn't think that this was any kind of laughing matter and didn't even crack a smile. Instead, she and Jacob continued to stare in disbelief. *Gott*, help us.

Drew leaned forward into Sarah's face. "It'll probably take a little getting used to but I'll learn how to handle it. But...I mean everybody has to start somewhere, right?"

The closer he came to her; Sarah could smell alcohol on his breath and smoke on his clothes. It was clear that baby John would not be going into the ideal environment for a baby and she held her breath throughout the remainder of the conversation.

"But what happens next?"Sarah felt foolish for having to ask this but it was necessary.

"I'll be in touch in a few days," Drew continued.

Then they watched him turn his cap backward and leave without another word.

Chapter Two

Jacob attempted to comfort his wife by putting his arm around her but Sarah still felt defeated. How could this perfect stranger march in, after having no involvement since birth, and take away their child?

Sarah felt sick in her stomach and after speaking briefly to the bishop, she felt even more sick; she didn't believe that I-told-you-sos were in order but the bishop certainly let them have it.

"Why can't he understand that we would be good parents to this child and a good example to the community; not a bad influence?" Sarah said to Jacob after they finally arrived at home.

Sarah put the baby down and began pacing the floors. "How can they do this to us?"

"I'm afraid they're the parents, not us. Therefore they have all of the rights," Jacob explained. "I'm not a lawyer but I'm pretty sure that there is nothing we can do."

"But Heather lied to us about the father being dead," Sarah spat out. "And now look at us."

"She did lie but it's not a crime to lie. We fell for it or wanted to fall for it."

"I guess you're right. But Heather said she would sign over her rights," Sarah said.

"Maybe she still does or maybe she has changed her mind. Maybe she and the baby's father are going to be a family…"

"I don't think so. Something tells me that getting his hands on that baby is less about his son and more about his own selfish gain," Sarah pointed her finger at John who was sleeping in his crib.

Jacob frowned. "And maybe he just wants his son. He has every right to have him."

"Whose side are you on?"

"I'm on the right side. John's side," Jacob said in a matter-of-fact tone.

"You know what I mean. I don't trust that Drew person. I know that he's the baby's father and all but I just don't believe that he wants that baby." Sarah bent down to nuzzle the baby. "Father or no father, I don't believe that he has honest intentions."

"But what reason would he have for dropping out of school and taking the baby? You'll have to let go."

Sarah rubbed the baby's back. "I don't know why Drew is doing what he's doing but I can guarantee you that I won't stop until I find out."

Chapter Three

The next day Sarah arose early to do her morning chores. After sending Jacob off to his doctor's office with a hearty meal, she decided to do some much-needed snooping. She loaded herself and the baby into the buggy and took off down the road, headed towards the city. She went down to Heather's apartment building, parked the buggy and went inside. When she arrived at Heather's door, she was hesitant to knock. She wasn't even sure what she would say but she prayed for strength and that the right words would come. *Gott,* help me.

By the time she raised her hand up to the door, it swung open. Sarah was startled and held the baby close to her chest. Then she stepped forward into the apartment. There was Heather leaning against the wall smoking.

Heather put her hands on her hips. "I'm surprised that it took you so long?"

"So long to what?"

"To come back here with him." Heather cackled like a witch.

"I came because I had to." Sarah walked straight towards Heather. "Why did you lie to us about John's father being dead?"

Heather shrugged her shoulders.

"You knew we wanted to adopt him..."

"And I wanted you to," Heather said.

Sarah raised her eyebrows. "You mean you still want us to have him?" Finally, there was a glimmer of hope.

"Of course. Where else would I want him?"

Sarah started to explain, "Well, his father came by and-"

"I know but I had nothing to do with that. I told Drew about the baby because he came by to see me and he started… well…anyway I told him we had a son. I told him he was going to be adopted. I didn't know he'd act like this."

"How can I believe you? "Sarah fought back tears. "Why did you tell me he was dead?"

"Because I wanted him to be dead, okay?" Heather balled up her fists and hit the wall.

"He never did anything except use me."

"Then why is he trying to take the baby away from us? He said that he dropped out of school to take care of a newborn and he doesn't look like the babysitting type…"

"But I didn't know he'd pull a stunt like this. Look, I don't know what he's doing; he hasn't told me anything. He ain't no saint but I guess he has his reasons."

"Is that all you can say? You guess he has his reasons? He is taking your baby out of a good home and bringing him to….to… I don't even know where and that's all you can say."

"He's not my baby anymore since I

signed him over to you so it's not my problem. Besides, Drew is his father so if he wants him then he wants him. Maybe Drew will be good for him; I don't know. All I know is that I can't take care of him." Heather began to cry.

Sarah put her arm around Heather. "Don't worry; everything will be all right." But the truth was that Sarah wasn't really confident in her own words.

Chapter Four

When Sarah arrived at home, Jacob was on the porch waiting. "Where were you? I've been so worried."

"I wasn't planning to be gone long. I'd hope you wouldn't worry if you noticed that I wasn't at home. I went to see Heather."

"Are you serious? You went over there by yourself? That was so dangerous. Are you all right?"

"I mean Heather didn't hurt me or anything if that's what you mean. But I'm not all right. My heart is broken. Strangers come into our home and threaten to take something dear to us."

Jacob sighed. "I know. I'm feeling a little sad as well but we have to let go. If the father of the baby wants this child, then there is nothing we can do about it. Can't you understand that?"

"Can't you understand that I don't believe Drew's intentions are honorable? I don't believe that Drew really wants to raise his son. And I can't, I don't trust him – not at all."

"Well, he has hurt you so it is understandable that you wouldn't trust him. I don't trust him but I don't think that changes our choices. We are not John's biological parents; that's the truth."

"We are his parents appointed by *Gott*." Sarah wiped a tear from her eye. "Have you forgotten that we've been a family all these months?"

"I haven't forgotten anything. You know I love him too," Jacob explained.

"Do you?" Sarah folded her arms across her chest.

"But Sarah, be reasonable," Jacob said.

Tears began to run down her face. "Reasonable? You want to be reasonable when a man has come to take away our child."

"He's not our child," Jacob said.

"But how do you know if you won't take a chance and fight for him. You fought to become a doctor against the odds. You even fought for me to become your wife. All of a sudden you've lost your will to fight? That is not the man I married." Sarah turned her nose to the ceiling.

"I came back to the community because of its values. I am tired of fighting." Jacob ran his fingers through his beard. "Drew said he would contact us in a few days and I suggest that you be ready to give him back. We will do this peaceably and in order."

Sarah shook her head in disbelief. "Just like that? "

"Just like that." Jacob went into the house, slamming the door behind him.

Chapter Five

The next few days in their household were tense ones. Sarah continued to take care of baby John as if he was her own while Jacob seemed as if he was trying his best to disconnect from the situation. She worked, she waited, and she prayed, hoping that something would come up, that something would cause Drew to have a change of heart. But every day there was only silence and she was grateful for another day to be a mother to her son; in her heart he was hers. And no court or letter of the law could ever change that.

Yet, the conflict was interfering with her marriage. Jacob spent most of his days working with his patients, many of whom were skeptical of being seen by an Amish doctor. Many were skeptical about seeing any doctor at all because they had gone all their lives without one. Either way, the stress was unbearable for both of them.

Sarah would help him in the office most of the day, while doing her household chores in between. She cooked, gardened, mended, washed clothes, churned butter, made jellies and jams, and took care of little John without complaint but she was exhausted and given the stagnant status of the adoption, she was also disillusioned.

Nothing seemed to be going right lately. She prayed that *Gott* would help her to not be upset with Jacob but she couldn't help herself. How could he just stand there idly by and let someone take their baby away? It made her angry every time she thought about it but she knew that she had to be submissive and accept the unacceptable.

One day when Sarah was tending to the garden, a strange person appeared behind her. She recognized him as the local mail carrier and he handed her a certified letter. She ripped it open and saw that it was from Drew's attorney. Her heart dropped and she braced herself. Sarah grabbed the baby who was sleeping in his stroller beside her and ran to Jacob's office as fast as her legs could carry her.

She burst through the door. "It has happened. They're finally coming to take him."

"Who? What's going on?"

"Drew's attorney sent this letter and…" Sarah was shaking.

Jacob read it, and then took his wife in his arms. "It's time," he said, gently rocking her.

She collapsed to the floor and refused to get up.

"Sarah, please. I have patients that are coming," he said.

But she ignored him, continuing to scream and cry. She could hardly believe that the nightmare was finally unfolding.

Every day she feared that this would be the day that she lost John. She moped around the house and hardly spoke to Jacob.

Later on that day Sarah started to pack John's clothes; each piece she'd sewn by hand except for the original outfits she'd purchased for him after finding him on that fateful night.

Each piece held so many memories for her. She could hardly believe that five months had gone by so fast. It was even hard to believe how her life had changed so fast from a carefree girl who wanted nothing more than to leave the community and be free - to a wife and now a woman pleading to take on the responsibility of motherhood. They'd only been married a few months so there was so much they had to learn about each other yet they had built a family from day one. It wasn't their plan but she thought that perhaps it was *Gott's*.

Jacob didn't have much to say and stayed as far away as possible. She was sure he didn't want to hear her sulk or complain about losing John.

Gott had given her husband and child of her dreams, only to snatch one away. Sometimes she felt she was losing Jacob too because they weren't on one accord. Why couldn't she just let Heather's child go? Because it was not Heather's child, it was hers.

The bishop had already checked on the situation and of course, Jacob had given him a full report. They would be giving up the child any day now and their perfect Amish community would go back to normal whatever that was.

Jacob came home and stood behind her. He hesitated, squeezed her shoulders and she cringed. She didn't really want him to touch her because she was upset. But when she did feel his strong firm hands, her heart began to turn toward her husband again. Jacob took off her *kapp* and ran his hands through her hair.

They were finally able to connect in a way that they hadn't been able to in a few weeks. There had been so much going on, concerning the baby. But now Jacob kissed Sarah softly and despite the needy newborn, he claimed her for himself.

Once they'd spent a while together, with tears of both joy and pain, it was time to continue packing.

Sarah stood up. "I'm setting the first box of John's belongings by the door but I'm still against it."

"I know you are and I know how hard this is for you," Jacob said. "But I am proud of you."

Sarah squinted. "For giving my child away?"

"No, for having the courage to let go."

"But I will never let go, even when they take him away from me." Sarah pointed to her heart. "I will always carry him in here."

It was true that she'd never expected to fall in love with the child but what was done was done; there was no going back.

When it was time to set lunch on the table, Sarah stopped packing. Jacob sat down to eat his chicken soup.

After Sarah served Jacob, she went back to her chores.

"Why don't you sit and eat?"

"I don't really have any appetite," she said.

Sarah couldn't hide her disappointment and although Jacob tried his best to help, she wouldn't smile. She brought the last load of clothes to the door and left it in a crumpled heap.

Suddenly, there was a knock on the door and Sarah wondered who it could be.

Knowing Sarah's condition was shaky; Jacob decided to answer the door.

She peeped around it as Jacob pulled the door open; and it was Heather.

Chapter Six

Sarah glared at Heather who was standing in the doorway. Jacob invited her in and stepped aside.

Heather looked beaten. Her face was red. Her eyes were puffy and swollen. Her hair looked stringy and dirty. Sarah immediately wondered what she'd been through.

Sarah took a deep breath and remembered his manners. "Hello, Heather. Please sit down," she said.

Heather came in, looking nervous and hesitant.

Jacob led Heather over to the kitchen table and pulled out a chair for her. Sarah slowly walked over and sat down in the chair beside her, turning her body so that they were face to face. Jacob didn't move and seemed frozen in time. For a moment there was an uncomfortable silence.

Suddenly, Heather said, "I know you're wondering why I'm here and sometimes I'm not sure myself but I have to do what's right for...for..."

"The baby," Sarah interrupted.

"Yes...the baby," she confirmed.

"What is it?" Sarah took her hand; it was cold and trembling. "Would you like some hot tea?"

"I thought you all didn't do electricity," Heather said.

Sarah smiled gently. "We don't but we still have an oven and a tea kettle. Are you sure you don't want some?"

Heather nodded. "In that case, maybe just a little."

Sarah stood up to pour the hot water and placed the tea bag into the cup. She served Heather, and then sat back down.

"I didn't think you would come," Sarah studied her face.

Heather looked back and forth at Jacob's and Sarah's faces. "I had to. I saw Drew again and I…he didn't seem like a father who loves his son."

Sarah gasped. "Oh?"

Heather nodded, and then went on to explain. "He just seemed cold, like what we had done was some kind of a business deal and like taking him from you was some kind of I don't know… conquest or something." Heather stopped to sip her tea. "I don't know; it just didn't seem right to me. I would still like the two of you to be his parents." Heather paused as tears began to roll down her eyes. "I never meant to fail as a mother…"

Sarah spoke sincerely. "You're not a failure. Any real mother would want to give her child a better life. I know you've had to make some tough decisions but I admire you for doing so."

Heather's bottom lip quivered. "You admire me?" Heather chuckled through her tears. "Ha, that's a good one."

"Yes, we both do," Sarah said, clearing her throat and signaling for Jacob to join in the conversation.

"Uh... yes, we certainly do," Jacob said, looking as if he hadn't been paying attention.

Sarah swallowed hard before speaking. "You see, Heather, we both know how hard it would be for you to raise this child alone and if Drew is not the devoted father that he claims to be, we definitely understand your concern."

"You don't understand; it's more serious than that," Heather said, closing her eyes as if the emotions were too much to bear. "I'm afraid that he may do something to purposely hurt John."

Jacob looked at Sarah and stepped forward. "I know he might not be the best father but why would you say that?"

"Because I found this...." Heather reached into her purse and pulled out a piece of paper.

Chapter Seven

Jacob reached for the paper before handing it to Sarah. "What exactly is this?"

"I don't know for sure but it fell out of his pants pocket the other day…"

Sarah read the newspaper article as Jacob looked over her shoulder. "It looks like this is an article about how selling babies on the black market is on the rise." Sarah shifted her eyes to Heather, then the article and back again. "You can't possibly think that Drew would be capable of something like that."

"You don't understand. I don't know what he's capable of. I've only known him for a few months before becoming pregnant and I didn't see him during that whole time. He was always…different but now he's just…I don't know…"

"So you think he's dangerous?" Jacob rubbed his beard.

"I'm not sure if he's dangerous or not but I just thought you should know and be prepared." Heather stood up and walked towards the door.

"Wait. John is sleeping. Do you want to see him?" Sarah asked.

Heather shook her head. "No, it's better if I don't."

"We understand," Jacob said as he opened the door for her.

Sarah followed her to the door and Heather threw her arms around Sandra.

"I'm sorry I haven't been such a good friend when you two have been so kind to me. I'm sorry that things didn't work out for you and now Drew will take him away forever," Heather said, pulling away.

"It's not your fault. There's nothing you could've done except what you did here today which is warn us." Sarah fought back tears. "*Gott* is in control now."

Heather walked out without another word, leaving Jacob and Sarah to their thoughts.

Sarah slapped her hands together. "I told you something didn't seem right. I knew it."

Jacob shook his head. "But what can we do?"

"I don't know but we're going to do something. We're not going to sit around and watch Drew come and sell this baby off," she said.

Jacob looked worried. "We don't know that for sure."

"Tell me what you feel in your heart," Sarah said.

Jacob was silent and cast his eyes downward.

"That's what I thought," Sarah said. "So we have to figure out what Mr. Drew is into and

I mean fast."

Chapter Eight

Sarah and Jacob's lives had taken quite a turn, from newlyweds to parents, to self-appointed detectives. They used some of the profits from Jacob's medical practice to help pay for the additional attorney fees and some of the costs associated with snooping. Sarah and Jacob couldn't afford to pay a professional to watch him so they did it themselves, leaving the baby with her grandmother, going into town at night, observing everything and they reported any suspicious behavior to their attorney.

It had been two days since the letter had arrived and Drew had not come for the baby yet, but they noticed that he had purchased a new car. Instead of preparing for a baby and buying infant items, he seemed to spending his money on frivolous things like jewelry, new clothes, gambling and a whole lot of drinking.

"We've watched him long enough and we're no closer to having any evidence of wrongdoing," Jacob said.

Sarah was very frustrated. "What are you saying? That we just give up?"

"No, I'm not saying that. I just wish that we had a way to get more," Jacob said.

"Maybe we do have more. We see that he just met with a middle aged couple," Sarah said.

Jacob failed to see the significance. "How does that help us?"

"They were wearing expensive looking clothes and jewelry. And did you see the car they were driving?"

Jacob raised his eyebrows as he caught on. "Do you think they're in on this?"

"They could be and it's worth a try. Maybe they're in the market for a baby. We've got their names so we can go to the police now with something and maybe they can check it out before Drew comes for him, Sarah explained. "It may be our last hope."

"Maybe you're right." Jacob nodded. "We will go to the authorities."

So Jacob and Sarah prayed before going to the police with all of the information they'd gathered. And as it turned out, there had been a string of baby kidnappings in the local area which had the entire department already on high alert. There was already an ongoing investigation so John's situation fit right in. After calling in Drew for questioning in relation to some of the other missing babies, they found out that he had a serious jail record and hadn't been registered in school for quite some time. Instead, he'd been involved in a variety of petty crimes in the area, including an assault, which he was awaiting trial for.

Jacob and Sarah held their breath as they waded through the legal system, wondering if baby John would be forced to go with his father or if he would get lost in the system himself.

Even with all of their hard work, the outcome was uncertain.

Chapter Nine

After weeks of investigation, Drew came to their house one day. "I'm turning over everything to you," he said.

"What do you mean by that?" Jacob asked, calmly.

"You know what I mean, man. You can keep the kid." Drew took out a cigarette and started to light it but saw the expression on their faces and stopped. "I ain't got no time for that anyway."

Sarah studied Drew's face. "Really? Do you mean it?"

"Really. The police are on my back. They think I stole some kid so they're going through my bank accounts and stuff." Drew looked nervous.

"Is that so?" Sarah asked but there was joy rising up in her spirit.

Jacob exchanged contact information for Drew's attorney with their own so that they could meet to sign the appropriate paperwork.

"Look, man, I just want this stuff over with. I'm not trying to go back to prison," he said.

Sarah couldn't believe their dream of adopting was finally coming true, after all they'd been through.

All that was left was to stand before the bishop.

Chapter Ten

Jacob took Sarah's hand and stood in front of the bishop, who surprisingly claimed that they were very brave for taking the matter into their own hands and saving a child from a lifetime of misery.

Six months later, little John's adoption was finalized and Jacob and Sarah couldn't be happier. As promised, Heather had signed away her parental rights with no problem, secure in the knowledge that her son would have a stable family life. And Drew signed away his, relieved that he would not have to serve time in prison. Jacob and Sarah were thrilled to be able to provide a home for the baby they considered their son from the beginning; it was a beautiful and happy end for a devoted couple.

Although things were a little shaky at first, with the bishop's approval, the community soon came to accept the *Englisher* boy as Jacob and Sarah's own child.

Sarah put John to sleep in his wooden crib, and then curled up beside Jacob. "I love you, Jacob."

"I love you more, Sarah," he answered, giving her a soft kiss on the lips.

"I'm so grateful that *Gott* has allowed us to become parents in such an unusual way,"

Sarah said.

"Now let's practice becoming parents in the usual way." Jacob grinned as he took his wife into his arms and showered her with his love.

THE END

6: HAVING SECOND THOUGHTS

The Amish Zooks Cast

Sarah Zook: Eldest Zook child

Joseph Zook: Sarah's younger brother

Abigail and Rachel Zook: Sarah's twin sisters

Zachary Zook: Youngest Zook child

Chapter One

Sarah Zook was eighteen when she underwent her baptism. She'd spoken about it heavily with both her parents, who had been baptized at different ages. She spoke to her grandmother as well, and a few of the elders who were willing to offer counsel. She studied for it, reading her father's old journals on his own baptism and reading records of baptisms that she could find in old archives.

When she was a child, she imagined herself getting baptized as early as possible. Baptism was the only way to a family, the earlier she did it, the earlier she could be married and begin a family of her own. Her mother warned her then, and several times later, that baptism for the sake of another was no true way to enter into a promise to uphold the *Ordnung*. She then sent her to study scripture on it.

"Why do the English undergo baptism as babies?" Sarah asked one morning over breakfast. She'd stayed up past her bedtime the night before reading by dim candlelight.

"They believe sin is an inherent part of existence," her father said. "They believe all people are born with a taint."

"Are they?"

"You tell me."

He was like this, an intelligent man who forced all his children to think. He encouraged learning for all them and refused to ever answer questions outright. It was frustration at times but also fun. Sarah enjoyed learning.

So she thought. She considered what the Bible said about sin, Adam and Eve's transgression in the garden. They had not been born into any form of sin. But were not their descendants for their ancient crime of disobedience? What was it that poisoned their existence? The snake?

The apple.

It was one of the first things Sarah remembered being taught, that their way of life exercised as much sinful knowledge as possible. And infants do not have any at all, so how could they make an informed decision to be baptized?

"They are without knowledge of good and evil," she said.

"Go on."

"They need to know first, and make the decision for themselves."

Her father smiled and offered her an extra piece of toast as a reward. She happily took it and slathered it with jam.

After that she thought heavily of baptism. She often prayed for guidance and understanding and courage. It took several years and she understood why her mother wanted her to wait, how important it was. So she did, until she was eighteen and watched several friends get baptism and turned a blind eye to the English life not far from their home. This was her calling and exactly where she was meant to be.

So she undertook the classes with the elders, hoping to be baptized in the fall before having to wait until next spring. For weeks while her parents sang the *Ausbund* in church services, she and several other young adults from the community huddled together under the direction of Elder Hostler and read about the *Ordnung*. That was where she truly met Aaron for the first time.

She'd known of him before, they'd played together as children while their parents threshed the fields together at the end of summer. She'd always envied him his energy but she learned quickly in classes that she had him beat in reading and study. He turned red in the face every time he answered wrong and she raised her hand to swoop in correct.

"Showing off is a sign of pride, Sarah," he said one day, after church services concluded for the day.

"Its pride to claim you know my transgressions and judge me for them," she shot back and she knew she had him. He turned that familiar shade of red again and she giggled. "I can help you if you want. You don't want to wait until spring to have the ceremony."

He shook his head and walked away with tight shoulders and hands shoved into his pockets. Sarah shrugged and the pattern continued for the next few weeks before Elder Hostler scolded Aaron one day for not being able to recite their assigned portion of the *Dordect* Confession to have memorized.

"Please let me help you," she said after the services. "We only have a few weeks left and Elder Hostler isn't very impressed with you."

"I don't need pity," he said.

"It's a kindness. No one has to know. You can come over to help my father stack firewood for the winter. And we'll study while you work. No one will ever have to know. My father's the smartest man I know, he can help too."

Ultimately, she wore him down and he showed up that afternoon with an axe in hand and a less than eager face. But Sarah smiled all the same and followed him with her books all day, reciting lines and asking him questions. Her father would help where he saw fit and answer Aaron's questions. By day three he was answering many of them on his own and reciting lines better than Sarah had ever seen.

By the next class, Aaron was raising his hand as well, sending small smiles to Sarah. They spent several more weeks studying together under her father's watchful eye and talked about life as a true member of the community. They talked about how they'd spend their weekends, the names they'd each want for their children. They remembered games they played together as children and laughed for hours. The repeated the process until the very day before the ceremony.

"This is your final chance to change your mind," Elder Hostler said. "Think carefully, the Amish church is not the only path to salvation and breaking the *Ordnung* will result in shunning. Only undertake this commitment if you mean to uphold it until the end of your days."

That night, Aaron came over for dinner at her father's invitation and they spent hours watching the stars from the backyard and talking. Sarah's siblings lingered nearby, asking questions in envy as their youth forbid them from entering the baptism yet. In the dark Sarah felt her face flush a few times and caught Aaron's jolly eyes, shining in the dark. And when he departed for the night he gave her a lingering look and wave.

The next day they bowed together before the bishop, answering his questions with assuredness. Aaron promised to commit to church service, should he be called upon it later in life. Sarah never felt happier than when she felt the rush of water fall over her head and the kiss of promise from the bishop's wife. Then she and Aaron rose together, beaming as they joined the community for the rest of the service.

And after it was over, and they were celebrating with a picnic in Sarah's yard. Aaron offered her a piece of China that had been in his family for generations and told her he'd already asked her father. He then asked her to be his wife.

At the time she said yes without even waiting for him to finish. And now, over a year later, she felt herself shake at the thought of it.

Because they had bypassed much of the courtship period, both Sarah's father and Aaron's insisted they prolong their engagement. Sarah tried not to hide her disappointment at first, but she also understood. And now, over a year later, she felt herself grow nervous when she truly thought about why.

She hid the fears well. But as the intended date grew closer and closer, Sarah felt herself grow sweatier at the thought of forever binding herself to Aaron. She was sure she loved him, but her mind was slow to be silenced when fears set in.

Things were not helped when her grandmother, suffering ailments from her bed for weeks now, insisted she see her first granddaughter married before she went to be with the Lord. Sarah felt trapped.

Chapter Two

Aaron was a man of the field. While he had friends who worked well in carpentry and some who were gifted with animals, his skills had always been in gathering crops and taking in the air of the fields at harvest time. It was an excellent time to think, to clear his head, and try to speak with God about things that were troubling him. And, lately, his most prominent trouble was the one thing that was meant to give him peace and happiness: his marriage.

He was sure he loved Sarah; his heart had never felt lighter than when she was near and when her attention was focused on him. Her laugh was the music in his dreams and he never wanted to go a day without seeing her.

But others had talked that way as well.

Johanna Miller and Zachariah Ziedler had talked of nothing but each other for months during their courtship. And then, as if overnight, they broke it off in melancholy and tears and insisted that their union was not the will God had planned for them. Aaron wondered if he and Sarah had been too quick, if they trampled over God's plans for them by being hasty in the after-joy of their baptism. Would God send them a sign that they were making the wrong choice? Were his fears the sign he feared?

It was difficult to muddle through everything that went through his brain.

"Are you asleep Aaron?" Abel asked from a row over.

"Huh?"

"You've taken a whack at that same corn stalk about three times, where's your head today?" he asked. "Still with your dear Sarah?"

He meant it as a tease and smiled all through it but he had no idea, how could he know the torment going on inside Aaron's mind? They had not yet made their engagement known in the church; that was coming at the end of the week and the ceremony not long after, though.

Aaron was sure his friends likely suspected it. While Sarah's parents had known about the engagement long before the usual time because Aaron had asked her father for his guidance, his own family was not yet aware either.

In short, Aaron felt the entire engagement had been a mess of tradition. It was not uncommon for uncommon things to happen, especially if God willed it. But was he arrogant to believe his unorthodox engagement was God's will? What if they were disobeying some sacred command they did not yet know about? Were they already breaking their vows by going at a pace the rest of the community did not?

These questions kept Aaron up at night

and his friends were beginning to notice.

"What's troubling you, Aaron? Truly?" Levi asked, walking over.

"Things I cannot yet say," he said.

He wanted to ask Levi about his sister, about how Johanna had broken off her courtship and engagement. But that would give away exactly where his fears were coming from. He could not go to Sarah's father for fear of the disappointment in the man's eyes when his future son-in-law was admitting to being fearful of marrying his daughter.

He felt truly and utterly alone, surrounded by friends and confidants.

But when the wind rustled around him and he felt the kiss of the sun, he thought of the Lord. He did not walk alone, and secretive as he was, the Lord knew of Aaron's struggles late at night and during the rush of the day.

"I think I'll take a short rest, if that's okay," he said, putting down his sack. Levi nodded and gave his shoulder a comforting squeeze.

The rest of the boys carried on, continuing their work and Aaron sat down on the cool earth. He looked up at the gorgeous blue of the sky and the softness of the clouds. He felt the gentle brush of the wind over him and took several deep breaths. He closed his eyes and thought of God and everything he read. He prayed that he might understand what he was and his friends were beginning to notice.

"What's troubling you, Aaron? Truly?" Levi asked, walking over.

"Things I cannot yet say," he said.

He wanted to ask Levi about his sister, about how Johanna had broken off her courtship and engagement. But that would give away exactly where his fears were coming from. He could not go to Sarah's father for fear of the disappointment in the man's eyes when his future son-in-law was admitting to being fearful of marrying his daughter.

He felt truly and utterly alone, surrounded by friends and confidants.

But when the wind rustled around him and he felt the kiss of the sun, he thought of the Lord. He did not walk alone, and secretive as he was, the Lord knew of Aaron's struggles late at night and during the rush of the day.

"I think I'll take a short rest, if that's okay," he said, putting down his sack. Levi nodded and gave his shoulder a comforting squeeze.

The rest of the boys carried on, continuing their work and Aaron sat down on the cool earth. He looked up at the gorgeous blue of the sky and the softness of the clouds. He felt the gentle brush of the wind over him and took several deep breaths. He closed his eyes and thought of God and everything he read. He prayed that he might understand what he was

It was difficult to muddle through everything that went through his brain.

"Are you asleep Aaron?" Abel asked from a row over.

"Huh?"

"You've taken a whack at that same corn stalk about three times, where's your head today?" he asked. "Still with your dear Sarah?"

He meant it as a tease and smiled all through it but he had no idea, how could he know the torment going on inside Aaron's mind? They had not yet made their engagement known in the church; that was coming at the end of the week and the ceremony not long after, though.

Aaron was sure his friends likely suspected it. While Sarah's parents had known about the engagement long before the usual time because Aaron had asked her father for his guidance, his own family was not yet aware either.

In short, Aaron felt the entire engagement had been a mess of tradition. It was not uncommon for uncommon things to happen, especially if God willed it. But was he arrogant to believe his unorthodox engagement was God's will? What if they were disobeying some sacred command they did not yet know about? Were they already breaking their vows by going at a pace the rest of the community did not?

These questions kept Aaron up at night

feeling, that he could silence his mind, even for a few moments, and see the Lord's will clearly.

He prayed for this for several minutes before getting up and rejoining the group at work.

Chapter Three

They announced their marriage, as customary, at a church service in October. Sarah did not attend the service, staying home to prepare the traditional meal to introduce her family to her fiancée. It all felt so terribly out of order and she tried not to think about it but every whiff of the meat cooking in the oven and the sour smell of the beets roasting in brine brought her back to the issue at hand.

Sarah could think of no one else she wanted to commit herself to, but that didn't mean she and Aaron hadn't been hasty. And any chance of trying to talk about it was dashed when her grandmother insisted on seeing the wedding before her passing. She could not blame her grandmother, nor was it right to. But the burden she felt on her shoulders was going to crush her if she didn't find some kind of release in it.

Aaron arrived with the rest of her family after services, all beaming and complimenting her on the wafting smells of food from the kitchen as she set out plates.

"Congratulations," her youngest sister said while her brothers beamed at her.

She smiled back as sturdy as she could manage and asked her mother to help put the food out for serving. They gathered around the table and her father lead them in grace before they dug into the meal.

"Elder Hostler was particularly excited," her father said. "He's also extremely proud."

Sarah gave a thin smile and didn't look at Aaron. He'd kept his head mostly confined to his plate. He spoke when spoken to, but his mind was clearly elsewhere. Sarah tried not to take it as a bad sign.

"Grandmother is anxious for the wedding," Sarah said, trying not to let her voice shake as she spoke.

"Well it'll be here in a few days. When are you extending the invitations?" her father said and turned to Aaron. He jumped in his seat and turned that familiar shade of red Sarah knew from their time together in classes. It calmed her a bit, to see the echo of the boy she met.

"Tomorrow," he coughed out. "Levy Miller is going to be helping me."

Sarah's father nodded and started telling a story about how snow had come early the month that he'd married Sarah's mother and had to trudge through a foot of it to deliver invitations. The family giggled and Sarah tried to join in.

What she didn't notice, trapped inside her own mind, was the eyes of her younger siblings on her throughout the dinner. She also didn't notice their looks to each other or the way they disappeared after dinner to commune together.

Chapter Four

Zachary did not often communicate well with his sisters. He thought girls were boring most of the time and their games in the yard were boring too. But he also knew all his sisters well, and Sarah had looked pale and nearly sick the entire dinner. When Joseph bumped him on the arm and nodded to Aaron, who looked nearly as ill, they looked to their sisters. They'd seen it too.

"I say we talk to them both, apart, see if they're going to be more honest that way," Joseph said.

"Do you think Aaron will really speak to you?" one of the twins asked.

"I'm his favorite," Zachary said proudly.

"I don't think so, but it's worth a shot," Joseph said.

So they made plans. The girls would get Sarah by herself, away from the rest of the family, and try to talk to her. Zachary and Joseph would do the same with Aaron, perhaps find him tomorrow during his travels to send out invitations or while he was working in the field.

Of course, they weren't exactly sure what it was they were looking for in their talks. Both Sarah and Aaron seemed downcast and hadn't said a word to each other all through dinner. Sarah had been smitten for Aaron since they met and he'd turned red in the face whenever she was around for as long as they'd known him. There were no lost feelings of love between the couple, so what was keeping them in such a state of anxiety? And a secret anxiety at that? They clearly weren't talking to anyone about their troubles.

Zachary knew he was no elder and they should perhaps consult their parents first, before meddling. But sometimes the wisdom of siblings could be more helpful. Sarah was nervous and their grandmother had taken a turn for the worse in her illness and it made her grow impatient.

But what, then, was Aaron's trouble?

Chapter Five

Aaron had never been particularly close to Sarah's siblings. His own mother had been struck with an illness after he was born and was unable to have more children. He was a unique only child in the community and his parents had believed it a miracle that he existed at all. He longed for the companionship of siblings though, when he'd been lonely in the winter with no one around.

But around Sarah's siblings he'd always felt nervous. There were so many of them and similar as their faces might seem, they all were incredibly different from the one next to them. It was hard, sometimes, to keep track of who was who, especially the twins, but they were to become his siblings soon too. He was finally getting the large family he longed for, and he worked hard at remembering individual things about all them.

They were receptive to his interest, if more outgoing than him. They occasionally invited themselves to help at his farm or invited him over. But it was something of a big surprise when Zachary and Joseph offered to go with Aaron to offer invitations to his wedding. He and Levy stood in the early morning light, yawning and talking, when the two boys came up the road, smiling right at them.

"We thought we might accompany you," Joseph said. "We're to be family after all; we should spend more time together before it becomes official."

Aaron tried to hide how taken aback he was lest he accidently offended his brothers-to-be. Levy seemed to find nothing strange about it, smiling and greeting them. He knew how rambunctious the siblings could be. He came from a big family too though, and laughed at Aaron's inexperience with siblings.

"Your brothers are good men," Levy said. "Well, this one will be a man soon anyway."

Zachary looked offended at the accusation and Joseph nudged him. Levy laughed and ruffled his hair, saying he'd make a fine man soon.

"How are you this morning, Aaron?" Joseph asked.

"Well. Tired. Nervous," Aaron said.

"All to be expected," Joseph said. "I don't know how I'm going to get through my own wedding one day."

Aaron swallowed hard at the heavy lump in his throat and felt himself begin to sweat at the collar when Joseph's eyes lingered on him in a look he could not quite place. As the sun was cutting through the trees on the horizon, they started their journey across the fields to offer out the invitations.

Aaron had many members of his church district, it didn't help his nerves that it meant the wedding would be huge. He'd have plenty of eyes watching him fumble through his own nervousness. That didn't raise the rate of his heart at all.

They first went to Schneider farm and spoke with Abraham Schneider. He smiled and clapped Aaron on the back and congratulated him. Then they went to the Rittehouse home and spoke with Elisabeth and Johann who both agreed with beaming faces to be at the ceremony. Aaron was beginning to grow nervous as the day wore on and the numbers grew.

It was around midday when Levy said he needed to stop to get something to eat from his family's stall at the market. It was also this time that, as Aaron had expected and been waiting for all day, that Joseph and Zachary sat down next to him while they rested.

"How are you Aaron, I mean truly?" Joseph said. His voice was much less jovial than it had been when they first met up that morning. He'd become serious and somehow older.

"Fine," he said. "Exhausted, as I said."

"I want you to know you can speak with us, we're to be your brothers after all," Joseph said. "We'll keep your confidence, whatever it is. We're as much your brothers as we are Sarah's and we want what is best for the both of you."

Aaron sighed. He had always been a terrible liar. And he felt guilty brushing away their help when they were offering so sincerely. Maybe this was part of having siblings too, learning to confide in someone.

"I have an anxiety about everything," Aaron admitted. "I've been feeling it for some time now."

"That much we guessed," Joseph said. "What has made you nervous?"

"I fear that we perhaps rushed into this," he said. "I love Sarah and I would be happy to spend the rest of my life with her but I fear we overstepped. I fear the Lord did not intend for our union and that perhaps Sarah will find herself unhappy with me by the end."

"If God wills something, no amount of worrying can stop it," Zachary said. Aaron nodded but did not feel comforted by it. It was the possibility that the Lord would destine them for separation that made Aaron quake.

"What's bringing this on?" Joseph asked.

"Time. I think," Aaron said. "I do too much thinking in the fields, overthinking. And I never had the benefit of a big family to talk to."

"Well you've got us now," Zachary said. "And we want to see our sister and you happy."

"This unease is your own making," Joseph said. "I don't pretend to know the Lord's will but I think this discomfort is coming from you and your mind, not from Him and your heart."

"It's hard to know the difference," Aaron said.

The brothers nodded in sympathy and they got quiet again, reveling in the sounds of autumn and the chirping of birds.

"Bring your fears before God and He will give you your answer," Joseph said. "And bring your fears before Sarah. You two are becoming one; you should face such things together."

Aaron feared that answer but he also knew in his heart it was true. Hearing it out loud only furthered his belief and fear of the inevitable. But if he could not talk to Sarah, then who could he talk to? Marriage and commitment meant he shouldn't have to suffer alone. Perhaps she would tell him he was being silly and laugh at him as she always did and then they'd be happily married. Or maybe she would be offended and reject him in favor of someone stronger and smarter.

Either was possible, but he would never know if he said nothing. And Sarah deserved to know everything before they entered into a commitment with each other. They could not truly be bound before God under false pretenses.

"I will speak with her after I have some reflection," Aaron said finally and Joseph and Zachary nodded in their approval.

Levy eventually returned with loaves of bread for each of them and greetings from his family. Aaron pushed away thoughts of Levy's sister and her broken engagement. He focused instead of the sounds of the land and the thought of Sarah smiling, giggling face. It was his home and place of comfort. In that he would find solace.

Chapter Six

Sarah spent her morning pouring herself into the project of sewing Joseph's work pants. He'd put a fourth hole in them over the summer and short of scolding him, Sarah silently continued her diligent work, hoping this time he'd keep them in better shape, but she wasn't betting on it.

It gave her time to think, as well. With each stitch she thought about her grandmother. She should go see her, speak with her, ensure her she'd get to see her first grandchild wed, just as she wished. But every time she thought about opening her mouth to talk to her grandmother she feared everything she'd push down to the depths of her would come out. She could never disappoint her grandmother like that.

Rachel and Abigail walked into the living room with a tray of tea and some biscuits, setting them on the ottoman in the center of the room. They sat on the floor before the tray and smiled up at Sarah who gave a small smile back and returned to her work. She didn't get far as she felt her sisters' eyes watching her from their midday treat. She wouldn't give them the satisfaction of giving into their staring game. But it continued over the next several minutes, causing her to miss a stitch so she huffed and put her work down.

"Just come out with it, you two," she said, frustrated.

"We just want to talk," Abigail said.

"That much I gathered for myself," Sarah said.

They were silent for a second, staring back at Sarah who was growing increasingly annoyed.

"What is it you wanted to talk about?" she sighed.

"We're afraid to upset you," Rachel said.

"You've already done that, might as well finish the job," Sarah said bitterly.

The twins shared the same, frowning, sympathetic look, and then turned back to Sarah. They had a knack for communicating with their eyes and seemed to take a deep breath and give off a sigh together, like they were connected in the mind.

"It's about Aaron," Rachel said steadily.

Sarah felt herself grow pale. Not long ago she would go red in the face at the mention of his name, now she dreaded it. How far had they fallen from what they used to be?

"What about him?" Sarah asked.

"In short: are you happy?" Abigail asked.

"Happy? Of course."

"We've noticed the anxiety," Rachel said. "We just want to help. You're the first one to get married and we want the best for you."

"Aaron is what's best for me."

"We agree, that's why we want to help whatever this strange nervousness is."

Sarah felt herself soften at that. She could see the sincerity in their eyes. They meant every word of it. And they looked like they might be as ready to cry as she sometimes felt. Her father once told her siblings were meant to stick together, like a pack. If one was wounded, the rest could feel it. And her distress had not only caught their attention, but worried them, just as her father had said.

If she could not be honest with her siblings, then who could she talk to?

"Do you think Aaron and I have been too hasty?" she asked, quietly, as if saying it out loud would bring down the sky by admitting her fear.

"Hasty?" Abigail asked.

"We entered into all this very quickly. We've been betrothed for a year but the engagement came quick after our baptism. I just fear we're overstepping God's wishes," she said.

"If you were, wouldn't God have already done something about it?" Rachel asked.

"Perhaps he wants me to suffer for a time before he truly delivers punishment," Sarah said bitterly.

"Careful Sarah," Abigail warned. "You shouldn't talk in such an ungrateful way. The Lord does things for reasons far beyond us. If that is truly what is happening, then you must accept it with grace and thanks. He's making you stronger. But I think you and Aaron are truly meant to be."

Their words were a small comfort to Sarah, she could admit that much.

"Hebrews 11:1, remember that much," Abigail said, coming forward and taking her sister's hands in her own in a show of comfort. "This is a trial, no way around that, but trying to guess its purpose or ending is only going to hurt you. Worrying about tomorrow's troubles will not make them go away; it will only ruin today's peace."

Sarah closed her eyes and let out a breath she didn't realize she'd been holding. They were right, they were both right. She'd been arrogant to think she could sit alone and deal with this without guidance or help. She should speak with her grandmother, and with Aaron.

Though it would be hard to bring it up to him. He was so stoic most of the time, it was nearly impossible to guess his mind. But she could not let that stop her, if they were to be husband and wife. This would not be the first or last time they would suffer some form of miscommunication and fear. The point of it all was to face it together. So she made a promise, to speak with him.

But first she thanked her sisters and let her knitting be done for the day. She was done with distractions, for now. So instead she sat and enjoyed tea and snacks with the twins. They would not be able to do this soon, as she was to move in with Aaron in a house he and his friends were building for them. She was excited about it; she couldn't wait to be in her own home with him.

So she focused on that instead of the fear bubbling underneath. She would take several breaths, return to her reading, speak with her grandmother, and pray for guidance. And when she was ready, she'd speak to Aaron and sort this mess out.

She refused to disappoint her grandmother's dying wish.

Chapter Seven

Aaron considered himself always something of a secret night owl. He enjoyed the daytime and all the energy and work that came with it. But ever since he was young and struggling to understand his studies, he stayed up late by candlelight reading and thinking. That only increased when Sarah had helped him learn to understand the scripture and his studies.

But tonight was not a night he was awake by his own will.

It was well past midnight at this point. He was tired from a day of traveling around town to invite members of the community to the wedding. His feet were sorer than they'd been in a while and the sun baked his skin and zapped his energy, even in the cool autumn air. So he'd tried to go to sleep at an early hour, just after the sun went down. But he found himself tossing and turning over and over. His bed seemed to no longer hold a comfortable spot and no matter how he positioned his legs and arms they seemed to want to do nothing but move.

So finally, he let them. At first he told himself he was simply going to get some water from the pump and see if he could calm himself down during the walk. But after drinking the water, his mind started buzzing; he realized sleep was something that was going to evade him for the time being.

He stared at the clear night sky; the stars twinkled in the vast openness. The English didn't have this, a perfect view into the world above. Their cities and electric lights polluted their air. Here, in the dark, with dazzling lights above, Aaron listened for the whispers from the Lord among the sounds of crickets. In his mind he unleashed his questions. Had they been too hasty? Was this the Lord's will? Were they simply arrogant and excited youngsters?

He tried to focus, tried to feel his answers. He was certain he loved Sarah and he would continue to love her unless God placed love for another in his heart. In the dark he tried to filter everything out of his mind but it was easier said than done. That's when he took to pacing. Elder Hofstadter once said that movement helped him think, that he wrote all his important papers on a board while he was pacing his own yard. So Aaron did the same.

He paced the length of the yard and then around the front and back again. He tried to work through each one of his questions. He rephrased them to himself and stopped a few times to try and think of a prayer that would befit his struggles. Ultimately, he decided there was not enough room on their land. So, barefoot and dressed in his night clothes, he started taking a walk down the lane.

He told himself by the first turn in the road he'd a have thought of the answer to at least one question. That didn't work. So he tried it with three more turns. Still he was left wondering and turning over thoughts and questions inside his head. It was not long until he found himself on a familiar stretch of road that lead to the Zook farm.

Had he unconsciously brought himself here? Had God steered him in the direction of where all his woes—and possibly all his answers—would lie?

He allowed himself to walk towards the farm and the closer he got, he realized he saw the flicker of a light around the back. A figure, shrouded by the dim light but very much present, was sitting back there, still and calm. He was cautious when approaching, in case he spooked one of Sarah's parents or her siblings who would no doubt then immediately tell her parents he'd been prowling on the farm in the dark.

As he came closer he recognized the familiar face and his stomach dropped. It was Sarah who was sitting alone in the dark on the back porch of the house. Still as she was, she was very much awake. She was pensive as she stared off into the night but Aaron dared not get closer to further investigate her face. He should turn back, he should head home and save this conversation for morning and daylight and chaperones. They took their oaths; surely this would be breaking some form of the *Ordnung*?

But God had also delivered him here in the night when he didn't know which way his feet were going to carry him. God alone was their chaperone, was that not the way things were supposed to be, now and again?

He let himself stop and feel again. He waited, patiently, in the dark and listened for something that could not be heard, it had to be felt. The Lord would not let either of them sleep, He lead Aaron to walk down this path and delivered him here. This was destined to happen, which meant it must be God's will to talk to Sarah.

So he stepped forward. He took a deep breath and held it and walked towards Sarah, without caring for noise, until she noticed him.

She didn't look frightened or surprised. Perhaps she felt it all too. Maybe she knew, in her heart, as Aaron did that the Lord had brought them together in the quiet, just for them.

"Hi Sarah," he said with a sheepish smile.

The smile she returned was warm and seemed to brighten up the night as he pulled her cheeks to touch her eyes in the most dazzling way.

"Hello."

She said it soft that anyone else would have never heard it. But Aaron knew that tone was meant for him. She'd always been soft with him, why should now be any different?

"Do you have some time? Can we talk?" he asked.

"By all means," she shrugged and sat back, getting comfortable in her chair. Aaron stepped forward and took a seat on the stoop.

Chapter Eight

Sarah knew before her head even hit the pillow that sleep would not come easy that night. Perhaps her own decision that sleep would be elusive was part of the reason it ended up being that way. She stared at the ceiling for quite some time before she realized she hadn't even closed her eyes. She'd been counting the splinters she could make out in the dark. They'd come from childhood games of tossing pins at the ceiling to try and get them to stick. Now they were make shift stars in her bedroom.

She had no concept of how long she'd been there, staring at the ceiling and hoping she miraculously found sleep. Eventually the sounds of the rest of the house grew quiet until they were gone completely. She knew it had to be late then and came to terms with the truth that sleep would be illusive to her the whole night on unless she did something about it.

So she went out to read.

As much as she enjoyed reading, it had a tendency to make her tired in the night. So she grabbed one of her old study books and went out to the back porch. She lit the oil lamp which cast a dim, orange haze over the wood.

The night was still and the sky was clear, she almost felt bad for disturbing it with her light. But she cracked open the book and began to read on the first page she could find. It was by the time she got half way down the page she realized she hadn't remembered a single thing she read and her eyes had glanced over the same line three times without her noticing.

Eventually she gave up on reading and instead stared off into the sky, eyes unfocused, just letting her mind wander through all sorts of scenes of her childhood, of Aaron, of her grandmother's smiling face. She would meet with her grandmother tomorrow, though what she would tell her was still a mystery and it seemed not even the stars or the protective blanket of the night sky could give her that answer.

That's when she heard the rustling and her eyes fell on Aaron, awkward, nervous, and tired looking in the dark. She couldn't help but smile. He hadn't startled her or scared her and his presence was somehow soothing for once. Perhaps it was because they were according a brief moment alone. Though her parents would never approve, he was here and she felt watched over.

They greeted each other and he took a seat on the steps leading up to the porch, his body half turned to her so he could look out over the rolling fields, glowing in the night.

"It seems I'm not the only restless one here," he said.

"How long have you been awake?" she asked.

"I never actually fell asleep," he shrugged.

She smiled and nodded and knew he understood.

It was moments like this that took away Sarah's doubt. It was natural, being with Aaron. He was her dearest friend and wise without realizing it. He was protective and calming for her. She watched his shoulders relax and he let about a sigh and she knew he felt the same, even if he didn't realize it.

"Why can't you sleep?" she asked.

"You first," he laughed, turning to smirk at her.

Sarah gave him a nervous smile and busied herself with pulling at a string on her apron.

"I'm afraid to tell you," she said, quietly.

"Would it make you feel better to know I'm afraid to tell you why I can't sleep?" he asked, lowering his voice to match hers.

She let out a brief laugh. It might, but it also might not. Perhaps he was nervous with complete and utter excitement; perhaps he was bursting at the seams, so anxious to marry her that he could not contain it. And she'd deflate all his dreams by telling him she couldn't sleep because she was petrified for the very reasons he was excited.

"How long were your parents courting for, before they got engaged and married?" she asked.

"Two years. My mother said my father was slow on proposing, he claimed he just wanted to get it perfect. Apparently that took two years. And your parents?" he answered back, calm and nonchalant as if he had no idea why she was asking.

"Three," she said. "My grandfather was very strict and my father said it took him two years to earn a spot in his good graces. He said he had to pray every night and then each day, grandfather seemed to like him more and more."

She smiled at the memory and could feel the air around her lighten as Aaron smiled with her from where he sat off to her side. They were silent for a moment after that, letting the stories hover between them, trying to figure out what it all meant.

"Our story is a bit different," Aaron mumbled, his eyes pulling away from Sarah to focus intently on something else. His nervous energy was back.

"Do you think that's a bad thing?" Sarah asked, fighting the shake and fear in her voice.

"Do you?"

Her instinct was to say no. How could it be bad? She knew Aaron was the one she wanted to marry and spend her days with. But what if the Lord did not feel the same way?

What if Aaron fell out of love with her or her with him? And then they spent the rest of their days in punishment of their own misery for not heeding the Lord's will? How could she possibly voice that to Aaron without making him hate her?

"Your fears are my fears," he said, quietly. "But I think your wants are my wants too."

She felt everything that had been weighing on her chest lighten at once. They looked up and their eyes connected in the dark.

"I think," Aaron began. "We should stop trying to think about it. I've been driving myself crazy trying to guess what should and shouldn't be happening. I haven't made time to really listen."

Sarah nodded.

"I'm not sure I know how to listen," she admitted.

"I think it starts when we stop trying to demand answers. The Lord provides what He will and we're made to know everything we're supposed to. Asking for more is prideful and arrogant. He brought us together. We should be praising Him in our thanks."

Sarah couldn't help but smile.

"You've come a long way from the boy who had not a single verse memorized when classes started," she said and he smiled, goofy, and shrugged.

"I had a good teacher."

They laughed quietly and talked some more, pointing out stars or the sounds of nocturnal birds. Eventually Sarah was yawning too much for Aaron not to notice and he politely bid her goodnight to return home.

She padded into the house and back up and into her bed into one of the most restful sleeps she had ever experienced.

Chapter Nine

The day before the wedding, Aaron and Sarah spent the morning—with her mother's assistance—baking a cake. She wanted to thank her siblings for their counsel, especially when she learned her brothers had gone to speak with Aaron. They were younger but, perhaps, wiser than her, or at least more willing to listen, as Aaron said. So they asked her mother for help with her old cake recipe and baked one large enough for her four younger siblings.

But before giving it to them, she took a portion of it when the pair went to go meet with Sarah's grandmother.

Though she was feeling better after Aaron's talk the other night, she felt the final test would be in what her grandmother had to say about the whole thing. She didn't plan on telling her every detail of their anxieties but the elderly woman had never met Aaron and she was eager for her grandmother to get the chance before she had to share their wedding with the rest of the community.

So, together, they entered her grandparents' house, cake in hand, and gently entered her grandmother's bedroom.

"Is that my little Sarah?" he grandmother called softly from the bed. "You're all grown after all."

"I'm getting married," Sarah reminded her grandmother with a laugh who smiled right back.

"Yes, yes, have you brought the lucky young man to meet your old Nana?"

"Yes, grandmother."

Aaron had been nervous about the whole thing. He'd pressed his clothes three times to relieve them of any wrinkles. He'd combed his hair and brushed any excess dirt off every part of him he could find. He stood up straight when they walked into the room and did his best to smile.

"Hello, ma'am," Aaron said, stepping forward and offering a slight bow of his head.

"You found yourself a handsome one, is he smart?"

Sarah giggled at Aaron's wide eyes and blush.

"Smarter than he realizes," she said.

"Good, good," her grandmother said. "We need plenty of smart men. You're all good at lifting hammers and farming, it takes a special one to be intelligent as well."

They made small talk over the cake and Sarah wondered if she should ask her grandmother about her own engagement period. If it all seemed hasty but she couldn't stop smiling at her grandmother's beaming face. She'd never seen the woman so happy before. It was like Christmas morning and childhood games all wrapped up into one, shining moment.

Her grandmother asked Aaron plenty of questions. She asked about his family, his farm, his time in classes with Sarah, his favorite food. And all the while, Sarah remained silent and pensive to the side.

This was God speaking to her now, she was sure of it. She did what Aaron suggested and she listened. She watched. She heard. There was so much happiness and warmth in the room and Aaron and her grandmother talked and talked and smiled as if they'd been family all along. She knew in her heart this was God giving her the answer she'd been seeking. This was exactly as it was meant to be.

She thought of what her mother used to say when they were kids and would ask questions about the English world for the first time. Man makes thoughts every day and wants to be praised; God makes feelings that last a lifetime and asks for so little in return. So she silently thanked the Lord with folded hands and smiled to herself.

The sun was setting and Sarah knew if she was going to get the chance to offer thanks to her siblings as well, they needed to leave. They departed the house with kindness and the promise that next time they saw her grandmother, it would be at the wedding and

Sarah had never been so happy to promise her grandmother her dying wish.

When they got back to the house, her siblings were already gathered.

"Mother told us you had a surprise for us," Abigail said. "Zachary's been impatient about it."

"I smelled cake!" he insisted and Aaron laughed.

"You smelled right," he said.

They pulled the cake from where it had been cooling and placed it in front of the younger Zooks.

"We wanted to thank you," Sarah said. "You were very helpful to us both and had quite a bit of guidance, especially for your ages."

"Father said we should all listen to the younger ones more," Joseph said with a smug smile and Sarah rolled her eyes as she began to cut the cake.

They laughed and ate cake and spoiled dinner with Sarah figured one night couldn't hurt in the interest of family and thanks. They played games in the living room and Abigail insisted on trying to show Aaron how to sew before he pricked his finger for the third time and she took pity on him.

He departed for the night and Sarah hugged each one of her siblings and offered them thanks in turn. The next time she saw Aaron, it would be at their wedding.

Chapter Ten

Sarah was awoken gently by her mother on the morning of her wedding, well before sunrise. It took her a few bleary moments to realize what day it was before she popped out of bed in excitement.

"It's today," she whispered, excited to her mother.

"It is indeed," her mother smiled. "Now go and wash up and start to get ready, I need to wake up your sisters. Your father and brothers are already eating breakfast."

Sarah did as she was told and hopped out of bed. She washed her face and hands and brushed through her hair. Her sisters and the rest of her *newehockers* would help her get ready properly but she wanted to make their jobs as quick and easy as possible.

She walked back into her room and saw her dark blue dress hanging by the window. Her mother had guided her in how to make it properly, how to make it last. It would be her church clothing for the rest of her life, and one day she would rest eternally in the dress when her body was sent to the earth and her soul went to join the Lord in heaven. The dress had to be perfect, or as near to perfect as they could get.

And in the early morning glow, the faint

light of the sun waiting just off the horizon, it seemed to be as perfect as possible. It glistened and caught her eye and didn't let go. She knew vanity was a sin and this was no time for it but she held quiet pride for her work and the dress she'd made for herself.

"Stop gawking, we've got a lot to do," Rachel said, walking into the room behind her. Abigail was with her. "Did you eat yet?"

Sarah shook her head.

"We figured as much," Abigail said.

She offered up a plate of warm bread and butter and placed a glass of milk on the dresser. Sarah took a few bites and a sip but was too excited to eat. She'd let her brothers have the rest so it didn't go to waste. Then she and her sisters got to work.

They helped dress her and smoothed out the dress. They brushed through her hair themselves and carefully braided and pinned it up. They chatted together about anything and everything, as if this wasn't one of the most important days of Sarah's life. They laughed and told jokes and by the time the sun rose, Sarah was nearly ready.

"Aaron's *forgeher* are already seating people," Abigail said. "You're almost perfect."

Slowly, Abigail helped place the black prayer covering over Sarah's head and she felt a moment of joy at the completion. She was dressed and ready for it all to begin. Her sisters smiled at her through their tired eyes and Sarah leaned forward to pull them both into a tight and warm hug.

"Thank you," she whispered to them. "For everything."

"Whether you're married or not, we'll always be your family," Abigail whispered back and huge her tighter.

They descended the stairs together, holding hands, and smiling at their mother who waited with their grandmother. The elderly woman looked worn already but had tears in her eyes as she smiled at the scene. Sarah stepped forward to hug her as well and her grandmother told her what a lovely bride she made.

"We'll see you soon, my dear," her father said, placing a kiss on her forehead as the family separated from her and Minister Weiss stepped forward, Aaron next to him.

Aaron was more clean and calm than Sarah had ever seen him. His clothes were pressed, his hook and eye jacket perfectly placed. The man who stood before her was a far cry from the boy she met in classes who grumbled about her knowing more than him. But echoes of that boy hid in Aaron's boyish smile.

Together, they walked with the minister who brought them in for counsel while the sermon commenced in the church room of the house. Minister Weiss spoke evenly with them, prayed with them, asked questions and took their own. The time past quickly and the more they talked, the more Sarah felt sure in it all. She considered, briefly, mentioning their joint fears to the minister to get his thoughts. But they had listened to God and the Lord had given them an answer. Faith in that would be enough.

When the hymns died down, the minister stood up.

"Are you ready children?" he asked.

"We are," they said in unison.

"Then follow me."

Together they walked into the church room and all eyes beamed on them as they took their place within the congregation. It was not unlike their baptism, only this time, Sarah didn't feel so alone. She and Aaron were in this together now.

"Sarah Zook, Aaron Bechtel, step forward," the minister said.

They obeyed together and kneeled before the minister. He asked them, quite seriously, about their commitment, about their marriage, about their plans. They answered honestly to all the questions. They vowed their commitment forever and their unwavering obedience to the Lord and the *Ordnung*.

Then the minister blessed them and it was done.

They were husband and wife now.

The flurry that happened after the

wedding made it difficult to get a moment to themselves to rejoice in their own way. Though Sarah didn't mind sharing smiles and congratulations across the yard as the table was set for the afternoon meal and Abigail insisted Sarah helped with the matchmaking.

"I'm not very good at it," Sarah said, setting a plate down at the table where both their fathers would sit, side by side.

"Nonsense, you managed to find your own husband," Abigail said. "I think this might be the year Zachary finally admits he'll have to marry a girl one day. He still thinks they're gross."

The sisters laughed together under the bright sun.

The air was a chilly November day but the sky was sapphire blue and full to the brim with gorgeous, soft clouds. The breeze was mild and only light brushed to let you know it was there.

"My famous roast," her mother declared, walking out with a pot in her hands and several women behind her with more. "And no Eli Raudenbusch, you cannot have the recipe."

The group laughed as they sat down to eat. Everyone told stories and jokes and the children played games after the meal while the women went back to prepare more food for the evening meal. Sarah and Aaron smiled to each other over the throng of people and Sarah couldn't imagine a happier time in her life.

Epilogue

Sarah and Aaron had spent their months until February visiting all their relatives. It had been an exhausting few months but Sarah could not remember smiling so much in her life before. Aaron's relatives were joyous, happy people and her own relatives were welcoming to him with broad hugs.

Aaron, for his part, felt energized by it all. And when they returned to Sarah's family home at the end of February he thought of Levy and his sister and how much she missed by not listening and seeking counsel with God. He prayed for her happiness and that one day she would learn the joys of everything he experienced in the past few months.

In May, Aaron began work on building their own home. He had help from Sarah's father, her brothers, from Levy, and a handful of other men. Despite Sarah's insistence, he did not let her see one inch of the property until it was completely ready. He wanted to offer her a dazzling surprise.

Difficulties came, of course, when the weather did not always cooperate but the house was coming along beautifully by the time they had to halt their building for the winter months. Aaron trusted it would survive the snows and winds and be waiting to welcome them come spring. Their winter was spent by the fire, reading, talking, playing games with Sarah's youngest siblings, baking things in the kitchen.

He didn't know it was possible to find himself even more in love with her but their second winter together proved that to be a possibility as they didn't have a bad day once during all the cold and dark months of the year. And when March arrived with the thaw of spring, Aaron went back to work on the house.

"Today's the day," he said the morning he decreed the work done and it ready for Sarah to see.

"Finally, I've waited a year," she said.

"Don't be impatient."

They took a buggy to the new house, at every turn Sarah looked around rapidly to see if she could spot the new home while Aaron chuckled at her efforts. She chastised him for teasing her and he shrugged. He may have decided to take the long way around just to mess with her one last time before he finally pulled up to the cream colored house with the black roof.

"It's wonderful."

Sarah was in awe as she stepped out of the buggy and up to the front porch — to their front porch.

They stepped inside together and Sarah threw her arms around Aaron in a hug that communicated how happy and grateful she was.

"Think of all the meals, this kitchen is so big," she said, eyeing the stove.

"I would say you're welcome but a big kitchen is more for my benefit than yours," he teased.

They explored the house together as Aaron showed her all the rooms and things he'd put in for her. He showed her some items from her parents' home that he'd snuck out to place here so it felt a little more like home. She smiled and thanked him and told him it would have felt like home no matter what because he was there with her.

It was several months later, when Aaron was planting the first seeds in their small fields, that Sarah felt their child kick for the first time in her stomach.

They had spent the night before debating names and whether it would be a boy or a girl. Sarah wanted a boy so she'd have another version of Aaron to teach and counsel and another place to find his smile. He insisted he wanted a girl so she'd be as smart and kind as Sarah had been when they were younger. They both decided they wanted as many children as possible. Aaron had always lamented his lack of siblings and Sarah was so grateful to her own that she could not deny her own child as many friends in life as possible.

"The child kicked," she called out to Aaron who was planting corn.

He came running over, tripping over his own feet once or twice, and was offering a huge, toothy grin.

"Really?" he asked.

"No, I just like to watch you trip," she teased and he rolled his eyes.

She took his hands and placed them flush to her stomach, his palms warm on the outside of her apron. They waited for a moment or two before another kick came from within and they laughed together.

"That's a girl for sure," he beamed. "She's already as feisty as you."

"Or it's a boy who's got your strength," Sarah countered.

They smiled and Aaron took a short break over tea with her while they talked about the crops and how many chickens they should get from the market the following weekend. They talked about names briefly and decided, should it be a girl, they'd name her for Sarah's late grandmother. She got her wish of watching their wedding but did not make it to her first great-grandchild. So she'd live on in their daughter who would bear her name.

Sarah couldn't remember why she had been nervous in the first place.

END OF PART 1

7: TWIN HEARTS

Chapter One

When Rachel Zook and Abigail Zook were born, their mother considered it a miracle that there were two of them. She said she'd always thought it might be twins, but was never truly sure until the moment they were both born on the same day. Abigail came first, screaming into the world before the midwife told her she had no time to rest. There was another child waiting to be born. Their mother was so exhausted and excited, she nearly fainted right there. But she worked again and a few moments later the second twin was screaming and crying into life.

They had the same room, the same crib; they shared clothes more than any of the other siblings. They played games together that no one else understood.

When they were young children, they used to walk together down to a creek no far from their house. They followed the twists of the light, clear water into the edge of the woods where they made their play area. It was a flat plain of land that was smoothed over and free of plants thanks to floods from the creek over the years. It served as a makeshift shore when the water rose and they made it their kingdom.

"We should call it Jerusalem," Abigail said, one afternoon.

Rachel nodded her head fervently in agreement.

They'd stored dolls there and toys. Sometimes they even hid snacks in hovels they dug out of the ground. They'd come home messy and their mother would scold them each time and their older sister Sarah would complain that she was the one who always had to help clean them up.

The last summer they spent together, in their hidden place in the woods, was much less fantastical than the days when they were young.

"You remember when you tried to convince me a lion lived in the woods?" Rachel asked.

They were lounging on the bank, their shoes off, the sun peaking through breaks in the leaves to touch the ground with spots of golden light. Some animals rustled in the leaves and twigs off in the distance and they laid back, hands propped behind their heads. Their mother made them clean their own clothes now.

"I wasn't joking," Abigail said.

"Oh come off it," Rachel laughed. "There are not even bears in these woods."

"But there are foxes. I see them in the winter. They stick out like a bright spot in the snow," Abigail said.

"That's hardly as scary as a lion."

"Why do you think I told you lion and not fox?"

The laughed together before getting quiet again. Rachel yawned and considered closing her eyes for a few moments.

They always finished their chores as early as possible in order to get out here and rest undisturbed. Their younger brothers had both tried, at different points, to follow them but had always been called back by their father or mother who noticed the cows hadn't been milked or the firewood wasn't stacked right. Sometimes they even brought their chores out here, knitting in the afternoon shade of the trees.

"We probably can't come back here next summer," Abigail said. "Sarah's getting married and mother will put all her chores on us. We're too old for it."

Rachel knew this was true but didn't like to think about it. She knew growing up was a part of life and becoming an adult was part of it too. Everyone experienced the growing pains, their father said so. It was not always easy going from days of games and fun to chores but the Lord expected it of them, of everyone, and they did not get special treatment. So they'd take what they could get on what they had left of sunny afternoons in the shade of the place of their childhood games.

"We're supposed to be married next?" Rachel asked.

"Not for a while. We're only just starting rumspringa," Abigail said.

"Sarah and Aaron got engaged fast though," Rachel said.

"And look how anxious it's making them. They're meant to be together but there's no need for a rush."

Rachel secretly wanted to ask who Abigail thought would get married first. She shuddered at the idea of being left alone while Abigail went off to get married but she also felt guilty about the idea of doing the same to her. Everyone had siblings and saying goodbye to them as their started their own families was not easy, everyone said so. But Abigail and Rachel were closer than siblings; they'd shared their mother's belly together and come into the world together. They shared a room and stories and games. For one to leave the other behind would be dreadful. But it was also, as their father said, a part of life.

Abigail might have had the same thoughts but she was quiet about them as the afternoon rolled along and they tried to guess the names of the birds they could hear chirping to each other.

"Do you ever think the boys will ever find this place?" Rachel asked as they got up to head home for the night.

"They're too dumb," Abigail laughed. "Besides, it's ours, they can't have it."

They walked over the fields together, waving when they saw friends and neighbors who greeted them constantly with jokes of how impossible it was to tell them apart. Their mother once tried to each get them to wear specific colors to make them more identifiable but all it led to were games where they pretended to be each other. Now their mother was adept at telling them apart, even if their neighbors and sometimes their siblings could not do it.

They walked into the house and silently washed up together before their mother could make a comment about the state of their clothes and hands. They tucked stray hairs away and silently understood it might have been the last time they could sneak away to their secret playground. They joined their family for dinner, clean and smiling. Their brothers glared at them, jealously knowing where they had been. Sarah rolled her eyes and their father said grace before they dug into their meal.

That night, they stayed up after everyone else went to bed. They sat on either side of the large window in their bedroom and looked out.

The full moon hid many of the stars that night but it created a wonderful silver glow over the land. They looked off into the distance at their woodland home away from home.

"Tomorrow we have to help mother take the bread and cheese to the market," Rachel said.

"I know. She'll probably make us do it again," Abigail said.

"Are you nervous?"

"A little. But I've never really been to market before."

They agreed there was some fun in getting older and growing up. They liked the idea of getting to do things they couldn't before, but they never forgot what they were losing. It was a part of life, and that night when they each retired to their own beds, they thanked to Lord for the chance at childhood fun and for always keeping them together.

Chapter Two

Rachel and Abigail had spent several months as their mother's designated helpers at the market. Every morning when their mother planned on opening the stall, they woke up before she did in order to get the items ready. They debated over who got to carry the bread versus the dairy products and their brothers would laugh and say girls were weak before they'd toss a pillow at them and threaten not to make them breakfast the next morning.

They enjoyed their early morning walks in the burgeoning sunlight, though the winter months could mean a fair bit of misery on the road. They didn't go often in the winter because the English didn't often like to trek out of their sprawling towns and into the country out of fear of the snow.

But Rachel loved the snow. She loved how clean it looked when it first lay on the ground, how millions of tiny little particles gathered together to create a blanket for miles and miles over the earth. Her mother once told her prayers were like snowflakes, in times of trouble, if enough people gathered their prayers together for one common goal, they could achieve something miraculous, like the blanket of snow. She remembered that every winter when the ground was invisible for weeks at a time.

This particular day was caught between the roughness of winter and the thaw of spring. They were walking in a chilly morning, evidence of winter snow still present in pockets that hadn't gotten enough sunlight to banish it away. They were wrapped up in cloaks as they carried the items to the market for their first time in weeks.

"Next time you carry the milk and cheese," Rachel said through panting breath.

"I'm older," Abigail sneered, not unkindly.

They teased each other on the walk to ignore the tendrils of cold that still got through their clothes and the strain of their muscles as they transported the items into the town.

Their stall was, luckily, part of the ones inside the actual market. Their aunt had a stall outside that they sometimes helped with in the autumn but they couldn't imagine spending hours there in the cold or in the blazing heat.

"Hester Speltzer told me a secret yesterday," Abigail said after they got settled.

"A secret you should keep?" Rachel warned.

"You don't count."

It was true. Whenever they'd been told secrets, they spilled them to each other quickly. No matter what, even if someone told them not to tell another soul, they told each other anyway. They kept nothing from each other, and understood that all these secrets and stories would stay locked between them.

"She's going to begin a relationship with Solomon Moore," she whispered.

And that marked another friend they had lost to the rising adulthood of the rumspringa. Several of their friends had gone off to start courtships with young men or even announced an engagement. They were far from too old not to be wed, but they felt left behind as their friends rushed into the world of community and adulthood and left them behind.

"Do you have your eye on anyone?" Rachel asked.

"I'd tell you if I did," Abigail said.

She knew that, she did. She just got nervous sometimes. They were quickly approaching the point where their lives might truly separate with the beginnings of maturity and their duties to their community and to God. They always knew it was coming and that through life they would remain close, but things could never be as they were, once they were married and with families of their own.

"If you had to pick one, who would it be?" Abigail asked.

Rachel pouted her lip and furrowed her brow in thought. She knew exactly who she'd pick, but she didn't want to appear too hasty and risk being teased by her sister.

"Jeremiah Bergey," she said, after a long time of pretend thought.

Abigail nodded.

"And you?"

"I don't know."

"That's not fair, I told you mine."

They giggled and bowed their heads together when their mother scolded them for playing around when they were supposed to be working. They silently got back to work through blushes and small giggles.

"I'm still deciding," Abigail finally whispered to her after a while. "You'll be the first to know."

"It better be."

It was when they took a short break for an afternoon meal that Rachel first noticed a boy she recognized, vaguely, from childhood watching her. When she met his eye, his face glowed bright red and dropped down quickly. She smiled, despite herself, and shrugged it off. She knew the boy to be Abel Fisher. He was a year or so older than her but they'd played together as children. They hadn't really talked since those days.

Abigail, however, did not turn away. She watched Abel's eyes return to her sister's face while she was oblivious and eating her meal of bread and butter. He looked at her softly and with a fair amount of longing. She had seen that look in many other couples.

She knew what it meant and she tried to ignore the gnawing jealousy in her stomach.

Chapter Three

Abel had known Rachel from afar for a very long time. He'd watched her play games with others as children. He'd always admired the way she managed to command a room. She'd always been the leader when they'd play tag or hide and go seek. It was hard to believe, sometimes, that she was the younger twin though Abel knew those things didn't truly matter much where a few moments were concerned.

It was that commanding presence she had as a child and into young adulthood that always made him far too frightened to approach her. He knew it was a crush, he'd known it for some time. His brothers, all of whom were already married, would make fun of him for it.

"Rachel Zook would clear the fields and you'd be making dinner," they'd joke and laugh.

It made his cheeks turn red with heat and his shoulders slump as he'd walk away to cut wood and try and prove something.

He was a small child. His mother said he'd been sick a lot in the cradle and still carried remnants of a nasty cough. While it only made his parents love him more for all he had to endure to reach his teenage years, his brothers found games in it. His mother swore it was their way of showing affection, of trying to include him in their pack. But it only made him feel more like an outsider.

Which made it all very strange that he would find himself so taken with Rachel, someone who seemed just like his own brothers in female form. He didn't want to analyze it; he only wanted to get to know her.

Rachel, her sister, and their mother would often go to the market. They had the best cheese in town and their bread wasn't far behind the Mueller's loaves. Once or twice he even bought some from them and she barely batted an eyelash at him.

But this morning he'd gotten up early. He'd tended to the garden for months in the hopes that it would yield some colorful flowers and plucked them. He tied them together neatly with a bow of twine and carried them with grace and the utmost ease to the market that morning.

Next came the waiting. It was a busy morning and he didn't want to interrupt her while customers flocked to their stall and their mother barked out orders and chores while they traded their goods for money and did their best to be polite to the English travelers or entered the town and talked loudly on their phones. It wasn't until very near the end of the day that he finally saw an opportunity and hoped his flowers hadn't wilted in the bustle of the day.

"Rachel," he said so softly that she didn't

even hear the first time he tried. He cleared his throat. "Rachel Zook."

He'd said it louder and she turned this time. Her face fell on his with mild confusion for a moment before she offered him the same bright smile she'd given to all the customers that day and he felt his heart sink just a little bit but he pressed on.

"I don't know if you remember me," he said. "We played games together as kids."

"I remember," she insisted, though it was clear from her face that his name was so far out of her mind that she didn't even know where to begin guessing.

"Abel Moser," he said. He felt himself hearten a little when her face light up with honest recognition and her smile turned a little more genuine. He was vaguely aware her sister was behind her, watching, but he kept his eyes on only her. "I brought you a gift."

He thrust out his arm, flowers in hand, so fast that she jumped slightly in surprise. He felt himself turn a little red and she smiled when she realized what he was offering. She nodded and took them from his hand, pressing them into her nose and smelling them.

"They're lovely," she said. "My grandmother had a garden of flowers for the longest time. Nobody tends to it now since she passed."

Abel nodded and tried to look solemn

and empathetic. He wasn't sure how to respond to that but he'd gotten this far and he needed to keep going. He'd thought about this for months, if not years, it could be the beginning of everything if he allowed himself a little courage.

"I was wondering if you'd possibly meet me this coming Sunday — before church," he said and felt like his insides were going to twist into twenty different knots with nervousness but he pressed on. "I thought we might talk. Catch up. We're both older than when we were children."

He wanted to smack himself. Of course they were both older than when they were children. That's the future of getting older. It wasn't smart. But maybe he'd get lucky and she didn't want an overly smart man. Maybe he can try and being funny, maybe he'd be better at that.

"Perhaps Abel," she said, not unkindly but the voice she used for customers was back. "Thank you for the flowers. They're truly a kind gift. I'll see you around."

And with that he was dismissed. He felt himself flush with all sorts of emotions as she turned away and didn't bother to make eye contact with her sister who was watching him closely. He made the decision, as he walked away, to try again tomorrow after a few short prayers while the morning sun rose.

Chapter Four

Abel did try the next day after praying for some guidance from the Lord. She accepted the flowers again and made small talk but seemed to know where the conversation was going and turned him away again, not without a heartfelt thank you for the flowers.

For the rest of the week, he watched carefully as she and her sister would talk and laugh together at the market. He wondered what it is they talked about and if he'd ever get to the point where he understood girls.

"The problem is," his oldest brother said. "If you think you know what's going on inside a woman's head, that's when it's all over for you. They're complex. The more confused you are, the better it is."

He tried to remember that and take it to heart as he spent the rest of the week planning on what he could say to Rachel. He was going to meet her during church service, regardless. There was no harm in that. They established they were friends, after all. And maybe outside the busy environment of the market and in the calm of a Sunday morning she'd be a little more open to talking.

So when Sunday came he was up even

before their roosters were crowing. In the dark of the early morning he picked what was left of the flower garden he'd worked on for months. He arranged the colors in the most interesting way he could. He thought about trying to think of something witty to say. Maybe she didn't like the vanity of how pretty the flowers were and wanted to hear something substantial. He wished he'd tried harder at memorizing Psalms when their mother read them to all the children at holidays. He was no King David, a far crime from an intelligent poet. But didn't heart serve as the beginning of poetry?

When the sun rose, he walked to church in his best clothes, pressed and polished. He held the flowers carefully as he walked. The air was mild and the sun was kind and he didn't sweat nearly as much as he feared he would when he got to the church yard and began scanning the crowds for signs of the family he was looking for.

The first person he saw was actually Abigail. He knew it was her because she always wore a light pink dress to church while Rachel wore a dark green one. They'd done it since childhood to help people in the community tell them apart at gatherings.

He waited nearby, knowing Rachel could not be far away from her sister and his patience was answered when she appeared with a bright smile.

Now was his chance.

"Hello Rachel," he said, as cheerful and happy as he could muster, with flowers in hand. "I brought you another gift. I hope your Sunday is blessed and your family is well."

He offered them to her and after a moment of hesitation, she reached out and took them. He gave her a nod and one last smile and walked away. Less could be more. And saying nothing was better than saying too much and making a fool of himself. So heartened, just a little, he walked into the throng gathered for church services.

***

Abigail had been watching all week. Where Rachel was always the loud one, always the one to talk first, Abigail had been quiet. Her mother joked that she was the reader and her sister was the doer. Like some version of David and Jonathan, put together they could do anything. For them, of course, anything meant winning childhood games.

But this was different.

Abel Moser was an odd boy, he always had been. He was quiet, but not in the same way Abigail always had been. Her grandmother called her "studious" and his brand of quiet came out of shyness and fear. She felt bad for him, in that sense, but never more so than when she watched him this past week.

Her sister had never been a huge fan of flowers and when they returned home, she handed them off to Abigail to put in water.

"Where do you want them?" she'd ask.

"Wherever you want them," Rachel would say.

"They're for you though."

To that Rachel would not answer and begin talking about something else. So Abigail started a collection of the flowers that Abel brought and worked to keep them fresh and alive as long as possible. She admired his determination as he brought her more and more.

But on the day of church, she felt something in her snap as she watched her sister take the flowers and ignore the boy's smile while he walked away to rejoin his family.

"Rachel," Abigail hissed. She motioned sharply for her sister to join her off to the side.

Rachel shrugged and followed her over while others began to file into the church doors.

"Why are you being so mean to him?" she asked in a whisper.

"Mean?"

"He brought you flowers several days this week."

"And I thanked him for it."

Abigail rolled her eyes and sighed.

"He wants to talk to you, not to be thanked by you," Abigail said. "You have to know that."

Rachel frowned and looked at the ground. She shifted her weight from one foot to the other. But before she could open her mouth to defend herself, they were called over by their father for services.

"We're not done," Abigail hissed as she walked away.

"You can be so bossy," Rachel said. "You're only a few minutes older."

"And clearly that much smarter."

***

They glared at each other through service when their parents weren't looking but both got a scalding look from Sarah where she sat with her husband. Abigail paid attention through the songs and as Elder Betchel spoke. When they bowed their heads to pray she asked God for patience in making her sister understand. It was a learning exercise, a lesson in maturity. Her sister would be better for it once she figured out the world did not always revolve around her.

When services let out, Abigail practically dragged Rachel back to the side of the building where she started hissing again.

"Why are you so intent on ignoring Abel?" Abigail said. "You've repaid his kindness the way you might talk to an Englischer at market."

"I'm just not interested in him that way,"

Rachel said. "He is a good friend, and I appreciate him, but I don't have any desire to take it beyond that."

"Can you at least talk to him about it so he stops getting his hopes up and destroying his garden for you?" Abigail said.

Rachel frowned at her but didn't outright have a comeback. She was always quick with those but not today. Maybe a part of her did feel bad. Abigail could see in her eyes there was something like pity there, and maybe guilt. But Rachel was also proud, sinful as it was.

"I told you before who I had feelings for," Rachel said.

Abigail felt her brow furrow as she tried to think back and remember. Eventually she landed on the conversation they had of teasing at market, earlier that week.

"Jeremiah Bergey? You were serious about that?" Abigail said. "He's older than you."

"Many women are younger than their husbands," Rachel defended.

Abigail groaned and shook her head. She could not force her sister to suddenly grow feelings for Abel. But she at least wanted her to treat him with a little more respect, quiet as he was. Jeremiah Bergey was older and all sorts of girls liked him. She'd get her heartbroken or grow out of it or both. Abigail just hoped she'd be a little smarter about it all by then.

Chapter Five

Rachel did not talk to her sister much for the next few days. It was the first time in a long time she'd given her any form of silent treatment. Last time this had happened it was because Abigail had broken one of the wind-up toys their grandmother had gotten Rachel on their birthday. That had passed when the toy had been fixed and they'd been forced to apologize to each other.

This was a little more complicated. And they couldn't exactly talk to their parents about it.

But Rachel stowed her annoyances at it and focused her energy on proving her sister wrong. She knew Jeremiah spent his days at the market, working the cattle auction. He'd helped his father with it since they were young.

She thought of all the ways she could find an excuse to say hi to him and what she would say once she had his attention. Ultimately, she devised a plan to burn a load of bread the night before. She wrapped up in cloth and she'd present it to Jeremiah as a rejected piece that she couldn't bear to waste. She knew her mother would be furious if she knew what she'd done but, in the end, it would be worth it. Her mother would understand when she came home with the promises of Jeremiah Bergey. He was well respected in the community.

The next day she hid the loaf of bread on the walk by offering to carry an extra crate. It was difficult, but she kept telling herself how worth it would be when it all worked out. And how much her sister would be eating her own words.

"Rachel, it's your turn to handle the money," their mother said as they set up.

"Yes mother."

"Abigail, listen to your sister today."

Rachel stuck her tongue out at Abigail when their mother's back was turned. Whoever controlled the money for the day was effectively the boss of the other. They traded off and no doubt tomorrow Abigail would have her revenge but for now, Rachel basked in being able to tell her sister what to do.

"Make them a pyramid," she said, when Abigail was stacking up the loaves of bread.

"They won't stay," her sister said back.

"Try until they do."

Abigail glared and did as she was told while Rachel tried not to snicker. She'd tucked the burnt loaf away, hiding it under the counter and refusing to move in case her sister or mother saw it.

Eventually, Abigail was in fact able to get the loaves of bread stacked in what Rachel had to admit was an impressive pyramid shape. But one loaf pulled out by a grabby child and all the work was for nothing when they went tumbling down. Their mother ordered her to help her sister clean up and they stacked them again, this time less ambitious.

They didn't talk through the whole thing and when their mother gave them a break for lunch, Rachel quietly went her own way with the burnt loaf of bread.

The auction grounds were a small walk across the field to the old barn. The men there always got to market early to get set up sooner. She hoped that meant Jeremiah would be hungry though she panicked for a few seconds, thinking he might have already ate and that she'd look dumb for trying to offer him food. But she pressed on.

She saw Jeremiah inside the barn. He was taller than most men and stood out. He had a bright smile on his face, even through the sheen of sweat and layer of dirt from this morning's work. She took a deep breath and walked up to him.

"Jeremiah," she called and he turned. His eyes fell on her without recognition but he looked at her kindly and with a smile.

"Hello," he said. "You're one of the Zook daughters, right?"

She smiled and nodded. That was a good start.

"I'm here every week, I see how hard you

all work," she said, nodding to the cattle. Jeremiah shrugged.

"We enjoy the work and I like to think we're good at it," he laughed and winked.

Rachel laughed as well and pulled out the wrapped loaf.

"My family sells loaves of bread and this one was burnt last night while baking," she said. "I hate to see it go to waste and it'll still be good with butter, if you'd like it."

Her voice was much sturdier than how shaky her insides felt. But it seemed to work as he smiled and nodded and took the bread.

"Thank you very much," he said with a nod.

He looked like he was ready to turn away, their conversation over, and Rachel panicked, trying to think of something to say to keep him talking to her when she heard her name called behind her. Abigail was marching over.

"We have to go back soon, mother needs to eat as well," she said.

For this, Jeremiah did turn around. Rachel watched, confused, as his face brightened.

"You are the other twin, right?" he asked. "Abigail."

Abigail looked as taken aback as Rachel wondered about Jeremiah knowing Abigail's name but everyone's surprise was short-lived when Abel appeared with another bunch of flowers in his hands and Rachel had to suppress a groan.

Before Abel could even open his mouth to offer them to her, Rachel turned away and marched out of the barn, lamenting how it all could not have gone any worse.

Chapter Six

Abigail watched her sister walk out of the barn in a huff and didn't know which boy to turn to first. Jeremiah looked mildly confused, holding a loaf of burnt bread in his hands for some reason. When Abel turned to leave the barn as well, Abigail turned to go after him.

"Wait, Abigail," Jeremiah called. "Can we talk, sometime? There's something I want to talk to you about."

"Yes, of course," she said with a shrug and walked out quickly to keep pace with Abel. Perhaps her sister's tricks had worked on Jeremiah after all. She'd ignore it for now and deal with it later.

"Abel, wait!" she called.

He was walking with shoulders slumped and flowers still in his hands. As quiet as he had been, he had never looked so small and defeated before. She truly felt sorry for him.

She called to him again when he didn't answer and was groaning inside at how late she was going to be getting back to the stall and how angry her mother would be but she couldn't leave Abel to sulk on his own.

"Abel wait," she said one final time, catching up to him and tapping his shoulder.

He turned around and frowned.

"What do you want, Abigail?" he asked. She knew he wasn't trying to be mean, he was just hurt. She couldn't blame him.

"I wanted to apologize for my sister's behavior," she said. "She has not been kind to you and it's not fair or right."

He shrugged. She knew it wasn't much consolation and she wished she could offer more.

"When we were kids she was always the more obnoxious one," Abigail said. "I didn't think it would turn her into this when we got older."

"I always admired the way she took charge," he said. "I should have known there would be very little chance she would look at the quiet boy and find anything of much value."

"That's not true."

They both took a seat on the bench.

"She's just going through a phase," Abigail said. "Which I know sounds weird since she and I are the same age but she'll be over this soon. I've been praying often for it. She'll grow out of the immaturity and this infatuation with Jeremiah Bergey."

"So she does like him? I was afraid she might, all the girls do," he said.

"And they all grow out of it sooner or later," Abigail said.

"Unless Rachel's the one he finally picks,"

he said.

"And if he does then we know it was the Lord's will, as much as we may not like it. We're all meant for who we're meant for. If it's to be then it will be."

Abel sighed and nodded. At the very least they could agree that one day Rachel would be kinder, even if it meant Abel was never meant to be more than a good friend to her.

"For what it's worth," Abel said. "I think you're a fine person and one day you're going to have a husband and family just as kind as you."

Abigail felt herself blush and looked down at the ground. All this bustle of boys around Rachel had left her feeling a little behind, but she dared not say anything and risk giving Rachel more ammo to make fun of her with, or make her angrier. Abel had always been smart though, for all his quiet tendencies. He was good at observing people.

"Thank you Abel," she said and meant it whole heartedly.

He smiled and offered her the flowers. She took them with a thank you. He truly was a nice person.

Chapter Seven

Rachel spent a lot of time thinking about what it meant that Jeremiah had not known her name but knew Abigail's on sight. They were twins after all. Knowing one meant generally knowing about the other. He'd looked at her like a stranger but saw Abigail and his face had lit up.

She'd have to get a chance to talk to Jeremiah alone. In her mind that would solve it. He was a popular man, always surrounded by friends. If they had time together to talk with just to the two of them it would be much easier.

The problem was, that was far easier said than done.

They saw each other in passing a few times at market but never more than a hello and it always seemed he reserved one for Abigail as well, whether or not she looked up or even noticed him there at first. Rachel tried not to seethe and gave Jeremiah the most dazzling smile she could. This pattern repeated for some time throughout the week.

Rachel finally saw her opportunity when Saturday night came. They were not going to market that day which meant Rachel had the entire morning and afternoon to finish her chores. Normally when she finished them she'd go up to her room and study or read or even play games with her younger brothers. Her parents left her to her own devices when she finished her chores for the day. Which made it a perfect opportunity to go out to the market and the auction barn and speak with Jeremiah, without her sister waiting somewhere nearby to steal the attention.

There ended up being one problem with the plan, however.

"We're having a family dinner on Saturday," her father said. "Sarah and Aaron will be there and all of you are expected to look your best for it."

She felt like a rock cracked by an unexpected wave and washed out into the ocean. She watched as all her dreams and visions she pictured for her future vanished in an instant. But she quickly regained her mental footing. She smiled and nodded to her father before heading off for the day.

She'd think of something.

In the meantime, she helped her mother with the delivery of a new piglet. Their family pig had been pregnant for some time and her mother had predicted every day that "today is the day" until finally, she turned out to be right today.

"The mother sow is doing well," her mother said when Rachel entered the shed with hot water and rags. "Going to have some healthy, new piglets."

"Can we name them?" Rachel asked.

"You know the rules," her mother said.

They had never been allowed to name the animals because their parents feared they'd be too attached when it came time to sell the animals or use them for food. In her mind, however, Rachel had named several of the animals.

Over the course of an hour, her mother worked with the pig gently, handing off squealing babies to her as they appeared. Rachel washed them and laid them down in a warm bed. They cuddled together and stilled after a while, drifting off into their first sleep.

"The Lord truly does grant wonderful things," her mother said when the final piglet was born. "All this pain and yelling for something so beautiful. Eve's first disobedience had a silver lining in this at least."

Rachel nodded and watched over the small pigs while her mother cleaned up the sow. She talked about how the pig would be down for a few days, resting, and they wouldn't worry about trying to get her out into the pen for a while.

And then Rachel thought of something.

She looked at the tired pig and then back at the small, sleeping piglets. That's when she forced herself into a coughing fit until her mother turned to look at her with concern.

"Are you alright?" she asked.

"Fine mother," she groaned out, possibly a little too dramatically.

"Are you feeling ill?"

"I'm sure it will pass."

It didn't pass. In fact, each day that Saturday drew closer and closer Rachel seemed to get sicker and sicker. She'd cough and cough and tickle her own nose until she sneezed. She stayed up late to make herself pale and tired looking in the morning. She pretended to lose her appetite and ignored the wailing growls of her stomach.

By Saturday morning her mother was insisting she stay in bed and rest, Sarah and Aaron would understand. Everything was going perfectly.

The one downside to this was that Rachel had to spend the day bored in bed and had to put on a show of being ill every time someone walked into the room. But it was a small price to pay for all the returns it would give her in the end. She justified it, in her mind, as her own form of test like the ones God delivered to the heroes of the Bible. Like Jacob once won his inheritance from Esau, destiny sometimes had to be achieved, more than given.

So she waited it out, thought about the good that would come from it, and prayed to the Lord for guidance. She didn't like that she had to lie, but she also remembered that Jacob had to do the same to earn his birthright from his father. Sometimes not every decision was pure but God worked in mysterious ways. She would not pretend to know any more than that.

So when the family all sat down at the table outside in the balmy afternoon air, she made her move. She dressed quietly and quickly. Anyone could come inside at any minute. Her mother might check on her once or twice before they truly got in to sitting down and eating dinner. She had to be quick and fast. So she dressed and padded down the stairs, holding her shoes in her hand to avoid letting them hear the soft click of her heel on the wood. She waited until she was out the front door—careful not to let it slam—before she put her shoes back on.

She was so wrapped up in her own joy at having her plan actually work, that she didn't notice the pair of eyes that looked exactly like her own, watching her from inside the kitchen as she left.

Chapter Eight

Abigail had wanted to believe her sister was sick. It wasn't because she truly wanted her suffering and ill, but she feared something like this might happen. Rachel was clever and ambitious. But Abigail had hoped she wouldn't resort to lying. But she couldn't deceive herself into thinking otherwise when she looked up and saw her sister, healthy as could be, sneaking out the front door.

She knew exactly where she was going. There was an auction every Saturday afternoon and Jeremiah and his father were always the head auctioneers. She was going to give it one last try and Abigail didn't know how to react first.

Their parents would be livid and her punishment would be severe. Lying was a sin, dishonoring her parents was a sin, attempting to meet a boy in secret without permission was wrong. So much of this would come down hard on Rachel and part of Abigail wanted revenge and wanted to see it happen just to teach Rachel a lesson. But she also didn't want to watch her sister suffer. Taxing as she had been in the past few days she was still her sister and her twin at that.

She could tell their parents or bring her home before anyone noticed.

She prayed silently, trying to figure out what to do and if the Lord would grant her some kind of sign.

It came in the form of Abel.

There was a knock on the door and Abigail jumped nearly three feet in the air in surprise but rushed to the door, hoping her sister had come to her senses and returned on her own. But it was Abel who was looking back at her, no flowers in hand, but a bright smile on his face. It didn't diminish when he saw Abigail but when he took an inventory of her and saw the concern on her face, his own morphed to match her.

"What's wrong?" he asked.

She stepped outside quickly and put a finger to her lips to tell him to be quiet. He nodded.

"I don't want to upset you but I need help and I was praying for the Lord to give me some kind of sign and then you came at the door so it has to mean something—"

"Abigail, take a breath," Abel laughed, just a little. And Abigail couldn't help but join him in that. She did take a breath before she started again.

"Rachel has lied and snuck out," she said bluntly and cringed because of it.

His face fell completely and he nodded,

attempting to seem unfazed by it. Abigail felt horrible for being the reason his mood had changed so quickly but there were more important things at stake here.

"What do you need me to do?" he asked seriously.

Abigail almost wanted to let Rachel get caught at this point. She didn't deserve someone as kind and loyal as Abel. But maybe he was part of the lesson she had to learn too.

"We have to get her back before my parents find out, or she'll be punished," she said. "And as awful as she's been these past weeks she's still my sister and I want to protect her. I believe she's gone to the auction market."

Abel nodded. He understood all of it and needed no further explanation than that. He stood up and nodded out to the road. They took off, without a second to lose.

Chapter Nine

Rachel found Jeremiah, quickly, like always. He was as tall and rugged as usual and she cursed herself for not thinking of anything to bring to offer him. She'd have to think of another way to start a conversation with him.

But she'd have to do what she had to do. She waited until there was a break in the bustle of activity at the auction to try and approach him.

"Hello Jeremiah," she said.

He turned to her, eyes settled on her face, and nodded with a polite smile. He then quickly turned back to the cattle he was standing next to; ready to bring out for the next auction round.

"How are you?" she asked.

"Perfectly well, I hope you are as well," he said.

He wasn't really looking at her, fixated with making sure the fur on the cow was properly combed and doing last checks to make sure she hadn't been lamed in any way. Rachel felt both anger and embarrassment boil up in her at once. Jeremiah was more interested in the livestock than what she had to say. She'd come all this way only to have him pay more attention to a cow than to her. It felt horrible.

She remembered the temper tantrums

she'd thrown as a child and this was the closest she'd come in a long time to throwing one again. But she'd be strong. This was a test and the prize was so close, she just had to navigate a little bit farther.

"I was hoping to get the chance to speak with you about something," she said.

"Now's not the time, Rachel," he said.

"I know, but perhaps after? It'll only take a moment or two," she said.

He seemed to perk up at that and Rachel would have been excited if not for the next sentence that he said.

"Is it about your sister?" he asked, quite earnestly this time before turning red. "Not that I — not that I'm — what I mean is."

"No," she said calmly. "I understand."

He hadn't even noticed her interest, which perhaps would make it better. She had nothing to be embarrassed of except her own actions. And how she had treated her sister and Abel. Her sister probably didn't even know Jeremiah was interested in her. Should she tell her? She fought down the slithering smoke of jealousy because it wasn't her place to be jealous.

She was still debating on what to do when someone hissed her name angrily and she turned and saw her sister marching up to her. Jeremiah was called into the ring with the cow in tow, leaving Rachel to face the anger of her sister alone.

"Have you completely misplaced your senses?" Abigail said. "What were you thinking?"

"I wasn't," Rachel admitted. "Well, I was, but only about myself. I'm sorry for that, I truly am."

"You lied to mother and father," she accused.

"I know, it's what I thought the Lord wanted."

"How could you possibly think such a thing?"

As Rachel opened her mouth to answer, another voice called and caught their attention. Rachel felt all the blood leave her face and her heart plummet into the earth when she saw several of the elders walking in their direction, eyes fixed on them. How were they ever going to explain any of this?

"Young ladies," said Elder Betchel. "What business do you have here?"

Abigail looked to be completely at a loss of explaining herself but Rachel jumped in quickly.

"Our pig recently took ill," she said and told herself it wasn't a lie. The pig was ill. "She's given birth and isn't quite herself yet. We're looking into possibly surprising our mother with a new pig."

She felt awful for the amount of lies she had to tell tonight and now she dragged her sister into it as well.

"Is this true?" Elder Betchel asked, turning to Abigail.

Rachel's sister was stone faced and terrified but was nodding. Rachel felt sick to her stomach. This was all her fault and she hoped the Lord knew that and didn't punish her sister too harshly.

"You are here without a chaperone," said Elder Ziegler.

Rachel had no idea how to save that when Abel appeared, as if from nowhere.

"I'm here with them," he said confidently. "Their father sent me, to help with the surprise for their mother and to keep an eye on them."

For all his quiet years, he did well when under pressure as he stared into the eyes of the elders and lied for Rachel. She felt awful, but she refused to let it show. They were almost out of this mess and she could go home and sulk in peace.

"I wonder why your father didn't warn us you were coming," said Elder Ziegler and for a moment Rachel feared it would all unravel. "But, a surprise is a surprise after all. I hope you bring your mother happiness and joy with your gift."

The three of them nodded vigorously and bid farewell to the elders as they walked off. Somewhere a crowd cheered as a cow was sold but all Rachel could hear was the guilt ringing in her own ears.

Chapter Ten

Abigail stepped aside, waiting off across the way, while Abel and Rachel took a small walk in order to talk alone. Abel knew that Rachel was embarrassed and probably a little scared he'd somehow still get her into trouble. And after everything she did a part of him wanted to see her punished for it all but in the end he liked her far too much to be petty with her. Everyone deserved happiness and a chance at forgiveness. They'd scraped out of that situation, if only just barely, and for that he would be thankful.

"I want to thank you," Rachel said. "Not just for saving Abigail and I back there but for everything. You've been so kind to me and so patient and all I've been is cruel end neglectful."

She said it so bitterly that he knew she must mean it. She looked so miserable and sad, she would be punishing herself in such a way that no amount of revenge Abel could ever want would compare. This was how the Lord worked. Her crime was for the arrogance of her mind so it was only fitting that her own heart punished her.

"You are welcome, Rachel," he said. "I didn't do it for a reward. Just hoping you'd notice. And you did. And I'm always willing to help you."

He smiled and that only seemed to make her shrivel more. She nodded though, in acceptance, and they continued their walk.

"Perhaps I can make it up to you? And thank you properly?" she offered. "Why don't you come over for dinner next weekend, we can walk back from market together. We can talk then, just like you wanted all along."

These were the words he'd wanted to hear for so long but, unfortunately, right now, they were also the last thing he wanted to hear. She was still nursing her emotional wounds and wanted only to repay a debt she thought she owed him. It was no way to start a relationship and would end poorly.

So he did the hardest thing he'd ever done and he turned her down.

"I'm sorry, Rachel," he said. "Maybe another time."

And then he turned and walked away and tried not to feel like he was breaking his own heart into dozens upon dozens of pieces. On his way out he passed Abigail and Jeremiah talking together and hoped that something good would come out of that. Abigail deserved that much.

Chapter Eleven

Abigail and Jeremiah had stood together in an awkward silence. They weren't sure exactly what to do as they watched Rachel and Abel talk. She got the feeling that Jeremiah was constantly on the cusp of trying to speak with her but couldn't seem to force himself to do it. She considered, once or twice, saying something to ease the tension but wasn't sure how to start. The situation was all so strange that wasn't sure what to say first.

"I've been hoping to talk to you for a while now," Jeremiah said. "You always seemed so busy though."

He laughed nervously as Abigail turned towards him.

"I knew who you were, you know," he said. "I know a lot of the kids liked to make jokes about how you and Rachel looked alike and you wear those dresses to church on Sunday and stuff but, I always knew when it was you."

Abigail wasn't sure what to say to that but her cheeks heated up and must have looked scalding red in the late afternoon sun.

"I don't know if it means anything to you or not, but I'd like to get to know you even better, if I can. I like you a lot and think you might like me too," he said.

Abigail didn't know what to say. For weeks she'd watched as Rachel was the object of one boy's affections while trying to win another's. She had no time to consider that fleeting moment of her own jealousy when all this began. And now a boy was staring her right in the face, saying he knew who she was all along.

All she could do was smile and nod and be thankful when they got home that their parents hadn't noticed a thing.

***

It wasn't for many weeks that Rachel came up with the plan, and Abigail had to admit, it was a clever one. They were in their old hideaway in the woods. Rachel had taken her sister there and prepared a cake and snacks as a way of apologizing.

"Nothing should ever come between us," she said. "We entered life together; God did not want us to be separated. It was my fault."

Abigail forgave her sister whole heartedly and they ate together in the shade of the woods while they chatted about life. Rachel began teasing Abigail about Jeremiah, who seemed unable to concentrate whenever he saw her. Once she watched him walk right into a fence post while trying to say hello to her.

Abigail found it endearing and tried not to show how excited it sometimes made her. She liked Jeremiah, quite a lot.

Rachel had been quiet and pensive for some time now. They'd been going about their daily chores and trips to the market as if nothing had happened but Abel was nowhere to be seen. If he had been at the market, he was good at hiding. And no more flowers had been dropped at their door. Rachel was saddened and Abigail was lamenting the loss of a friend when Rachel had an idea.

She'd been sitting quietly after they ate when suddenly she sprang up like a wind up doll and shouted.

"I've got an idea."

"About what?"

"Abel."

She hopped up and started pacing in front of Abigail as she spilled out her plan. Abigail had to admit, there was some cleverness to it. Rachel had always been clever though. It may not completely win back Abel's affections for her but at the very least it showed how earnest she was. It was a heartfelt attempt, if nothing else. So Abigail agreed to help her with it.

They spent hours picking flowers they found from their garden, promising their mother they'd help the rest grow back when the time came. It was one last sacrifice they had to make to, hopefully, make everything right again.

They laughed while they did it, tossing clumps of dirt at each other and playing games they hadn't played since childhood. When their siblings walked by and rolled their eyes, it felt like their childhood all over again. Everything was as it should be. Well, almost everything.

They found as many colorful and bright flowers as they could and arranged them in a rainbow outside Abel's house one morning. They told his parents about the plan and they laughed and agreed to keep him occupied for a time while they set up their gift. It took a few hours and few more games, but eventually they had an overflowing garden of flowers waiting to greet him when he stepped outside.

This is when Abigail bid her sister farewell to watch what was happening from off to the side. She offered her sister one final smile for good luck before disappearing behind a tree in another yard.

As they planned, Abel's parents sent him outside to get something while Rachel waited patiently. He stepped outside and as soon as he lifted his head, walking off the last step, he gawked. His eyes washed over the small sea of flowers in the backyard. It took a few moments before his eyes finally found Rachel and she offered him the biggest smile she possibly could, clouded over with uncertainty and some obvious fear. But at least it was genuine.

"Hi Abel," she said. "I missed you at the market."

He looked speechless so she stepped

forward. He'd been a good friend to her for a while now; this was the least she could do in return.

"I wanted to try again," she said. "I know last time didn't go so well and you said no but I thought I might ask you again if you wanted to come over sometime. I'd like to spend more time with you. I hope you like flowers as much as I liked the ones you gave me."

She then held her breath and watched and waited. He looked around at the flowers some more and then back at her with degrees of confusion and shock. The longer it took him to speak, the less and less confident she felt about it all. But she stuck to it.

Eventually, his face broke out into a huge smile and she felt herself relax.

"How could I say no to something like this Miss Rachel Zook?" he asked with a laugh and she returned it.

Eventually Rachel called for Abigail to come out of her hiding spot and join them. Abel thanked her and they shared a look between friends and she winked. The new pair then quickly devolved into teasing her about Jeremiah when Rachel suggested she bring him to their next family gathering and they could all sit together.

"Our brothers will never stop teasing us now," Rachel said, that night when the sisters returned home.

"They're just jealous," Abigail said. "And young."

Rachel agreed and they walked inside together.

They didn't go to bed for hours, instead staying up and pretending they could count the stars and played with old games they dug out from when they were younger. They told spooky stories and tried to keep their laughing as quiet as possible in case they woke up their parents.

In life they'd find friends and they'd find love. They'd face hardships and trials. They'd go through a lot of things but they knew, the best way to face it all was together. They were sisters and twins, and that's what God had wanted for them all along.

END OF PART 2

8: GROWING UP IN LOVE

Chapter One

Joseph Zook never liked having to go over to the Weidler farm. His parents always made him dress up and gave him all sorts of lectures on being as polite as possible and he was forced to play with Rebecca Weidler in the yard. His oldest sister Sarah got to help make dinner with the adult women and his younger brother was allowed to do whatever he wanted. The twins took to playing weird games of their own making that they never let anyone else in on. And he was left entertaining Rebecca Weidler.

"You're doing it wrong," she said in that usual voice. "Hold the ball like this and you'll throw it better."

Joseph always turned red in the face and seethed whenever she told him what to do. He refused to let a girl boss him around. Girls were gross and mean and here was one his parents always forced him into playing with the most annoying person he'd ever met, and he had to deal with his younger brother as an infant. It wasn't fair.

"That is a part of life," his mother would say when he complained. "Few things are ever fair. Remember the story of Job and just take heart in getting through it all. This is nothing compared to the trials you'll have to face in life when you're older."

So he did as he was told and sucked it up every few weekends they took a trip to visit the Weidlers.

They'd been old friends of his mother. Johanna Weidler had been a childhood friend of his mother's back when her name was Johanna Wentz. Her husband, Jacob Weidler, had also been a friend of theirs. His mother often liked to tell the story of how Jacob and Johanna never liked each other and only tolerated being around each other because they were both friends with her. And then something changed when they were older and they found that their repulsion for each other was masking something beautiful that the Lord had planted in them long ago. And so they married and had children of their own and his mother said she'd never seen any two people happier.

Joseph thought it was a nice story and continued complaining and avoiding Rebecca whenever possible.

One day, she insisted they play a game of hide and go seek and then told him he had to seek. He groaned but agreed because he knew his mother was watching and she'd expect it of him.

"Go over there and count," she said, pointing to a tree.

"How do I know you won't run off into the fields or the woods or something or just hide in your room and I'll be stuck trying to find you all day?" he asked.

"I'll only hide somewhere in the backyard."

He nodded and went to his tree to begin his counting. She told him he had to count to 25, out loud, before he could come and find her. So he did just that, proudly, because he was pretty sure she wanted to make fun of him for not being able to count or something. When he hit 25 and turned around to begin looking for her, she was, of course, nowhere to be found.

He started in the usual places. He looked behind the pile of cut wood, he checked in the shed that held all her father's tools. He looked in the gap underneath the porch in the back. He checked underneath one of the tables that had a tablecloth hanging over it. Eventually he was running out of places for her to be hiding and became incredibly sure she had broken her promise.

He was walking on the edge of the backyard, by where the cornfield began, when something lunged out at him from the stalks and knocked him over. He yelped and turned to see

Rebecca laughing hysterically on the ground.

"That's not fair!" he shouted. "You said you'd stay in the backyard."

"The cornfield is the back yard."

"You didn't say so."

She shrugged and skipped off back towards the house where her mother was bringing out a tray of biscuits and cookies and tea for everyone. Joseph was angry but knew he couldn't do anything about it, his mother would be furious.

It only got worse when his siblings started talking about it on the way home.

"Everyone knows the number one way to show you have a crush is by being mean," Sarah said.

"You like Rebecca Weidler," Abigail chorused in.

"I do not, stop it," he huffed out and put his arms over his chest angrily, crossing them tightly. He walked ahead of them and into the safe sphere of his parents.

"Just ignore them son," his father said. "You know your truth. Teasing is just the way with siblings."

It didn't make Joseph feel any better. Especially when he thought about how angry Rebecca made him all the time. She was infuriating and mean and Joseph didn't understand how his mom's friends could have ended up together if they were anything like that when they were kids.

But he tried to tell himself God had plans. Maybe Rebecca was just a test for harder things to come, like his mother said. In a couple of years his parents would probably stop making him go over there or maybe at least stop making him play with her constantly when they did.

It didn't end though. He was sent over there several weekends a month and every time forced into the unkind company of Rebecca who never seemed to let up on games that she always won at. Joseph hated it, but endured, thinking of how one day it would all go away and Rebecca would be off married to some man who had to deal with how mean she could be.

Things have a strange way of changing though. And for them it happened when they were both just shy of twelve years old.

It was strange, the way a girl could go from being a bratty, mean child to a beautiful young woman right before your eyes. Joseph had never understood the draw his father talked about. Sure, Joseph thought her mother was pretty but his father gushed about how beautiful he thought she was.

"It's not just the outside, that would be vain," he said. "It's how the inside reflects the beauty within. God grants gifts like that to only the kindest on the inside."

He thought that would mean Rebecca would grow up to be some gnarled old hag. But instead, after a few months of not seeing her or the rest of the Weidlers during the winter months, spring brought several surprises.

She dazzled in the virgin sunlight of spring while the world was still melting of winter around her. Joseph was willing to admit she'd gotten pretty and he'd gotten old enough to notice when a girl was pretty. But what truly shocked him is when instead of dragging him off to play some humiliating game, she sat under one of the trees in the yard and read, quietly. There was something so wonderfully graceful about the scene. And when Joseph approached her, she smiled brighter than the sunlight on a stream.

"Would you want to know what I'm reading about?" she asked, sounding completely sincere. There was a time she would have followed it with an insult, but she meant this. She truly wanted to share it with him.

"Uh, sure," he said.

She patted the patch of grass next to her and he carefully lowered himself down. She held up the book to him and started explaining about how it was about a man lost in the wilderness who finds salvation through his prayers to God. He goes days without eating, believing God will save him in the end and his faith pays off when he's returned home to his Amish community in Ontario.

The content of the book meant little to

Joseph but the passion with which Rebecca talked about the story enthralled him too. She was excited and knowledgeable and wanted nothing more than to share with him. Winter had changed her into something else entirely, something pretty amazing.

But he wasn't going to admit that to anybody.

Chapter Two

The spot beneath Rebecca's tree in the backyard had become their spot. Whenever Joseph would come over, he'd find her nestled back there and quietly move to join her while she read silently. Once he was there, she would sometimes read out loud to him until he could convince her to put down whatever book she was reading and they'd talk about things.

Rebecca may have lost her tendency to tease and provoke him, but there were other ways she could show her dominance.

"Don't you know the story of Esther?" she asked, laughing.

"There's no need to make fun," Joseph said.

"I'm not making fun. If you spend more time reading than running around the cornfields, you'd know," she said.

"It's my job. One day I'll be the man of a house and I'll have to provide for my family."

"Yes, but you also need to provide spiritually for them as well," Rebecca said. "And you can't do that if you don't know a single thing to teach your children."

Joseph sighed and plucked angrily at the grass beneath them while Rebecca shook her head. He hated that she was right but also didn't know where to start. He was not nearly as smart as her or as passionate about picking up books. But he imagined a future where his children were spiritually lost because of his own shortcomings.

"It's not that hard to learn," she said. "You used to think I was awful and then learned I wasn't so bad."

"That's not how I remember it," he said. Now it was his turn to tease her. "I remember a girl who would do nothing but play mean tricks on me all day long. If anyone learned anything, it's you who learned to not be so mean."

"You may have a point, but you also thought girls were gross and got over that. We both grew up," she said. "You can borrow my book if you want, you can start learning now."

Joseph shrugged and smiled as he took the book from her hands and tucked it under his arm. They talked the rest of the day about random things. Well, it was mostly Rebecca talking about things and Joseph watching in awe at the way the light caressed her face or how dazzling her smile could be when she was excited.

He thought about what his siblings had said when he was younger, about his irritation masking a crush. At the time he thought they were crazy, and he still did. He could never have a crush on the girl like that, he was sure of it. This girl was someone else entirely, that's who he was admiring.

He bid her farewell, as he always did, and walked home for the night, smelling dinner cooking from even far down the road. Waiting for him was a barrage of snickers from his family.

"Stop it," he said through gritted teeth, stepping into the kitchen where the twins were smiling to each other and Zachary was laughing.

"We're on your side," Rachel said. "We promise. It's just cute, the way things have changed between you and Rebecca."

"Nothing has changed," he said. "She's a good friend now and that's it."

"A good friend you can't ever take your eyes off of," Abigail said. "And every time we're at the table it's always 'Rebecca said this, and Rebecca did that.' It's nice that it's not about complaining about her for once in a long time."

Joseph felt his face reddening. He turned around so that no one could observe his face. "I'm going to get more firewood for the oven," he said and marched off, letting the back door slam behind him to the sounds of giggles.

It wasn't until he had bent over and began picking up wood that he realized he'd been followed.

"Do you really have feelings for her?" asked the voice of his oldest sister Sarah.

Joseph looked up at Sarah. He always felt good around her. She had turned just as mature as his mother, her kindly and soft face urging him to share his thoughts.

"I don't know," Joseph shrugged and went to piling up logs in his arms.

"It's not something to be taken lightly," Sarah insisted. "As children it's just games but now it means something. If you feel something now, you need to think on it, talk to father and pray on it."

"Why? What makes it so different?" he asked.

"Because you're becoming a man and God does not place feelings in your heart for no reason," she said. "If the feelings are there and they're true, you need to do something about it. Speak with father; he'll help you pray on the matter.

She walked away and it took Joseph a few extra minutes to collect the wood before following her back in.

Chapter Three

The problem that arose, however, was that it took quite the heartbreak for Joseph to realize just how much his feelings for Rebecca meant. He was out one day with his mother and sisters at the market, purchasing some produce from a farm stand owned by the Schwartz family when he spotted Rebecca across the road, book in one hand, and a young man on her other side.

Joseph recognized him. He was a tall, athletically built boy named David. He was broad shouldered and incredibly sturdy looking. What was worse, however, was that David, like Rebecca had always been something of a bookworm, quiet and shy and nose pressed to pages so he didn't have to talk to other people.

And she was smiling and laughing with his stoic, but content face. And Joseph understood, for the first time, what it meant to have pain in your chest that you felt on another level entirely. It didn't bruise or blister or bleed but it ached beneath his breastplate.

He could no longer deny that the time spent with Rebecca were indications of a casual friendship. It was more than that. He wanted her to be his and him to hers. Joseph wanted Rebecca to play tricks on only him, share the stories from her books with only him. Not David Meyer.

"Joseph, Joseph," his mother called pulling him from his trance. "Help your sisters with these crates."

He did as he was told and lifted a crate of cabbage into his arms. The walk back was silent. If Abigail and Rachel had noticed his melancholy or the reason for it back at the market then they did not say. They talked about other things, church services, gatherings that friends were planning. Once or twice Joseph was pulled into the conversation but had only grunts and one-word answers to offer as he seethed silently, thinking about David and Rebecca walking together all day.

When they returned to the house, Joseph put down his load and walked out to the field where his father was shearing crops. He shoved his hands in his pockets and tried to keep his head up, like his father always said, but he wasn't feeling too tall at the moment. He walked up to his father who seemed to sense his presence and put down his tools.

"That's a long face," his father observed. "It's a beautiful day Joseph, there's no cause for taking it for granted with a sad face and sadder heart."

"You don't understand," Joseph said.

"Don't I? I'm far older than you and been through it all, try me son."

Joseph sighed. It sounded silly, in his head, to think about it, to be so mopey over a girl. A girl who he spent much of his childhood complaining about, loudly and often, to his family. But important things in life required courage, his father always told him that. If it was worth it, you worked for it. And admitting to his father he had a very strong crush on a childhood enemy was not going to be the most difficult part about any of this. If he couldn't even overcome his nerves now, he didn't deserve to be sad over what came next.

"I think I like Rebecca Weidler," he said.

"Okay." His father grunted.

"Like, really, really like her."

"I see."

His father removed his hat and squinted up at the mid morning sunlight. He took a seat on a fair sized rock in the clearing and patted a small spot on it next to him for Joseph to join him. Joseph obeyed and took of his hat as well. When they sat side by side, people always told them how much they looked alike. It gave Joseph strength, to feel like his father.

"These things aren't to be taken lightly, and if you're discussing it with me I know what that means," he said. "Have you spoken with Rebecca?"

"No, I'm too nervous but I saw her today walking with David Meyer and I got so jealous. I know that's not right, but its how I feel."

"If the Lord decides Rebecca and David are meant to be together, then you must respect that and move on."

"I know, but shouldn't I at least try?"

"There's nothing wrong with that."

His father smiled and squeezed his shoulder before pulling him into a hug.

"Take heart, son," he said. "Everything in life is a trial, pray and God will be on your side."

Joseph nodded before walking away and letting his father get back to work. He felt a little taller and a little sturdier as he walked back into the house, ignoring the glances of his siblings as he took to beginning his chores for the day. Things would turn out okay. All he had to do was be brave.

But bravery couldn't defend against the possibility that David had been braver first.

Chapter Four

Joseph first learned the truth about Rebecca's relationship with David from Rebecca herself. There was a certain amount of privacy that went into relationships in the community, but Joseph was an old childhood friend. Of course he would be the person she wanted to confide in. And, as much as it hurt, he took it like a good friend.

"He's really very smart," Rebecca said one afternoon under the tree. "He's quiet but when he does talk he says these profound things. I've never met someone so intelligent before."

"Interesting," Joseph said with a deadpan face.

"He does say some odd things though, from time to time. He knows a lot about English life, which is odd. He says he does it for research. He knows about their philosophies and religions," she said.

"I'm sure it's safe."

"He does speak of it almost reverently sometimes, it's odd. A little unsettling at times—"

"I need to go."

Joseph couldn't do it; he couldn't sit there and listen to her gush about a man who wasn't him. Even if this was the Lord's will, he wouldn't be put through torture for it. He would pray and ask forgiveness if he was defying God's plan but he would not get hurt without cause.

"Oh. I'll see you tomorrow then?"

"I've got a lot of chores."

And with that, he walked off.

He took the long trek back to his house. He cut off the road and crossed some fields and went through the woods. Nature was always a friend to him, when he needed it most. His mother would say you could hear God best in the rustling of the wind and the sound of birds. He wasn't sure exactly what he was listening for, but it was better than walking down the lonely, dirt road.

Besides, he wanted time to think. He knew that was dangerous too. His grandmother always said thoughts could be poison; it was the snake that had given Eve thoughts. But perhaps the sounds of God all around him would protect him from the dangers of relying solely on what was within his own head. He walked along the soft tinkling sound of the creek, leaping over it, carefully not to disturb the flow of the water. He stepped by and heard squirrels rush back into their trees in a rush and heard birds calling.

When he was back within sight of his home he was relieved. All he wanted to do was stop and rest for the day and try not to think about anything. But the second he got inside the four walls of his house, it was like he couldn't block out the sounds of his own thoughts.

Abigail and Rachel found him pouting in the living room, glaring at a book in his hands without actually reading it.

"What has you looking like such a sourpuss?" Abigail asked.

"Don't worry about it," he bit back.

"Is this about Rebecca?" Rachel asked.

That only aggravated him more. He huffed and lifted the book higher up to block his face and make a point. Neither girl seemed to accept that as an answer, however. They both sat down right in front of him and silently stared. They didn't push him to talk; they didn't fidget or say anything. They just stared and waited. They did this often. They could get the inside story out of anyone by simply sitting there and making them uncomfortable.

"Can you leave me alone?" he whined.

"Not until you talk about why you're so grumpy," Abigail said.

"It's about Rebecca, okay? Happy?"

"No. Tell us more. Did something happen?"

"Stop prying."

But they didn't leave. When he finally did turn to look at them he saw their faces were calm and kind. They didn't glare or storm off when he was mean. They patiently waited for him to tell them. He sighed. Maybe it would be helpful to have someone to talk to about it. He was too embarrassed to tell his father what happened and feared what he would say.

"Rebecca and David are together," he grumbled.

Their faces morphed into ones of understanding and empathy. They both nodded solemnly.

"And I kind of stormed off from her house unkindly," he said.

"You can't hold it against her if she chooses someone else," Abigail said.

"It could be God's plan."

"I know," Joseph growled. "Everyone tells me that and I know I'm selfish and prideful but I can't just turn these emotions off. I don't know."

Both girls got up as one and sat on either side of him. They each offered him a comforting arm around the shoulder. It was warmer than when his father hugged him.

"God does not expect you to simply stop being you," Rachel said. "But you need to amend for the things you do wrong and the way you mistreat people, especially your friends. You cannot stop jealousy and envy, but you can take responsibility for them, and ask the Lord for help."

Joseph knew they were right, he also knew what came next. They'd tell him that

Rebecca choosing someone else may very well be part of God's plan and he had to abide by it. And he would. He was an obedient child of the Lord but he knew it would not be as easy as everyone expected it to be. It was part of growing up, he thought, learning to cope with your trials in this way.

"Thank you," he said. "I'm sorry for being unkind."

"It's okay. We're all unkind sometimes," Abigail said.

Helpful as the talk had been, he was not completely consoled on the matter. And it weighed on his mind through dinner and through his dreams that night. Everyone was a child of God and he loved them all equally, so when something was granted to another person and not him, he had to learn to rejoice for his brother for the blessings they'd received, not be jealous for not receiving some of his own.

He told himself that every morning for several mornings that followed.

Chapter Five

He decided the best way to go about getting over his feelings would be to try and find something else to occupy his mind. He started first with trying to take up a craft. He'd be expected to develop some kind of trade. Many of the boys his age had already found some. He was a natural farmer but he needed something else, something that wasn't a chore.

He decided on carpentry. He'd always admired the craftsmanship of the woodwork he saw at market by carpenters. Perhaps this was all just God's way of pushing him in the right direction for a useful profession. His grandfather had once given him a small wood carving of a cat that he'd admired on his shelf for many years. It'd be a long way before he could craft something like that, but he could start by fixing the kitchen table. One of the legs had become wobbly.

Joseph carried the table through the backdoor and laid it flat on the most even surface of the grassy backyard. He used the end of the hammer to remove one of the bent nails from the wobbly leg and pulled the leg off. He inspected it for damage, found a solid place to drive the new nail in, and reset it. He began hammering until it was firmly locked in place.

He lifted the table up, set it upright, and tested its abilities by applying some of his own weight to it. It bore the weight with grace.

It wasn't a bad first start. Fixing a table leg was nothing compared to building one from scratch or getting the materials for a barn. But it was one step in the right direction. And it was something to occupy his mind without clouding it with thoughts of Rebecca and a life of hers without him.

Joseph went into town to try and find more supplies to work on building a small end table to gift to his mother. He was looking over the wood pile when he spotted Anke Spiels. She had been a fixture in his childhood life, occasionally a playmate at large community events where the children were gathered together while the adults spoke of more important things.

On a whim, or because of the creeping loneliness, he stepped forward.

"Hi Anke," he said far too quietly and with a crack in his voice. He cleared his throat as powerfully as he could and tried again. She turned and smiled when she recognized him.

"Joseph Zook," she said. "I haven't properly seen you in years."

"We see each other at market and church sometimes," he said.

"It's a far cry from our games of tag where you would always yell at Rebecca

Weidler for cheating," she laughed.

It did not have the intended effect. Joseph was right back to thoughts and talk of Rebecca. Perhaps it was God's way of not letting him get out of his own trap so easy. Or maybe he needed to try harder.

"How have you been?" he asked.

"Well, I hope you and your family are as well," she said and he nodded. "I actually spoke with Rebecca a few days ago. She mentioned you been acting strange and was afraid you were ill in some way. She misses you. You two became surprisingly close after all those childhood spats."

He couldn't win. Anke's face was one of pity and kindness but he couldn't handle seeing memories and thoughts of Rebecca swimming in his eyes.

"I need to get back home," he said and nodded his head, waving goodbye. She seemed to understand and nodded, not stopping him.

He backed out of the market and tried to smile but it felt stretched and forced across his own face. He'd have to try again elsewhere.

When next he decided to speak to a girl, it was someone he did not even recognize. That made the chances that she didn't know Rebecca, or at least wouldn't bring up his friendship with her, much higher. One such girl was a young woman, about his age, whom he didn't recall ever seeing before.

"Hello," he said carefully, walking up to her. She turned to look at him. "I'm Joseph. Joseph Zook. I don't think we've ever met but I wanted to say hello."

He probably sounded so stupid but she was looking at him with a kind smile and nodding her head.

"We wouldn't have met before. My family is new to the community. We moved here from our community in Ontario," she explained.

It was not common, but it did happen that families would transplant to new Amish communities. It happened for a variety of reasons; many of them were not pleasant for the family for one reason or another. It was possible a member of this girl's family had been shunned and brought their name into disrepute. Or perhaps someone had become the victim of a terrible illness or accident and the memories were just too painful. It was best not to ask.

"Welcome," he said. "What's your name?"

"Ruth Bauman," she said.

He nodded and repeated it in his head. This could be the answer. A new girl, from a new land. She never met Rebecca and had no idea of the torment going on inside his head. This could be the solution to all his woes.

"You and your family are welcome at our home, anytime," he said. He felt guilty for speaking for his entire family but he also knew his mother would want to welcome them. She might even be proud of his hospitality, if it was not rooted in such selfish motivations. Still, he was doing good for someone and that had to count for something. He still felt the gnawing guilt in the pit of his stomach, however.

"Thank you, I'll relay your kindness to my family," she said. "Thank you, Joseph. I've been feeling a little lost my first few days here."

"What are friends for?"

He smiled and she smiled but none of it felt like it should. She could be a good friend for him and maybe even some to talk about his troubles to. But she was not Rebecca and she never would be and his heart was far too aware of that.

Chapter Six

Abigail did not like seeing her brother so melancholy. Rachel agreed immediately when she brought it up to her one night.

"He's always been hot blooded," Abigail said. "Seeing him like this, so mellow, it's unsettling."

"I think father has noticed but he's too afraid to bring it up," Rachel said.

"It's still this Rebecca business, do you think?"

Rachel nodded.

They were whispering across the expanse of their room that separated their respective beds. As children their mother would make rounds to make sure they weren't staying up late into the night, conversing about various things that crossed their mind. As teenagers she seemed to be inclined to let it happen or realized she couldn't stop it.

"Should we talk to him? Rachel asked. "He didn't seem very happy about us trying last time."

"I think we're approaching this the wrong way."

Abigail got out of her bed quietly and tip toed over to Rachel's, careful to avoid the loose floorboard that creaked under pressure. Their mother had always been a light sleeper. She sat down on the edge of Rachel's bed as Rachel sat up, bringing her knees to her chest and resting her chin on them.

"What's your idea of the right way to approach it?" Rachel asked.

"We get to the root of the problem." Abigail said.

"The root?"

"We will talk to Rebecca." Abigail explained

"That sounds like an absolutely terrible idea."

"No, listen."

Abigail grabbed Rachel, who was turning away, and forced her to look back and pay attention.

"We know how Joseph is feeling and we know he's going to stay that way. But no one has asked Rebecca what she thinks. We can just talk to her about it—"

"And go behind Joseph's back?"

"We won't say anything about how Joseph has been feeling. We'll just talk to her and see what happens."

Rachel sighed and slumped back against her headboard, picking at a loose string in the comforter over her body.

"Well we don't have any better ideas, even though any idea would be better than that."

Abigail shrugged.

"So, we agree to try and talk to her tomorrow?" she said.

"Sure."

Abigail quietly crept back to her bed and felt herself fall into a much more calming slumber now that they had some semblance of a plan to get a smile back on their brother's face.

The next morning they ate breakfast quickly, hoping to get over to Rebecca's before their mother insisted they begin their chores for the day. Rebecca always liked to read early in the mornings, out by her favorite tree, Joseph had told them as much once. So they planned a small walk over to the Weidler farm in the hopes of catching her during her usual morning ritual.

They put on some cloaks to deal with the slightly brisk morning and quickly walked out and onto the road. They walked with a hurried pace. It was too early to truly pass anyone who might stop them but they were on a tight schedule and if their mother found out she'd drag out of them the reason and then Joseph would never forgive them for spilling his secrets.

They came in sight of the Weidler farm and, as expected, Rebecca was sitting in the back, propped against a tree, a book to her nose and her eyes actively moving across lines on the page, devouring what she could.

"Rebecca," Rachel called when they got close enough.

She looked up surprised and her brow

furrowed for a moment before she recognized the twins in front of her and relaxed into a welcoming smile. She placed a finger in the book to hold her spot and set it down on her lap.

"What a pleasant surprise," she said, getting up, her page folded over to mark it. "I haven't seen either of you in a while."

"We thought we'd stop by and say hello before we started our chores for the day," Abigail said. "We've heard rumors about you and David Meyer."

She said it with a smile and a tease, to make it seem casual. But Rebecca's face fell slightly as she nodded.

"Yes, he's a kind young man and we have a lot to talk about," she said.

The frown on her face caught the attention of both the twins and they shared a brief look before stepping forward and sitting down, Rebecca joining them on the ground.

"Something's the matter?" Abigail asked.

"A few things, I suppose. David is kind and smart, but he says the strangest things sometimes."

"Like?"

"He talks a lot about English books and English life. At first I thought it was just his way of researching things, making their way of life known to him so he could avoid it with the English town nearby. But he seems to almost delight in talking about it and that worries me."

Abigail and Rachel looked at her solemnly. That was a problem. And it could turn into a bigger problem if left unchecked. But it seemed like the tip of the iceberg inside Rebecca's head and Abigail reached out her hand to take Rebecca's. She squeezed it firmly, trying to convey her care and encourage her to continue.

"My other troubles, I'm afraid, are too close to your own hearts to talk about," she said.

"Why is that?"

"They concern your brother."

Both twins tried not to look too excited as they leaned forward, just slightly. Rachel took her other hand and squeezed it as well, nodding.

"He is our brother but your secrets will be ours to keep should you wish it," she assured. "If you need someone to talk to then we're listening."

Rebecca nodded.

"He's been distant with me. He fled the last time we were together and I haven't seen him since," she said. "It hurts, to lose such a close friend like that and not understand why. I know he is your brother and you might have his confidence but if you could hint to me what I did wrong, I could fix it."

They looked at each other. Through eye contact alone they tried to converse on what to do. They said they would not spill Joseph's secrets to Rebecca, but if his depression held answers for her and a possible solution to their problem, shouldn't they try it? Rachel nodded and Abigail turned to speak.

"Joseph is a little distraught at finding out you've begun a relationship with David Meyer," she said. "For reasons you can probably guess without us having to reveal our brother's heart."

Rebecca looked taken aback as her wide eyes took in the information. Her cheeks turned a light shade of pink and her neck bobbed as she swallowed thickly. She let go of both of their hands.

"I always thought he saw me as another sister," she whispered, it seemed, mostly to herself.

"Do you share his dismay for the same reasons?" Rachel pressed.

Rebecca did not answer but the blush on her cheeks seemed to give them all the answer they needed. And the entire situation became a lot more complicated.

"You need to pray and think on this, Rebecca," Abigail said. "Seek counsel on the matter. If you have feelings for another and you fear you will lose David to the temptations of the English life, you must find some sort of counsel with your parents or even the elders. It's a serious matter."

Rebecca nodded and thanked them for visiting. She told them to return any time and gave them one last smile before stepping back

into her own house, book in hand.
    They hoped they were doing some good.

Chapter Seven

Joseph had spent time with Ruth Bauman over several days. He'd see her at market and speak with her, though she had yet to make good on his invitation for her to visit his house. He didn't mind though. It was nice to have someone to talk to, outside of his present situation, who had no idea of the strife inside his head. He could forget about Rebecca when he was with Ruth. It was easy to brush everything aside and explain to things about the town, about what she could expect from the change of seasons, about what crops worked best in the climate.

"You certainly know a lot," Ruth said.

"I'm just observant," Joseph shrugged. "I only sound smart. My dad would make me look incredibly stupid."

She'd laugh and he'd laugh. Their friendship was easy in a way that his with Rebecca had never been. And somehow, that was making all the difference in the worst way imaginable.

"What was your home like, in Canada?" he asked one afternoon.

"Generally colder than here," she giggled. "But smaller, the fields didn't roll there like they do here. Everything up there is colder and there are more mountains. The terrain is less suited for the kind of farming you can do here."

"What are the people in the community like?"

"Not all that different from here. Everyone is kind and helpful, but my father couldn't bear the stares and talk after my brother fled to live with the English. After conferring with our elders they decided it would be best if we came here."

Joseph nodded, already forming a plan in his head without even realizing it. The spark for this came when he caught sight of Rebecca talking seriously with David. They were tucked away in a corner, and perhaps thought of themselves invisible to the world but he saw them and felt his stomach turn.

He couldn't stand it, not for the rest of his life and not for five more minutes. He'd have to get away. He could go north, to the Amish communities where Ruth had come from. If they were kind and understanding like she said then surely they'd take him in. He could have his baptism there; promise to be a leader in the church in his adulthood if the lot fell upon him.

He wasn't sure, of course, how he would get there or how long it would take. But he could do it. At least he'd be far away from here.

Unknowingly, to him, on that far side of the market, Rebecca and David were not discussing things as he might have assumed.

"But David, do you even know what

you're saying," Rebecca hissed.

"I know it sounds strange and maybe even a little vile to your ears," David said. "But I haven't been baptized yet, I haven't made a pact to abide by the laws of the Amish community and everything in my heart is telling me not to."

"And what do the English have to offer?" she asked.

"I don't know. But I can't live my life wondering."

"That is called temptation, David."

"To you, perhaps."

She could not believe what she was hearing. David was planning to leave the community, face a possible shunning to join life with the English. He would never be able to return. It was not even a matter so much of the moral depravity of English life but he had no idea how to exist in their world. He would be swallowed up or get hurt. Whatever Rebecca felt or didn't feel for him, she couldn't stand by while he got himself in trouble looking for adventure.

"David, please reconsider this," she pleaded.

"I've thought long about it and I know you've had your suspicions about it," he said. "I wanted you to know first because I made you a promise—"

"And now you're breaking it."

"I will think on this for one more night.

And by tomorrow when my decision is made, then it will be made."

Rebecca felt helpless. She could try harder to stop him. She could ask someone for help, but would that be betraying his trust? To whom did she owe her first allegiance in the matter? Why did everything have to be so terribly confusing when you became an adult?

Chapter Eight

Joseph packed up what little he had. He gathered his favorite clothes, the boots that stood up well in the winter. He packed up a few books and the journal his aunt had given him once. In hindsight this would all look incredibly silly. He was a teenage boy overacting but in the moment it made perfect sense. He had to get away from the source of all his bad feelings. He had to find a place of quiet where his thoughts could not intrude on his prayers to God and guidance could finally reach him. This was the only way.

So he flung the heavy bag over his shoulder and stood as proud as he could in the dark, deciding to run away from home. He wondered if Rebecca would miss him, if perhaps she would guess his reasons for leaving. Maybe that'd make her change her mind and one day they could be together again. It was drastic, but plenty of things in life were and he read story after story in childhood of heroes of the Bible making dramatic choices and God seeing it through in the end.

Maybe this could be his.

He very carefully began to move out of his room. He was never any good at avoiding the tiles that creaked but he hoped luck and the Lord would be on his side this time as he moved through the dark with as much care as speed would allow. His mother was a light sleeper; she often caught the twins awake and chatting far past midnight. This would certainly wake her if he made one wrong move.

He moved down the stairs and was in sight of the door. Everything was coming together and the freedom of the end was in sight. All he had to do was cross the floor, maybe three steps across, put his hand on the handle and pull. He'd be out in the chilly night air and free to run from every single problem he was facing.

"What do you think you're doing?" a voice hissed.

And just like that all his plans went up in smoke and, for a brief moment, he saw them for the stupidity they must look like, for the unthought-of impulses they were. He sighed and turned around to see two mirrored faces looking at him. The twins, dressed in night gowns and robes, where staring at him with glares and arms crossed over their chests. He felt his shoulder sag. Their faces looked so much like mother's disappointed face that he felt his face heat up in shame.

"Joseph," Rachel said. "Please tell me you were not about to do something as stupid as leave home because of all this?"

He didn't say anything, keeping his eyes down and hoping they didn't notice the flaming red in his cheeks at his embarrassment. It seemed God's plan, as it often was, was far different than the one Joseph had thought up in his head.

"I just need some space to get away from all the thoughts and things," he said.

"And that meant packing up everything you have and taking off in the middle of the night?" Abigail asked.

He shrugged, dejected and embarrassed.

"Where were you planning on going?" Abigail demanded.

"It's dumb," he said.

"All of this is dumb," Abigail said. "I just want to know where you would have gone if we weren't here to stop you."

"To where Ruth Bauman came from, in Canada. Somewhere far away."

They looked at him with so much pity and kindness, he felt guilty. For a moment he pictured their faces if they had found him gone and reproached himself for his shortsightedness. What was he thinking? Going away from such a loving family.

Joseph knew they truly cared, and for that he would be grateful for as long as he was granted time on Earth with his sisters. They were kind and protective and sometimes he took that for granted, but right now he appreciated the softness of their faces.

"Running away from problems will never

solve a thing," Abigail said, softly. "Do you remember what Joseph did when he was locked away in Pharaoh's prison, falsely?"

Joseph swallowed and shrugged.

"He prayed to God for answers before realizing that answers is not our right and asking for them is not our place," Abigail said. "The Lord taught the birds to fly and the winds to blow. He knows far better than you or I what lies ahead on the path. Running from it is an act of cowardice and a betrayal of faith that he will see you through."

"I'm sorry," he murmured.

And he meant it. He felt terrible. Even in the night time when the eyes of the world were asleep, God knew what he was planning and sent help in the form of his sisters to keep him from doing something he'd regret forever.

"It is not us you need to apologize to," Rachel said. "Go back to your room. We won't tell mother or father but you need to pray on this. The Lord stopped you tonight, let Him in and you'll find the answers you seek and the calm you desire."

Joseph nodded and moved to go back up the stairs.

"And Joseph," Abigail called. "Please, whatever you do or however it makes you feel, talk to Rebecca. Promise me that."

He nodded. He meant that too. He would keep that promise. Abigail deserved it, Rebecca deserved it, and it seemed to be where God was pointing him. So he walked back up the stairs with more cares for quiet because the last thing he needed was saving from his sisters only to be found out by his mother on the way back into his room.

He dropped the bag on the floor, promising himself he'd put everything back tomorrow, and he dropped himself into bed, still half dressed. He thought he might have fallen asleep the second his head hit the pillow but he dreamed of nothing. It was a fitting punishment for the grave mistake he'd almost made.

Chapter Nine

Rebecca had never been so nervous in her life. By morning David came to see her. He told he had made his decision: he was going to leave Amish life, forsaking the baptism and promises to the community, to enter into the English world. Rebecca wanted to cry. He would endure so much hardship there and possibly never be able to return home to the community for protection when he needed it most. But his face was stern and his eyes were resolute.

So she went with him, her family, and his to the elders.

She felt sick. She hadn't been able to stomach eating a thing, standing before the elders. David relayed an impassioned speech about his desires and why he wanted what he wanted. He spoke eloquently and strongly, but about all the wrong things. The elders stayed quiet for a time, after he spoke, before getting up to offer their response.

"It is common that many youths in the community face the temptation of the *Englischers*," said Elder Brecht. "It is part of the trials and lessons of the *rumspringa*. But giving into these temptations, that is a sign of weakness. I do not think you are a weak young man David Meyer; think on what you are saying."

"I have, for a long time," he said. "I did not choose this life. I want the chance to choose a life for myself."

"You were born exactly as you were meant to be," said Elder Breman. "God makes no accidents. He chose the Amish life for you, and you are forsaking his gift out of pride."

"My decision stands."

There was a deafening, ominous silence in the room. Rebecca was sure everyone would be able to hear her heartbeat echo across the pews and stone of the church. She hadn't said a word all morning. Though occasionally glances had been thrown her way, no one had called on her yet. She was forced to bear witness to all of this and feel queasy the entire time. She wanted nothing but to run away and find somewhere to hide. When she thought of comfort and home, the face of Joseph formed in her mind.

She hoped he would find it in his heart to talk to her again. She would need a friend to cling to after all this was over. She felt somehow tainted by David's words. They were not betrothed, not even close. But the town knew of the nature of their relationship. If his name was in disrepute, if he was shamed, would they look at her with similar disdain? Would Joseph be her friend then?

"Rebecca Weidler," said Elder Brecht. "Do you have anything to say on this matter?

You entered into a relationship with this young man. You have the right to express your feelings on this matter."

Rebecca swallowed thickly and stood up. She wondered if they could see her heart beating through the fabric of her dress. It certainly felt that way.

"I have relayed my concerns and objections to David when I first feared this was the path he was choosing," she said. "I can offer no more objection that what I already have. I do not support his decision and wish desperately for him to choose another option. But I cannot force my will on another."

The elders nodded. "Well spoken."

She shakily lowered herself back down into her seat. Her mother discretely grabbed her hand and squeezed. Out of the corner of her eye she saw her mother give her a small smile and a nod. She felt, for the first time in a long time, that things might be okay. So she took a breath.

"When this is done, it cannot be undone David," said Elder Breman. "You will be defying the Lord's plan for you. Like Miriam you will be cast out and left to fend alone in the wilderness."

"I understand."

Rebecca felt her heart breaking. She may not have had the feelings for David that she harbored for Joseph, but David was her friend and she cared about him. He would be alone in the world and she wanted to cry for him. He was too proud to see what he was doing, too blinded by temptation. And there was nothing she, or his parents, or the elders could do to stop them. As she watched David's mother cry at her son's resolute declaration, she felt even sicker than before.

The elders concluded that David would be cast out of the community, unable to return. He nodded and thanked them for all they had given him in his early life. And then he walked out of the church doors, never to return. The last of David she would ever see would be the marching back of his head as he disappeared from her world forever. And it did hurt.

"You are not implicated in this," Elder Brecht said to her. "David has said as much, how you petitioned to get him to pray and see the reason of his decision. For that we thank you. Your kindness to save his soul was not a match for his pride, but your efforts have been noted by us and by the Lord."

Rebecca swallowed. It was some consolation. But her heart still hurt and her stomach was in knots. She stood and her mother kept a comforting, steady arm on her as they moved to walk out of the church doors. Behind them the weeping Meyer family stayed behind to speak with the elders while Rebecca hoped for nothing more than Joseph's comfort and friendship again, even if he could offer her nothing else.

She walked home with as much dignity and bravery as she could muster before collapsing into her spot underneath the tree in the backyard. She wept silently and was sure she felt God wipe her tears away with the gentle breeze of the afternoon wind.

Chapter Ten

Joseph took several days to himself. His sisters had showed them a secret spot in the woods they would often go to as children to play games alone. It was a quiet little clearing on the bank of a creek just inside the woods. It was peaceful there and Joseph prayed and listened to the sounds of nature for the advice God was giving him through the soft sounds of birds and rustling leaves.

He had almost made a terrible mistake. And in contrast, David Meyer had actually made the decision to go through with his own terrible decision. Perhaps there was some poetry there. David, shunned and alone now, was what could have become of Joseph if his family had not been there to save him from his own despair. His sisters had rescued him from an unforeseeable and dangerous future. David had not listened to anyone's counsel; he pushed out God's words in favor of the ones inside his own head.

Joseph took solace in that lesson. But he could not bring himself to approach Rebecca. He felt embarrassed. She did not know about his brief attempt to run away, but he would feel the guilt and embarrassment for quite some time when he looked at her. And he felt she deserved some space during it all. She had been called before the elders and had been out of sorts for some time, distraught over David's choice. Joseph expected as much. They had been in a relationship; of course she would miss him terribly.

So he sat on the bank of the creek and lazily played with a straw he popped in his mouth to chew on. How could David give up a life like this? Everything here was so beautiful and free and clear. Nothing in the world the English had made could compare to Joseph's love for his home and the land God had granted him by his birth.

Even if he never got the chance to be with Rebecca as he wished, at least he would have the lovable Amish community until the end of his days. He would make sure of that.

"I hope I'm not disturbing you," said a small voice that Joseph knew instantly.

He heard rustling and turned to see Rebecca standing there, sheepish and with the smallest smile he'd ever seen. Her face was too dazzling to ever be adorned by small smiles. She should only smile bright. And it hurt him to think that she was hurting too.

"Hello," he said evenly, sitting up. He patted the ground next to him and she accepted the invitation instantly.

"I haven't spoken with you in a long time," she said.

"I'm sorry for that," he said. "Especially after all that you've endured these past few days. I was selfish and I should have been a better friend."

"I understand why you did it," she said. "There was a lot of confusion between us."

"Confusion?"

Joseph turned to look at her and her eyes and face were becoming bright as her smile grew. She nodded to him and reached for his hand, gripping it gently. He felt his heart begin to pound and saw pink lightly brush over the peaks of her cheeks.

"I thought you would always see me as just another sister to you," she said. "We'd been friends for so long I assumed you saw me as only an old friend."

He felt his throat getting dry.

"And so when David Meyer asked to begin a relationship with me I said yes, hoping that it was the beginning of a plan God had for me, even if it was a life without you," she said. "But, clearly, that was wrong."

Joseph wondered if he was dreaming. Was she actually saying everything he had hoped she would say since the day he realized what his feelings for her meant? Was God rewarding them for all they had endured?

"I understand now the reasons for our silence these past few weeks. You felt the same way about me and assumed the same things," she said. "And for a while after things happened with David I wanted nothing more to be alone.

But every time I pictured a place to hide and be safe from all these awful feelings, it was your face I pictured. So I came to find you. Your sisters said you would be here."

Joseph didn't know what to say. So he didn't say anything. He looked at the undone laces of his own shoes and gripped her hand, hoping it would be enough to convey what he was feeling. She squeezed his hand back and they remained together and silent for a few minutes, listening to the sounds around them.

"I'm sorry for my cowardice," he said when he was finally able to form words. "I could have saved you a lot of pain and confusion if I had been brave and honest."

"This would have required a much different type of courage," she said. "And I don't blame you for your fear. But now that we're here, together, and we know what we both want. Can we—maybe—try to see what becomes of this?"

For the first time in a long while, Joseph smiled. He smiled bright and real and could feel the warmth spreading through his body. He turned his head and nodded and watched her face split into a dazzling smile as she squeezed his hand.

He stood up and pulled her with him. Together they walked over the rolling hills and back towards that spot in Rebecca's back yard, under the tree, where their story had began.

However, this time everything felt perfect.

END OF PART 3

9: TRUTH OR BARE?

Chapter One

Church was always one of Zachary Zook's favorite times. He loved being surrounded by other people, he loved doing things in the community, and the sermons from the ministers were always much more well crafted and helpful than his father's occasional attempts to impart wisdom (though he appreciated the gesture). He always said the community would cringe the day the lot fell to him to take up the mantle in the church and he hoped, for the sake of all, it never came. Still, he read and prepared himself just in case, no matter how much his children agreed that he should leave the sermons to the ones God had chosen for such things.

"We turn our attention now, to the youth of the community," said Minister Macht. "For this I will yield the floor to Bishop Zweifel."

Bishop Zweifel was the youngest bishop the area had ever seen, according to Zachary's mother. He claimed to have felt his calling early and strong and took on the burden and the blessing of leading the church. He spoke mostly during important sermons and important holidays.

The bishop rose and looked around at the faces gathered and eventually settled on the young teenagers. Zachary tried not to gulp too loud as he felt, like many of his friends around him; the attention had been turned to him with the bishop's piercing blue eyes.

"Many of us here who are older and wiser will recall the time of our *rumspringa* with fondness and maybe even moments of embarrassment," the Bishop said and earned a chuckle from the rest of the congregation. Zachary smiled, small and quiet, thinking he might feel like he was joining in on the joke. "But, many of the youth in the community today do not fully understand what *rumspringa* represents and what its purpose is."

Zachary had been feeling his palms get sweaty all week when he thought about his own *rumspringa*. It was upon him, fast and without warning and upon his friends as well. They took it in their stride better than him, laughing and leaving behind childhood games for more mature ways of having fun. But for Zachary, *rumspringa* meant something very different. He'd spent hours in the field with his father, working on the crops while his friends teased him for not understanding how the *rumspringa* works.

"This time is, yes, a time when the rules of our community relax to allow the youngsters to experience freedom of choice and the consequences therein," the Bishop said. "But the purpose of this time is to prepare you for the rest of your life. You come out of the *rumspringa* a fully-fledged member of the community, baptized, and with a spouse or the promise of marriage. *Rumspringa* has less to do with 'running around' and more to do with preparation and dangers."

Zachary looked up at that, chancing a glance at the bishop's strong, pale blue eyes. He was not an unkind looking man, just a scary one. He had a hard, strict face. According to Zachary's mother his own *rumspringa* had been very short, two years at most.

"You will be tempted, as we all are in turn," he said. "The things that will tempt you are plenty. The call of the *Englischers* is always present but you may find yourself tempted by feelings of despair, of anger, of confusion, as well. This is a time where you learn not to give in, where you learn to seek out God through prayer when it seems your head is telling you to betray your values and our rules."

There was some mumbles going around of agreement Zachary sunk down in his seat slightly, wondering if the nervousness he was feeling now was one of the feelings the bishop was referring to. Perhaps he was already falling into the dangers of *rumspringa*.

"Some communities within our faith and lifestyle allow for grossly lax customs during this time. Some of the adolescents of these sects of our culture will dress like the English, operate English vehicles, ignore their home prayer, or even engage in drink or food that is forbidden," he said, sternly. "Whatever you feel or fear during *rumspringa*, feel blessed and protected in knowing that you have been born into a community that will guide you through this time."

The sermon went on for a little but longer before the bishop concluded to sounds of approval from the adults and even some younger teenagers and they were dismissed.

As they filed out into the bright sunlight of the afternoon, his brother Joseph asked, "What about you Zachary? Are you prepared to face the wiles of the *rumspringa*?"

He laughed and poked Zachary in the ribs, causing him to jump. It earned a chuckle from his twin sisters who came over.

"You've been practically dreading this time all your life," Abigail said. "You've basically been a little adult from the day you were born, maybe you'll learn to have some fun now."

"I do have fun," Zachary defended. "It's just different than what you do for fun."

"And different from what everyone else

does for fun," Rachel joined.

"I think what you're really scared of," Joseph said. "Is finding a girl."

That caused a round of snickers from his siblings as they walked off from church and Zachary felt his face practically catch fire with embarrassment.

"Girls don't interest me," he said.

"They will soon."

Zachary walked ahead to the sounds of further teasing and jarring from behind him. He heard his parents catch up with his siblings and the sounds of scolding. He didn't feel much better though.

He'd finished school and he knew what he wanted. He wanted to work in the fields with his father. The idea of running about and bending the rules as much as this time period would allow was not something that drew interest from him. The idea of hunting around for a girl to one day ask her to marry him was equally unsavory in his mind.

Girls were annoying and giggled too much and he wanted nothing to do with them. He wanted the tools in his hand and the smell of dirt and earth out while he worked.

He did not need an entire *rumspringa* to tell him this. And he didn't need his siblings to tease him about all they thought they knew about what went on inside his head.

He'd be fine, even if his life took a

different path than theirs.

Chapter Two

Elisabeth Bauman sighed.

It was the third church service that Elisabeth and her family had been to in this community and she still didn't feel any better walking out after the church service concluded. They were not like the sermons Bishop Houser ever gave. This bishop was scary looking and very stern. She found it hard to concentrate on the sermon and was afraid to look into the bishop's roving eyes. It was a far cry from the gentle looking wrinkled eyes of Bishop Houser whose sermons were filled with inspiration and benevolence.

Even the outside looked different.

"Isn't it gorgeous?" Her sister Ruth asked as they walked together over the quiet dirt roads leading away from the church and back to their farm.

The hills here seemed to roll in all the ways Elisabeth had only read about in books. They were green and stood in solid waves, like an ocean caught in time. The trees were lush and covered everything with a softness. The sky here even seemed like it might be a clearer, sharper blue against the puffs and curves of the white clouds. Objectively it was a beautiful place; God had taken his time here to craft a beautiful home for his Amish children.

But it was not familiar.

Elisabeth thought about the flat expanse of their home in Ontario, the way she could see for miles and miles, uninterrupted. Here she could see for miles as well but the land blocked her vision far too soon. Ruth said the hills were needed, that this place had more English towns than they did back home and that temptation could be worse here. Perhaps that's why God crafted the hills here, to protect them.

"It is very pretty," Elisabeth finally agreed.

"Elsa," Ruth said, using the nickname that only she was ever allowed to call her. "You much learn to be grateful."

"I am very grateful," she said. "There are bad memories of back home, I understand that and I felt the shame too. But this place is new and strange. The land is beautiful but it's not home."

"What would it take to make it feel like home?"

That was a question that Elisabeth knew the answer to but it would not do any good. What she missed, more than anything, were her friends. Eli and Johann and Sarah. They'd shed tears when she told them her family was leaving, though they understood. Their own parents had started to forbid them from coming over to Elisabeth's house and doing things together in town.

But at least they had the chance to see each other; they'd been close enough to walk to. Now they might as well be a world away and Elisabeth feared she was never going to see their faces or hear them laugh ever again. It was painful.

"I don't know. I miss my friends and the familiar neighborhood." Elisabeth replied.

"I miss my friends too," Ruth said quietly.

"But you've already got new friends," Elisabeth said. "Joseph Zook is your friend. I have no one."

"Then use your time during *rumspringa* to make new ones," Ruth said.

"I don't want new ones, I want my old ones."

Elisabeth knew she was being difficult now, and probably resembled a child more than she resembled a young woman entering into *rumspringa*. And Ruth's face showed as much when she frowned and furrowed her brows and looked exactly like their mother when she was ready to deliver a lecture.

"This is the path the Lord has chosen for us. Not all things in life are pleasant or easy, but they are given with a reason," Ruth said. "You must make the most of it. Pray, if you need to, for guidance and help. But this is a test that will lead to a new view on life. We must accept the challenge and be grateful for all the good it will bring."

It was hard to believe so fully in something that felt so arduous at the moment. Everything felt rough and painful, like trying to cross a frozen river in winter over thin ice. It was so tempting to go rushing across because the goal was right there, but one wrong step and the ice would crack and you'd be at the mercy of nature and all the world's harms. The best thing Elisabeth knew was to stop and pray and cross carefully and as the Lord willed it. He would reveal the safest route, even if it wasn't the fastest or the easiest.

Elisabeth took a breath and nodded.

"I'm sorry for my ungratefulness," she said. "I'm just very sad and very lonely."

Ruth put her arm around her and pulled her into her side as they continued their walk, home in sight.

"I would be concerned if you weren't feeling sad. That is not a fault. The fault will be if you choose to make poor decisions because of how you feel," she said.

The bishop's sermon on *rumspringa* hadn't done much to help Elisabeth's thought process on it all. Temptation and responsibility and a sprinkling of fun. She wasn't sure what she was supposed to do, how she was supposed to go about entering into it and making friends, or even finding a man to one day marry. It had always seemed like a given thing, like steps to check off a list, but now that it was real and here, she saw the work required for it. These things would not just come to her, even with all the praying in the world the Lord would not deliver to someone who asked without putting in an effort on their end.

"Can I go with you when you go to market this week?" she asked.

Ruth seemed to understand exactly what she was thinking and smiled, nodding and hugging her a little tighter. It was a step in the right direction, even if it didn't feel completely comfortable.

Chapter Three

Zachary had thought about the *rumspringa* sermon often over the next couple of days. When he was working out in the field with his father, his mind was prone to run every which direction, thinking about a hundred things throughout the day. All his thoughts this week returned to the *rumspringa*.

"Father," he said as he pulled up an ear of corn.

"Hmm?" his father grunted from his position bent over, trying to get at the root of one of the stalks.

"How long was your *rumspringa*?"

"Well," he said, standing back up. "Not very long compared to most of my friends. But your mother and I knew we were meant for each other earlier than most. In many ways we were just waiting for the *rumspringa* to come so we would be able to explore what we knew was always there. Once it did come and our feelings confirmed, we felt we were ready to move forward with the blessings of your grandparents."

"I see."

"That doesn't mean that's how it is meant to be for everyone, however."

He walked over to Zachary and placed a

firm and squeezing hand on his shoulder.

"Everyone is unique and their experiences in life will be different. That doesn't make any one experience or choice of path better than another," he said. "You will understand more about yourself soon and the Lord will deliver you to exactly where you're meant to be."

Zachary nodded and swallowed a thick lump in his throat. He returned to work and felt his mind continue to buzz over the same thoughts and fears. It would be to go against God's will if he never found a woman to marry. The Lord had commanded to be fruitful and multiple, he would be disrespecting that command if he did not find a wife.

They took a break for lunch, walking back towards the house with heavy bags of corn for his sisters to begin peeling. The sisters had already set out a lunch of bread, cheese and milk. Zachary first dunked his hands and head under the water pump and shook the droplets off as he walked over and thanked the Lord before shoving several pieces of bread in his mouth at once. He didn't realize how hungry he was until he tasted food for the first time since breakfast at dawn.

"The English would never need tractors if they did work as hard as you do," Joseph said, walking over and clapping Zachary on the back.

"Don't make fun of your brother, he's a

hard worker and every generation needs plenty of those," their father said.

"No teasing father. It's impressive how dedicated he is," he said.

His siblings had left the issue of the *rumspringa*. Zachary assumed they quickly got bored of it after church. They'd find something new to pick at soon, he was sure. As the youngest he got the brunt of all their jeers. But the lunch passed out without event and he was left over to his own thoughts. Zachary barely heard the customary small talk that took place within their family over lunch. He went over to wash his hands at the water pump.

"How are you feeling?" Joseph asked, pulling Zachary off to the side. "Your face still looks distant and I know how working in the field gives you time to brood."

"I'm fine. Just thoughtful," Zachary said. "Well, maybe not fine. I'm not sure."

Zachary washed his hands and dropped down onto the stump of an old tree nearby. Joseph kneeled down on the ground next to him.

"I've always dreaded the *rumspringa*, you knew that. I'm just not very good at making friends or even interested in understanding how girls work and I don't understand why I can't just keep things as they are and I can work in the field with father all day," Zachary gushed out all at once, afraid that if he didn't get it out he'd be too nervous to continue.

Joseph nodded in understanding.

"*Rumspringa* is meant to be a fearful time," he said. "Very few people experience it with ease or total joy. I was convinced I'd never find anyone to be happy with and then the Lord delivered on my prayers. It will come. You need only be patient and try not to let your own thoughts cloud your understanding of what God is trying to tell you."

Zachary nodded. These things were easier said than done. But he stood up and then rejoined their sisters and father on the other side of the yard.

"I actually came to ask you for a favor," Joseph said. "Mother is at the market and I need you to drop off a few loaves of bread she forgot this morning. Won't take long."

Zachary turned to his father who nodded.

"I can get a head start on some work and you can rejoin me when you come back," he said.

Zachary nodded. Joseph handed him the small bag of bread and patted his shoulder. Zachary waved goodbye to his family and made his way down the road.

He was grateful for the chore. He liked to be alone in the country, sometimes. He was always taught to listen to the wind and the birds and the rustling of trees to feel closer to speaking with God. And he did just that as he thought of all the questions that had been plaguing his head over the past few days. The sounds around him offered no clear answer but at the very least he did not feel so alone when he heard them. God walked next to him and would not leave him. In that he could be sure of his faith.

He got to the market and found his mother's stall. She was surrounded by English customers in their strange dress and loud talk. Zachary quietly shuffled past them and dropped the bag off to his mother who gave him a grateful smile and a quiet thank you as she juggled customers.

As Zachary turned to leave he very nearly collided with a girl he had never seen before.

"I'm sorry," he sputtered out quickly. "You didn't drop anything, did you?"

The girl was completely unfamiliar to Zachary and just as wide-eyed and startled by the whole thing as him.

"I'm sorry," he repeated. "I don't think I've ever met you before."

"My name is Elisabeth," she said quietly, tucking her hands firmly under her bags. "Elisabeth Bauman, we just came here from our home up north."

Zachary had heard about the Baumans. Joseph had made friends with their oldest daughter, Ruth.

"I heard about that," he said. "I think it's brave, you know, coming to a new place and I'm sorry for the hardships that brought you here."

He rubbed the back of his head nervously and stood awkwardly. Elisabeth was nodding, clearly too nervous as well to truly say anything back. They stood there in a strange bubble of silence while the sounds of the market crashed around them before Zachary decided to take a leap.

"Do you need help getting your things home? Since I very nearly knocked you over I think it's only fitting."

He tried to smile as best as he could and thought about all the times his brother told him how to be "charming." Some part of it must have worked because Elisabeth was smiling back, small and nervous, but smiling nonetheless. She gave him a strange look and he suddenly felt nervous under her gaze.

"I don't need any help," she said firmly.

Involuntarily, he felt his head jerk back in surprise. He knew it must have looked like a rude gesture, but he couldn't stop it.

"I see," he said. "I hope I haven't offended you in any way. I've just never seen you before and my brother Joseph is good friends—"

"With my sister, I know," Elisabeth said hastily, clutching her things tightly and turning around to leave.

"Yes, well, I was wondering if you might want someone to talk with in town, show you around. Or something."

Zachary was quickly losing his nerve as his heartbeat picked up, the longer she rebuffed him. He nervously rubbed the back of his neck and started busying himself by pretending his attention was drawn elsewhere.

"I'll see you around, I guess," he said and left, cursing his brother for ever giving him advice and cursing himself for ever trying to make something out of the spark of a feeling.

Chapter Four

Elisabeth, for her part, did feel bad about rejecting the boy's help. He had a kind face and talked so nervously that there was nothing ulterior in his attempts to offer her help. He was purely kind and she'd treated him poorly.

But she had to. He didn't understand.

As she lugged her items down the road, trying to remember all the turns and the directions that would lead her back to the house, she thought of all the reasons it was a bad idea to truly begin to make friends here. It meant, ultimately, that she was accepting that this was the way her life was now, that she would never return to her home up north and nothing would be as it was. Letting the Zook boy help her, show her around town, acquaint her things, would mean that there was something permanent about her being here.

Elisabeth couldn't stand that. Not even for all the nice things the Zook boy said or the possibility of friendship that he brought. This was not a place she wanted to make friends in; these people were not hers, no matter their shared lifestyles and worship of the Lord.

Her father promised her this was temporary. He said they'd go back soon; it was just a way to take a breath, to show the elders they were willing to wash themselves clean of the shame. Like Miriam in the desert, they would be cast out for a time before they returned, refreshed and new and willing to obey the Lord's commands.

She recalled the moments as they left and how badly she cried...

"I won't do it," she'd insisted, clinging tightly to the railing of the stairs. She liked these stairs, and the railing, and the creaking floorboard outside her room, and the familiar smell of home.

"We must go," her father had said. "This journey south is to cleanse our souls and find a home."

"We have a home," she insisted. "There's no reason to go."

"We are no longer welcome here," he said. "Our family has brought sin and temptation into this town and for the sake of the others in the community, and our own immortal souls, we must follow God's path and journey to where he will bring us better skies and clearer hearts."

He always spoke so softly but so surely, it was impossible not to give in to his words. Elisabeth felt her heart stir but thought of all the things she'd leave behind: the sunsets she was used, the smells that comforted her, the friends she'd known all her life. Why was she being punished? She wasn't the one who broke the

Ordnung.

"We are leaving only for a little bit," he said. "After a short time, our path may lead us back here. I promise you this."

Elisabeth held onto his words with all her heart. She thought about it before she went to bed at night and remembered it first thing in the morning when she dragged herself awake and out of bed. It was her mantra and at the forefront of her mind when she prayed to the Lord and asked Him for help each day.

Her father had promised her. And so it would be. And kind as the Zook boy had been to her, his friendship and smile was not worth risking the chance at happiness she had back up north, in her own home. Surely, if he knew, he'd understand, he'd agree.

So she walked home alone, assuring herself today had been a test of her will and desire to return home. She had passed, she was sure of it.

Chapter Five

Zachary saw her again. It was a few days later when he was sent out again, this time to collect feed for the pigs. He went to Noah Wilder's store, ready to lug back several pounds of feed to get them through the fall for one last trip to get feed before the winter when he saw her again.

This time she wasn't carrying anything, but she looked sad and tired as she stood there in the store, nervously rubbing her arm and looking around as if trying to find something to fix her attention on. Zachary debated just letting it be, walking away and letting her have her nervousness as she would want it. But her face was blotchy, as if fighting between an embarrassed red and a fearful pale. He knew that feeling well and his heart twinged seeing someone in silent distress.

"Hello again," he said, quietly, and with a small wave and smile.

Elisabeth turned to look at him with wide eyes. They settled quickly though, as she recognized him.

"Hello," she said tersely, with a nod.

"Is this your first time to the Wilder shop?" Zachary asked.

Elisabeth nodded.

"You should see it on Mondays. Packed to the walls with people. Best supply shop in the town," he said.

She nodded again and didn't offer any more interest in the subject. Zachary frowned, wondering how could he reach her or if he should even keep trying. She was stubborn and it all was feeling like more work that it was worth. But something in his heart told him to keep trying.

"I could show you around, if you want," he said. "Today sometime or when you're free of chores for the day. I'm not sure about the community you came from but this one is big and fairly close to English towns. Having a guide might be helpful, I know my brother showed—"

"My stay here is temporary," she said, suddenly. "We'll only be here for a few days more perhaps and then going back home."

"But...your father has already begun to till the ground in the farm," Zachary said.

"A few days, it is part of our penance and punishment for raising a member of the family to make such mistakes," she said. "So it is best if I do not get comfortable."

"Your sister has gotten comfortable."

"That is her own choice."

Zachary sighed and nodded.

"Well, I hope you enjoy your stay," he said. "Short as it may be."

She nodded to him a small thanks, not meeting his eyes, as he turned to leave.

Zachary spent as much of his time after that in the fields as he could. He avoided chores that would take him into town and avoided talking to his siblings whenever possible. Joseph had several questions waiting in his eyes, Zachary could tell. No doubt he and the older Bauman daughter were talking often about their attempt at matchmaking their siblings. But he didn't want to hear it.

He still saw her everywhere though, the few times he did go out. As much as he wanted to stay hidden away in the wilderness of his own backyard, she seemed to crave the social atmosphere and the buzz of the town. Perhaps where she came from was more populated, more "urban" as some might say. Maybe it made her feel closer to home.

It was during this time that Zachary had become exceptionally good at observing her. She had tendencies, and soon he found himself looking for them, and counting them like stars. It was a pattern he looked forward to seeing as he watched her nervously tuck loose and rebellious hairs back under her *kapp*. She'd rub her left arm with her right hand whenever it seemed she didn't know how to stand for long periods of time. She pretended to read things when someone got close to her, like labels or directions, or the annual farmer's almanac.

But most of all, what he noticed, was that her eyes were not at all unkind. She was not a mean person or a proud one. She was simply scared and nervous. She was a lone girl in a new place and he couldn't blame her. Though her belief that she was somehow going home interested him, from what he could tell from Joseph's conversations with Ruth; that was not happening. But he didn't bring it up, if it's what she clung to, to feel safe then he would not take that from her.

It was on the night of a community event at the Weidler farm that Zachary's stomach bottomed right out of his body as he discovered what a crush felt like. He realized it as the Baumans arrived at the party, Elisabeth sparkling in the lowlight of the backyard and the twinkling stars. Everything that seemed to torment her within only made her glow brighter in the night and there was the ghost of something that may one day become a smile gracing her lips as she took in the sight of the party and her sister leaned down to whisper something in her ear.

"You must be the youngest Zook," said Elisabeth's father, suddenly a few feet in front of him. He'd been so lost in his own thoughts he hadn't noticed them approaching.

"Yes sir," he said stiffly.

"You've got the look. All robust jaws, the lot of you," he laughed.

"Yes sir."

"You can say more than that, you know."

Elisabeth's father chuckled and his eyes seemed to exude warmth and calm but Zachary felt his throat closing up as Elisabeth looked at him with curious and confused eyes.

"Yes sir."

He felt like an idiot. He mumbled something and rushed off as fast as his legs would carry him. He had to get away from the Baumans; he could not look her father in the eye while he knew how his heart was pounding for his daughter. Further, he couldn't handle the eyes of Elisabeth on him so focused, for the first time in several days.

"You certainly are charming," said Joseph, coming up behind Zachary who had retired to the edge of the party.

"Please don't make fun of me. Let me be," Zachary practically whined.

"This is your wake up call to sort your feelings out," Joseph said, arms crossing over his chest. "You remember that sermon and what father always said, *rumspringa* is a time for discovery. Something to be embraced."

"That sermon said *rumspringa* was something to be feared," Zachary countered.

"Then you were not listening right."

Joseph stepped forward, placing a hand firmly on Zachary's shoulder and squeezing the way their father always did. It was not quite the same but it was comforting all the same.

"Understand that many things during this time in your life will be scary. Becoming a man will require more bravery than you think you have in you," he said. "But God will never lead you astray, nor hand you a trial He does not believe you can overcome. Pray on it all and talk to Elisabeth, when you're ready. All will be well in the end."

Zachary wanted to believe his brother's words were just wind but they struck something in him and he felt his resolve waxing behind his chest. Perhaps he could do it. He thought about the fable his mother often told, of the person walking on the beach who cries out in despair because they see no footprints in the sand beside them and how could God abandoned them like that? And God replied that where they saw only one set of footprints was where God carried them.

He took a breath and squared up his shoulders. He could do this. He nodded to Joseph who smiled and clapped his back encouragingly.

But when they returned to the party, the Baumans had already gone.

Chapter Six

It was not that Elisabeth did not adhere to her parents' insistence of a time for going to bed. She did go to her room and put out the kerosene lamp. She did not, however, go to bed right away. Sometimes, when the sky was clear, she'd stay up and read by the light of the moon. Sometimes she'd pray or spend the time thinking about her readings for the day. Occasionally she took up some of her knitting, hoping to get a head start on tomorrow's work. Her sister had called her the little owl when she was younger, for all the hours in the night she tried to stay awake.

Tonight was no different from the others. She was perched upright in her bed, her mind occupied with other things as the stars hovered above, twinkling without offering any real advice. The stars here were not so beautiful as the ones from back home, even if her father and sister insisted it was the same night sky.

This night, however, she was overcome with a heavy thirst from their salty dinner of stew. She'd gone to bed without a cup of water from the pump and spent several minutes devising a plan to tip toe out to get some without alerting her parents, who were still downstairs. They spent time together, reading or talking, after they sent their children to their bedrooms for the night.

So she crept out, slowly and surely. She thought of all the things in her old home, her real home, that would creak under her weight and make a noise. She was blind to everything here, and once or twice very nearly gave herself away with a poorly timed step. But eventually she made it down the stairs and took a pause at the bottom, listening for how close her parents' voices were.

"...don't know what to do," she heard her father's voice.

They were in the kitchen, directly in the path of her attempts to get to the water pump. She held in a groan of frustration.

"The truth, Ebenezer," her mother said. "It should have been the truth from the beginning, no matter how hard it was for her to hear."

"You didn't see the despair on her face," he said. "I couldn't prolong that or make it worse. May the Lord forgive me for my sin but understand for what reason I have done it."

She leaned in closer with curiosity, careful to not to fall from the effort and alert her parents.

"It is also Elisabeth's forgiveness you need to seek," her mother said. "It is her you have wronged with your actions."

"I will speak with her tomorrow. She was

just so sad, all she wants is to go home and it wounds me in a way I never thought possible to tell her that we will never go home."

Elisabeth felt her stomach bottom out and the cool press of fear coming up her spine. *Never go home?*

"What I said, I did to protect her then, but I need to protect her now. She refuses to make friends or integrate into the town because of this. I'll see to it that the truth is laid out."

Elisabeth couldn't believe what she was hearing. The memories of her home and the neighborhood rushed out in a blinding cascade of emotions.

No! Her tormented mind screamed in the darkness of the stairs.

Chapter Seven

Zachary was put off by missing his chance to talk to Elisabeth at the party. He felt cheated for all the work he'd put into preparing himself to speak with her only to have it thrown back in his face by her vanishing act, yet again.

Both his father and Joseph were sending him on errands in town, daily. He knew these were frivolous things, their way of getting him out of the house and perhaps into the interested social sphere of a girl or at least some friends. Joseph in particular was adamant that he somehow run into Elisabeth again. So far it was having no real effect. But he was seeing Elisabeth nearly everywhere they sent him. In fact, he was beginning to seek her out, wherever he went and found himself disappointed on days when she hadn't appeared in his line of vision, rare as it was.

And when he was not out and around in town, he was distracted with thoughts of seeing her. On his walks home he tried to figure out what it meant, going back each time to her rebuffs at his attempts to even get to know her better. When he was at home, the distractions filled his head as he swung the axe, cutting wood in the backyard.

One day, his wandering mind caused a

lot more trouble than simply a headache and some confusion in his heart.

He'd been working on fixing a spoke in the buggy in the stable. He was, by no means, the family's resident carpenter but he was the only one home and had to make do with what he could do and the tools he had at his disposal. It was going alright; he was hammering the new spoke in as a flash in his mind took him to Elisabeth's face and her sad eyes. He thought about the frustrations hidden there. Every time she ran off after catching his eye only drew him to her more. He wanted to get to know her the more she tried to push him away.

It was in this mindless rambling that he missed a swing of his hammer and brought a serious crack into the wheel. He jumped back, startled by the sound and looked at the busted wheel. The crack passed right through the wheel and one of the spokes. There was no way he could fix it.

Zachary growled and kicked the wheel before tossing the hammer. Of all the stupid things that could happen, this was the worst.

In a few seconds, his fuming was over and he was left to stare at the handiwork of his anger, frustration, and distraction. His father had always told him a wandering mind was a dangerous one and the proof of that was sitting right before him. He wanted desperately to blame Elisabeth and her continued ignoring of him but knew, in his heart, he was the only to blame for his mistake.

Zachary evaluated his options. There was only one thing he could do, purchase a new wheel. That would mean he would have to confess to his father what he had done. He looked down at the broken wheel and dreaded to think how his father would react. No, his father should never know about his slip-up. His father would think of Zachary as incompetent.

In the end, he shoved the wheel away, and hid it from view in a remote corner of the stable. Zachary took a ration of the corn from the stock in the family kitchen. As he propped it under his arm, guilt stabbed his conscience. *I am taking this without my father's consent.* He squared his shoulders resolutely. It was better than being caught for his blunder with the wheel.

But it was easier said than done. Zachary dreaded every step as he walked with the corn into town to trade it for a new wheel. He looked around every now and then hoping that he wouldn't run into his father. The guilt weighed down his ankles as he walked. If it were the sea, he'd be dragged down to the very bottom and drowned.

"Hit another pothole?" asked Johann Waltz as he offered him the corn and he dug around for a wheel that would fit their buggy.

"Yes."

He felt the sting of lying. It only made the

bile boiling in his stomach even worse. He hated every second of this and felt sweat begin to form in a ring around his head at the edge of his hat. Johann produced a wheel and took the corn in return and Zachary nodded in thanks and scurried home as quick as he could with the new wheel, praying no one noticed and his father was not lurking somewhere, watching.

Back at the stable, he reattached the new wheel. It spun beautifully on the axel without the hint of a squeak. It looked like it belonged. Something new perfectly integrated into the old. This was something he could easily hide away. Until his father's kind and trusting voice send ripples of dread through him.

"How did it go today?" His father entered the stable. "First time as the man of the house, all alone with your chores."

"Excellent," he said, voice cracking and clearing his throat. "I did well. Everything got done as you asked. Done almost perfectly."

His father smiled and it made him feel sick to his stomach. He ruffled Zachary's hair and gave him a look of pure pride.

"You're growing into quite the young man. Any woman in this town will be lucky to have you as a husband and provider one day," he said. "And before you say I don't mean it, just between you and me, I didn't tell your brother that during his *rumspringa*."

Zachary tried not to gulp too obviously as

he nodded and forced a laugh. His father pulled him under his arm and they walked back into the house for dinner. Zachary hoped that his past was behind him. But the words of Abigail as he entered brought out fresh pangs of guilt.

"When I counted early in the week, I was sure there was more," Abigail said from the container that held their corn. Zachary thought he might cry.

"Maybe you're just a bad counter," Rachel said with a shrug.

"Sure, make fun of me when we run out before winter is over."

"Settle down girls. All will be well. Just get dinner ready for tonight, worry about tomorrow's dinner tomorrow. And the end of winter's dinner at the end of winter," their father said, kissing each girl on the crowns of their heads.

"Yes father," they said in unison and grabbed the portions from the container before shutting it.

Zachary couldn't escape his conscience gnawing at him. It had been a terrible mistake. He should have never taken the corn. He should have never hidden the wheel. He should have never let himself get so distracted that he'd make such a mistake. He should have never tried to talk to Elisabeth that day. He should have just hid away from the world and avoided *rumspringa* altogether because now he was not only miserable from his own thoughts, but he was a liar, a sinner, to his own family. The Lord would not allow it to stay quiet and hidden away for long. One way or another it would be brought to light.

And he had no one he could think to talk to about it. Everyone knew his family and might very well tell his father before he had a chance to formulate an apology and explanation.

But wait... *Elisabeth*.

She didn't know his father; she had never wanted to get to know them. Maybe there was a light hiding in her stubbornness after all. He could ask her for help without fear of repercussions. He would find her again tomorrow and ask for her help.

Chapter Eight

It did not occur to Zachary that Elisabeth might be seeking him out for similar reasons. When he saw her next, a few days later, she made her way straight toward him and he thought he must be dreaming or perhaps she didn't seem him. She was never eager to see him, nor did she ever seem to actually want to get near him. He was struck speechless as she approached and stood before him.

"I will never see home again," she said, suddenly and resolutely.

Zachary's mouth opened and closed like he was doing an impression of a fish. His mind was blank as he tried to remember why he had sought her out.

"I had to tell someone," Elisabeth continued. "And you are the only person in town I'm—well, I'm comfortable with you. I know it probably doesn't seem that way with how I've been treating you but…"

This was not at all how Zachary imagined this conversation going, especially as her cheeks turned a shade of pink and she avoided his eye. Maybe his feelings weren't completely one sided. Perhaps there was something hiding beneath all the stubbornness after all.

But no, he came here for advice. He

couldn't get caught up in his own crush.

"I—uh," he stammered. "I needed to ask your advice about something—"

"What do you think I should do?" she said. "I like you Zachary, I do. That's what has been so hard about all of this. I was afraid giving into that meant that I was getting too comfortable here. I miss Ontario and want nothing more than to go back but now that will never happen."

"I think," he said, clearing his throat and regaining his bearings. "That you should accept the path that God has laid at your feet. You have a home here, a farm, your family is well, and you have me. These are all blessings because the Lord will never leave you alone. It's not always easy to understand why things happen but the best thing you can do to rest your mind and spirit is to stop trying to understand his will and accept it."

Zachary wasn't sure where that wisdom had come from. Maybe he was talking to himself too, just a little bit. It's something his father would say or Joseph. He felt a swell of pride in it though; maybe he was becoming a good man after all.

"My father was untruthful, Zachary," she whispered. "He lied to me. How do I forgive that? How does God forgive him when he continues to lie and does not right his wrong?"

Zachary felt his stomach turn as he

remembered the broken wheel and the missing corn. Her words could have been about him as well. For all the forgiveness he might have asked for, God would not help him until he sought truth and forgiveness from the ones he had wronged with his sin.

"I lied as well," Zachary mumbled. "That's why I came to find you. I needed advice on what to do. I broke the wheel of our buggy and traded away a portion of our corn to get a new one before my father could notice. I didn't want him to be disappointed in me."

He watched Elisabeth's face turn from despair to an outright scowl. She shook her head at him as her nostrils flared.

"You as well? I am tired of being surrounded by lies," she said. Then she turned on her heel and marched off, leaving Zachary standing there, ashamed and alone and feeling no better about any of it.

Chapter Nine

Elisabeth's angry and determined feet took her straight home to where her father was working in the front yard. He was mending the fence, hammering it anew. The work of a man who intended to stay put for a long time. She should have known all along.

"You lied to me," she said, marching up to him. She had never spoken to her father like this and was half afraid he would reprimand her for her tone and lack of respect. But he had lied to her and she was nearly an adult, surely it was justified.

It must have been because his face looked sad instead of angry. He let out a great sight and all the weariness was evident across his face and the way his shoulder sagged.

"It was for your own good," he said.

"No, it was so you could get your way. I didn't want to leave and you made me with a lie," she accused.

"That town was no longer a home for us, they didn't want us there," he reasoned. "If you stayed you would have been alone, no family, no husband, no future. Here we have a future. It's new and scary but we have something to look forward to here."

Elisabeth shook her head. She knew what

he was saying was true but that didn't mean she was happy about it all. She wanted to cry but refused to break down here, in front of her father.

"You've been handed a gift," he said. "What you need to focus on now is finding a young man in town. A match between you and a young man here will cement our place in this community. And then all will be well again."

"I don't know why the burden is on me when I never wanted to come here in the first place," she huffed and then walked off.

She heard her father sighing behind her but he did not come after her. This day had, perhaps, been the worst one she'd endured thus far since moving. And now there was no light at the end of it all, only more darkness.

Chapter Ten

It took a long, lonely night for Elisabeth to truly come to terms with her situation.

She was angry at her father for how he had deceived her, angry at the turn of events that caused her to be punished for something she had no part in, she was angry that her sister was conspiring against her with the older Zook boy, and angry that God seemed to be silent when she asked for understanding on all these matters.

In the end though, anger earned her nothing. It did not grant wisdom or greater vision. It only brought her misery and discomfort and dreamless, unhelpful sleep.

So she looked to the sky and thought about it all. She thought about home and looked at the moonlit landscape around her. It was beautiful and calm and had welcomed her in and kept her safe thus far. It had not betrayed her yet. Perhaps that was where her answers lay. She could move and people around her could change but the Lord was always with her and it was evident in the beauty of the silver sheen across the land and the sounds of night that met her ears.

It was then that she thought of Zachary.

The boy was nervous, and quiet, and, above all, kind. He had sought her out and offered to help her upon the first moment he met her. Many people would have turned away, ignored her, let her go through town alone and ignorant of the place around her, without a friend. But he approached her. And what's more, even after she rebuffed him, refused to acknowledge him, and treated him little better than the very dust from the road beneath her feet, he still came back to help.

He was a kind boy who was going to come out of his *rumspringa* a good man. She didn't deserve to call such a person her friend, let alone the man she might one day marry. But she couldn't stop herself from thinking it.

She'd taken her anger out on him because his constant presence and quiet nature was an easy target. That had been wrong too. He'd been a friend, receptive to her needs, and she'd repaid him with punishment the very way she herself had been punished by her old town for the wrong doing of others in her family.

No more.

That night, she got the first good night's sleep she'd had since they moved south. She awoke before the sun and moved swiftly to get dressed and prepare breakfast and get a move on. Her mother would understand her pushing back her chores in the effort of righting wrongs.

So she stepped outside and made her way quickly to the Zook farm, hoping that Zachary was as early a riser as she was.

***

Zachary had woken his brother just as dawn broke. Joseph opened bleary, unfocused eyes and looked at his younger brother.

"I need to talk to you about something," Zachary hissed.

"What now?" Joseph groaned.

"Please? It's important."

Joseph rubbed his eyes, "Not more girl trouble I hope."

"No."

Joseph sat up and stretched his arms. "Okay. Tell me what is it?

"Not here. Please come with me. I want to show you something."

Zachary led him outside and to the barn, hearing him grumble under his breath at the early morning chill and him still in his sleep clothes. They stepped into the barn and Zachary moved to the place where he had stowed the broken wheel, he pulled it out and set it before Joseph.

"So?" he yawned.

"I broke it."

"And?"

"And I took some corn from our rations to trade to get a new one so father wouldn't be disappointed in me."

Understanding seemed to wash over Joseph's face as he woke up, slightly, at this information. He was nodding slowly.

"I see," Joseph said. "Well if you thought father was going to be disappointed before…"

"I know, I know," Zachary growled. "It's been eating me alive and I had to tell someone and I don't know what to do."

"You've already committed a wrong, there's no way to go back on that," Joseph said. "Too often we try to hide where we went wrong, thinking it will somehow magically make the unfortunate deeds disappear. But life does not work that way and even if you hide it from others, you cannot hide it from God or yourself."

Zachary nodded, shoulders slump, head lowered in humility. He gripped tightly to the broken wheel.

"You must take time to pray to God, it was Him you offended first with your actions. After that, confront your deed to father. God is forgiving and he will make father be forgiving too," he said. "Learning these things are part of the *rumspringa* and one day you'll be wise enough to know when to pray to God yourself and to know when and whom you have wronged."

Zachary nodded, sitting down. Joseph gave his hair a ruffle before walking out of the barn and back into the house. Zachary bowed his head and understood that he should ask the Lord that He help him through this first test, and needed His guidance in all future follies he may commit.

He took a deep breath and prayed for deliverance.

Chapter Eleven

Elisabeth knew eavesdropping was wrong and rude. But she felt as though the Lord had delivered her to the Zook brothers at that moment, simply to listen. Joseph, whether he knew it or not, was speaking to her too. She thought on his words and quietly, though Zachary did not know it, joined him in prayer from her hiding spot across the barn.

She listed off all the things she'd done wrong, all the things she believed had been done wrong to her. She heard the rustle of the leaves and felt it in her very spine. She had been childish and she had been prideful. Her father had tried to comfort her with a white lie and she repaid God's offered path with her wants and her own desires. She had been ungrateful to all her blessings.

As she realized this, she felt a calmness come over her and looked up just in time to see that Zachary was letting out a similar, longing breath. Perhaps he had felt it too. Maybe this was God's work and will after all, for them to be together in this barn, in the early hours of the morning, praying as one.

But her road to forgiveness was not finished yet. God was with her, but she still had her parents to apologize too. So she got up and crept back out of the barn, promising herself she'd return to speak to Zachary again soon, as she needed his forgiveness as well.

Elisabeth rushed quickly back over the countryside and to her father. She heard the familiar, rhythmic sounds of the axe hitting the wood and splitting it in two. In the distance, she saw the figure of her father cutting wood in the front yard. When he saw her, he looked confused and worried.

"Elisabeth?" he said. "Where have you been?"

"Praying, father," she said. "I went out this morning to right a wrong and realized I have in fact many wrongs to right."

"You snuck out?" he asked.

"I did. And for that I'm sorry, but if I hadn't I wouldn't have received the wisdom I have now," she said. "I understand why you lied, I know you were trying to protect me and do what was best for our family. I also know I was ungrateful for that and too assuming of my own prideful opinions. I think the Lord has forgiven me, but you must too, if you can find it in you."

"Oh my child."

Her father put down his axe and kneeled on the ground. He offered his arms and she walked into them, accepting his tight hug. She hadn't truly hugged him since she was a little girl back in their old home. Now, for the first time, this place felt like it might truly be home. And perhaps that was the secret all along. The material things like her room and home and even the landscape did not mean home. Her father and mother and sister were home, and they were with her, even now, even through such a trying time.

"I've got more apologies to make," she said. "But I think I might be on my way to making friends."

"I'm glad for it," he said. "Do what you must and follow your heart, the Lord will always lead it home."

Chapter Twelve

Zachary approached his father as they walked out and into the fields for the day. It hurt him to think he might be disappointing his father with the truth but he knew that Joseph was right: his father would be far more disappointed to find that Zachary had lied to him.

"Father, I need to tell you something," Zachary said, shaky but resolute.

"What is it?"

"The corn missing from our stores is my fault," he said, unable to meet his father's eyes. "I took a portion to trade for a new wheel for the buggy because I broke the old one and was too afraid to let you know. I let you down on the first day you trusted me to work on it on my own. And now, because of that, I've certainly let you down."

His father stopped walking and turned to look at him. There was no malice or anger or sadness there. There was no punishment looming behind his eyes.

"Would it shock you to know that I knew the entire time?" his father said and Zachary gaped. "You've never been good at hiding things. I found the broken wheel and will admit I was confused about where the new one came from, but after Minister Macht said he saw you hauling corn in town, I put the pieces together."

"And you didn't say anything?" Zachary asked.

"I wanted to know if you would come to me about it yourself," he said. "I wanted to give you the chance to choose honesty, rather than force it out of you. If I did nothing but punish you, you would never learn. Sometimes doing wrong is like that: you need to learn rather than repent."

"I see."

They continued their walk out into the field, the sun rolling high above them.

"Life is not an easy thing, Zachary," his father said. "Especially for people like us. We hold ourselves to a higher standard than the rest of the world; our morals are absolute and designed to be for the good of all, despite any selfish thoughts that might creep into our heads. You must learn how to combat these things and deal with consequences so that when you are older, you can mend them yourself. No one will be there to scold you when you're my age and making mistakes. Learn young what to do when you've done wrong. And then one day pass it on to your children."

Zachary nodded, feeling lighter than he'd felt in days. They walked out into the field and he didn't break a sweat, he even smiled. Maybe he'd been wrong about his father's ability to preach. Or maybe his father was just very good at knowing his own son well and offering him help. Either way, Zachary was more grateful than he could truly comprehend.

Zachary promised himself several things that day. He would never again lie to his family. He would never again run away from consequences like a child. And he would find Elisabeth and speak with her, because through all the upheaval and emotional discord of the past few days, he was still convinced she might be the only one for him and he felt more worthy than ever to pursue her.

Chapter Thirteen

"I am sorry for treating you so rudely." Elisabeth looked at Zachary. She had just explained how her father had told her their stay in town was a temporary arrangement, and how she had discovered the truth, and eventually asked her father's forgiveness for her immature behavior the past few days. She had concluded by asking for Zachary's forgiveness.

Zachary said. "My father told me that it's best when we recognize and own our mistakes. We are not perfect and will never be. It's best that we not fall in the trap of our own pride and infallibility. The acceptance itself is atonement; you do not require to seek forgiveness from me."

Elisabeth smiled as she listened to Zachary's words. It was the first time she had truly thought of a lasting friendship and as he spoke she realized the invaluable gift that the town had given her in the form of Zachary. She was finally coming to terms with the beauty of the place and the knowledge that she would reside here permanently.

Elisabeth said, "You are right. But still... how do I make it up to you?"

A grin escaped Zachary's face. "Do you want to go on a buggy ride with me?"

"And why should I?" Elisabeth teased

him.

"Well, it has a brand new wheel that I would like to test." Zachary chuckled.

THE END

Read other books by Sandra Becker:

Amish Forever

Amish Second Chance Boxset

Amish Siblings Boxset

Waiting For My Beloved

and more...

Made in the USA
Lexington, KY
01 March 2019